Satisfaction Guaranteed

Satisfaction Guaranteed

LUCY MONROE

BRAVA

KENSINGTON PUBLISHING CORP.

BRAVA BOOKS are published by

Kensington Publishing Corp.
850 Third Avenue
New York, NY 10022

Brava and the B logo Reg. U.S. Pat. & TM Off.

ISBN-13: 978-0-7394-8103-5

Printed in the United States of America

For Jack and Van because out of your marriage came one of the greatest gifts in my life . . . my husband. I love you both. And, Vannie . . . if you recognize certain things about a feisty Vietnamese lady character in this book, what can I say? You are a true inspiration.☺While no character is ever patterned wholly after a real person, there are people in my life who embody the things I admire most and those elements are bound to show up in my books. Hugs and much love to you both.

Chapter 1

W hen the subjects of Beth Whitney's favorite fantasy and worst living nightmare walked through the office door together, the day from hell took a nosedive.

And really, that shouldn't be possible. Only Beth's shocked vision was telling her that it was. In Technicolor.

It wasn't bad enough that she'd woken extra early to avoid the alarm clock only to discover that rather than sleeping like good kittens, Mozart and Beethoven had spent the night shredding the perfect silk drapes she'd installed on her condo's living room window only a month ago. The toaster had burned her bagel, and her mom had called with yet another candidate in her campaign to rejuvenate Beth's nonexistent love life. All before eight-thirty A.M., and her arrival at work hadn't improved a thing.

Her in-box had been filled with the usual urgent requests, but two messages had sent her head spinning. They were hiring a new agent and her boss wanted the new recruit's office ready by early afternoon. And Ethan Crane was back from his latest assignment and working out of the home office for the foreseeable future. Which meant that she was back to catching glimpses of him that sparked erotic fantasies no good girl would admit to . . . even to her very best friend. Even to her cat.

And he would tease her . . . just like he always did, making her notice him. Upping feelings she'd rather pretend did not exist and none of which she would ever allow herself to act on. Not only was the man way out of her league, but he was all wrong for her. He was an agent. He was also too sexy for words and the one man she didn't think would balk at her most secret daydreams.

She balked at them though.

They scared her to death. Almost as much as he did. And there he was.

Maybe she should have let her mom fix her up with Mr. Eligible. Beth needed some kind of diversion to stop her body reacting so strongly to Ethan's presence.

The only problem was, no other man measured up. Not even her worst waking nightmare. If seeing her former fiancé for the first time in three years could not tamp down her body's response to Ethan, nothing would.

Following the two men and wearing a look of benign benevolence she knew was a better cover than sand camouflage in the desert was her father. He was also her boss, which was why she didn't leap from her chair and demand to know why in the heck he hadn't seen fit to warn her of Alan's arrival.

Okay, so it wasn't as disturbing as Ethan's, but her dad had no way of knowing that. For all he knew, seeing her former fiancé for the first time in years was shredding her wounded heart. She almost laughed at the image that thought provoked. Her dad was neither maudlin, nor poetic.

She would settle for marginally sensitive, but that seemed a far off dream, too.

All three men were talking and didn't notice her reaction to their arrival. Thank goodness. Her dad saw far too much as it was. She managed to school her expression into a cool smile just as Ethan's green gaze landed on her.

Even mentally prepared for it, her heart ran wild and the secret desires she'd been fighting since coming to work for her father nearly two years ago pooled low in her belly.

However, she managed to keep her breathing and her voice relatively even as she said, "Good afternoon, gentlemen. Ethan, you have two critical messages on your voicemail and a follow-up on e-mail. I assume you had your phone off during lunch?"

The subject of her most private fantasies smiled in a way that always sent shivers to interesting, if embarrassing, places. "We didn't want to be interrupted."

Darn.

"I assume I've got a few messages that can't wait either." Her dad's faintly narrowed gray gaze said he'd noted her slight in dealing with Ethan's stuff first.

Good. She'd meant to annoy him. Not unduly. She was a professional after all, but there was no way that he could not know that he should have warned her that he was bringing Alan Hyatt into the office. Only as usual, he'd ignored her feelings and done things his own way, no doubt with some scheme in mind. He never did anything without a plan, but whatever it was, she had no intention of falling in with it.

She and Alan were done. Period.

A man who stood you up at the altar did not deserve second chances. And if her dad could not see that then he was blinder than she'd always believed. A man that vision impaired shouldn't even have a license to drive. And she'd tell him that, too, when she got a chance.

Right now, she would do her best to project professional decorum. "Yes, Mr. Whitney. You have several messages, but the most pressing is probably the one from the White House."

His jaw clenched. He hated it when she called him that. He agreed she couldn't call him "Dad" in the office, but he insisted she at least use "Whit" like the agents did. When she called him "Sir," he knew she was annoyed. When she called him "Mr. Whitney," he knew he was in deep trouble.

His eyes were acknowledging that truth now. Smart man.

"I'll leave you to show Alan to his new office while I go take care of it then," he said.

"He's working here?" she asked, her composure cracking

slightly as the reality of why the other man was with her father sank in. "*He's* the new agent?"

"That's right," her dad affirmed with subtle punitive relish. "I'm sure you'll do a fine job of making him feel welcome."

She'd make someone feel welcome . . . like the State Department's internal auditor . . . in her dad's private files. Her eyes glittered with promise her dad chose to ignore as he bid the two agents a good afternoon and headed to his own office.

Oh, he was so going to hear about this later.

"If you're busy, I can show Hyatt his new digs," Ethan offered as the silence stretched on after her dad's hasty exit.

She looked up at him and then at Alan, her usually quick thought processes sluggish in the face of a situation she'd never, ever, not in a million years and a day, expected to face. Her dad had hired the man who had humiliated her in front of friends, family, and political hangers-on.

"Are you too busy, Beth?" Alan asked, his dark eyes probing, his tone implying more to the words than was on the surface.

He was tall, dark, and dangerously attractive. He knew it too, but for a while she had been someone special to him and vice versa. If he really was going to be working for The Goddard Project (TGP), then she would have to learn how to deal with his daily presence. She might as well start now.

Besides . . . it might be a good idea to set a few things straight. She didn't know what her dad had told Alan about her, but whatever it was, she wanted him to know the truth.

Their past would stay in the past.

She smiled at Ethan, though her jaw felt like cracking from the effort. "Thanks, but it's fine. This is part of my job. And you have phone messages to answer."

Ethan nodded, but didn't turn to go immediately. His green gaze was locked on her with disturbing intensity, as if he was trying to see inside of her to that place she kept hidden from everyone else. She couldn't imagine why. As far as she knew, the sandy-haired, to-die-for good-looking agent considered her a talking piece of office furniture.

And that was exactly the way she wanted it, too. "Did you need anything else?"

Ethan shook his head and turned to leave, no indication of discomfort at being caught staring in his manner. His tall, muscle-honed frame moved off down the corridor with easy grace she both admired and envied. The man was too confident for words. And too much of everything else besides.

"Do you two have something going on?" Alan asked.

Beth's gaze jerked back to him. "Me and Mr. Cool? I don't think so. You, of all people, should know I don't date agents."

"Anymore."

"You were an exception I lived to regret."

"I'd rather you regretted walking away."

She stood up, unwilling to rehash the past in such a public setting. "Well, I don't. Sorry."

He sighed. "People make mistakes, Beth."

"And most of us try to learn from them. I certainly learned from mine." She started walking toward the office that had been prepared for the new agent. For him. And darn it all anyway, her dad had known that. "Come on. I'll show you your space and explain the computer system and pass codes."

He didn't reply, but he did follow her.

Once they were in the office, she showed him his graphic interface computer.

"Everything is biometrically coded. Once your fingerprint is logged into the system, you can change the computer so only you have access."

She pressed her finger over an electronic eye on his desk and a flat screen rose into view. "Right now, I have access to your system, but it doesn't have to stay that way."

She touched the screen and the log-in box appeared in the center. "All computer systems have a triple security level access. Your fingerprint brings up the screen and then you log into the basic operating system with a password that changes daily." She typed in the password on the keyboard that had appeared when she touched the screen. "To get into your personal programs and files, there is another password that you can change as frequently as you feel the need, though the agency suggests doing so at least weekly."

"Do the other agents have you coded into their systems for access? Does Ethan Crane?"

"Most of them do, but some don't," she said, ignoring his reference to Ethan. She didn't know why he was fixating on the other agent, but she wasn't going there. She did enough fixating of her own in that direction. "I don't care either way. The accessibility of your system to me is mostly for your convenience, not mine."

He touched the screen with his finger and the application he'd brushed over opened up. Another touch and a picture on the screen zoomed to twice its size. "Holy shit. It's completely touch interactive."

"It gets better." She touched some things on the screen and a holographic three-dimensional model of one of their latest lab gadgets appeared in front of the screen. She dismantled it before his eyes by touching the right places on the mirror image on the screen. "You can go 3-D with any graphic with the capability."

"Incredible."

"It will probably be another year or so before even the screen is available on the consumer market and longer than that for the holographic imagery to make it to market, but we have access to some of the world's most advanced technology."

"So do the bad guys . . . or so I've been told."

"Right. That's the point of our organization. To stop technological advancement making it into the wrong hands."

"Your dad told me The Goddard Project was put together during World War II when it was discovered that civilian scientists who our own State Department were ignoring were being spied on by our enemies."

"And their technological advances were being taken advantage of while we dismissed them as crackpots."

"Like Robert Goddard."

"Yes. His rocket propulsion concept made it into German hands without his knowledge and we didn't even have a clue until our own military spied on their experiments."

"That's when we started taking rocketry seriously."

"And a host of other things."

"Hence the name The Goddard Project?"

"Didn't Dad tell you that?"

"We were discussing my first case actually." Alan leaned back against the desk, crossing his long legs, encased in slacks, at the ankles. "He told me you'd be happy to fill in the blanks on the background of the organization."

Of course he had. She was going to kill him. "There isn't much more to tell. TGP never got disbanded, but it stayed ultra top secret over the decades. Unlike a lot of agencies, it never got top-heavy with political brass either. I find it amazing that in a town like D.C. the secrecy thing has remained so strong. Our funding comes from the State Department, but almost no one knows we exist."

"I sure as hell didn't."

"Which just goes to show that the FBI doesn't know everything."

His lips quirked. "No, I guess it doesn't."

"Don't feel badly. Until I got clearance to work for him, I thought my dad just worked for the State Department. I'd never even heard the initials TGP. I don't know if my mom knows to this day what agency her husband works for."

"And you haven't told her?"

"No way. We sign an airtight privacy policy before we get briefed to work for the agency."

"I know."

"Yes, of course. Anyway, I keep my word."

"I do, too, honey. When I can . . ."

"You would die rather than give up state secrets, I know."

"I'd die for some other things, too."

"The past is over, Alan. Please don't bring it up again and please don't call me honey. We're coworkers now. Nothing more." Three years ago, the way he was looking at her would have melted her bones, but she didn't feel anything anymore.

Nothing at all and she was really glad. Fantasizing about Ethan had been good for something. She had to stifle the grin that thought brought.

"I'm sorry about what happened, you know."

"You said so at the time and I believed you, I really did." She sighed. She guessed it had to be said once more and with feeling. "But I also knew that if you could stand me up at the altar for the sake of a case, there would be a lot more situations in which I'd come a poor second to your job. I wouldn't have tolerated that very well. For both our sakes, I'm glad I realized that in time."

"It could have been good, damn it."

"No. I'm not forbearing like my mother. I would have insisted on coming first sometimes . . . most times if you want the truth. You could never have given me that."

He ran his hands through dark hair cut short to FBI standards. "What I do is important."

"I'm not denying that. I'm really not, but the relationship between a man and woman is important, too. Face it, there just wasn't any hope for us."

He sighed. "I didn't want to believe that then and I don't like it now, but I can see you still mean it."

"You haven't spent three years pining, I know you haven't."

"No." He smiled, his eyes acknowledging the hit. She was sure he'd had a much more active love life in the past three years than she had. "But I've never felt the same about another woman and I spent that time wondering what could have been."

"Nothing good. Nothing truly permanent. Not even if we had gotten married." She'd never even shared her deepest fantasies with this man.

Fantasies she sensed Ethan would understand and maybe even get into, but ones she doubted Alan would have taken seriously or been willing to act out.

When she'd realized that, she'd also realized that she'd held a lot of herself back from him. Lack of trust because he was an agent . . . or just a man? She'd never decided which, but it didn't matter. He hadn't loved her enough to put her first and she hadn't loved him enough to tolerate his job or trust him with her innermost being.

They were actually pretty lucky they hadn't ended up married. They would have hurt each other. She was sure of it.

"If you say so." He stuck his hand out. "Friends?"

She smiled and shook the proffered hand. "Friends."

She finished explaining the computer system and how to access central agency intelligence to him, then took him on a tour of the facility. He was impressed with the gadgets lab. All the agents were. Men and women alike, they didn't get recruited for TGP unless they were well versed in and enamored of the high-tech world.

He reached out to touch a pen that had a microcomputer and phone in it.

Vannie, the head of the lab, smacked his hand. "Don't touch. We're still testing that one."

Alan yanked his hand back and grinned down at one of their best developers. "Hi, my name is Alan Hyatt. I'm the new recruit."

"I'm Vannie and I'm busy." She looked at Beth. "You got that supply thing worked out with the chip manufacturer?"

"They're working on it, but we're probably going to be getting our product from Kulim. Is that a problem?"

"I need it now. How long is that kind of shipping going to take?"

"They can get here the day after tomorrow."

"Good." Vannie turned to go.

"She's surly."

"I heard that," floated over her shoulder as she disappeared in one of the lab cubicles.

"Watch it. Vannie isn't just one of our best developers, but she's in charge of assigning gadgets for field operations."

"In other words, don't piss her off or I'll be carrying last year's technology into battle."

"Something like that."

"She's cute."

"I heard that," came out in a growl over the cubicle wall and sounding ten times more menacing than Vannie's reaction to the surly comment.

"She may be diminutive in stature, but she makes up for it in attitude and she's too shy to be comfortable with comments on her looks."

"Her? Shy?" Alan asked in disbelief as Beth led him from the lab before he really annoyed the other woman.

Beth just laughed, but she wasn't kidding. Not really. In the lab, Vannie was a fire-breathing dragon, but out of it, she was quiet and definitely wary of men.

"I always wanted to be 007 when I was a kid," Alan said as they walked back toward the main office and her desk.

"I think most of the agents here did."

"Even the women?"

"Hey, don't knock Jane Bond . . . when they run out of movies to make on James, they're going to start on her."

"Is there such a thing?"

"In someone's imagination and in our department . . . yes. We've got a couple of female agents that would make Old James look like a has-been."

"I believe it. I'm looking forward to meeting them," he said with a wink.

They were both laughing when they reached her desk.

Ethan was standing beside it, his six-foot, three-inch frame towering over her empty chair. His sandy hair looked like he'd run his fingers through it and his green eyes were watching her with barely concealed impatience. "There you are."

"Um . . . yes."

She was used to his impatience, but not the unnerving way he was looking at her. Like he was really seeing her. She'd been noticing him for over two years, but the reverse . . .

well, it was a totally new sensation, and not altogether pleasurable.

Those feelings zinging along her nerve endings weren't pleasure, they were trepidation. Right. Of course they were.

"I was helping Alan to settle in."

"For over an hour?"

"What? Have you been buzzing my desk every five minutes, or something?"

His lips flatlined, but color scorched his sculpted cheekbones, confirming her teasing suspicion.

She stared at him in shock. "I've got my cell phone on me. All you needed to do was call it."

"It wasn't that important."

It had been important enough for him to come and hover over her desk, waiting for her return.

"I didn't think you'd be gone that long," he added.

"She was just giving me a tour of the facility," Alan said, measuring the other man with an indecipherable expression.

"Impressive, isn't it?" Ethan asked, with some pride, his tone and expression as if the antagonism had never been there.

"Very," Alan replied.

Ethan had been recruited for TGP right out of special agent training and had been with the organization for nine years already. The possessive pride made sense . . . the antagonism did not. Unless he saw her as an extension of the agency and thereby as belonging to him first and the new recruit second. Strictly in a professional capacity, of course.

But she'd never seen this kind of territorial behavior in him before. It was really odd . . . and just a little exciting. Even if she knew it had nothing to do with her as a woman, or even being a person really.

Too much about this man excited her.

In her opinion, he was the best operative they had. Which also made him the worst candidate for her sexual fantasies imaginable, but she couldn't stop thinking about him that way. She was just glad he didn't have any idea about the thoughts that went through her head when he was around . . . or when she was alone in her bedroom at night.

Ethan fixed his attention on her and her whole body tightened with primal anticipation she fought to hide. "I need some things from you."

Now why all of the sudden did that very frequent and very normal request sound so indecent?

It was all she could do to bite her tongue and hold back an offer of anything he wanted.

"I'll see you later, then," Alan said, drawing her eyes back to him.

He saluted her with two fingers like he used to do before saying good-bye. She nodded distractedly and scooted around her desk to take her chair. Ethan was back to watching her with that strange, inner-shiver-inducing expression. And he was standing much, much too close.

"What?" she finally asked in exasperation after several seconds of silence.

"What's going on between you and the new recruit?"

"Nothing."

"I don't think so. Earlier, you could have cut the undercurrents with a knife and just now he was looking at you intimately."

"Intimately? I don't think so." She knew Alan's intimate look and that hadn't been it. It had been more his "just friends" look. She was pretty sure. Three years was a long time . . . his looks could have changed.

"You're wrong. He was looking at you like he knew you intimately."

She rolled her eyes, putting on a good show of humored indifference, but inside she was gasping for air. Where was all this personal interest coming from? She couldn't afford for Ethan to start to notice her as a person. Her feelings for him were precarious enough as it was.

"You're imagining things," she dismissed.

"I'm a good operative, Beth."

"The best."

He smiled in acceptance of the compliment and leaned back against her desk, his strong thighs only inches from where her hands had automatically gone to rest on her keyboard. "I got that way by relying on my instincts. I'm not imagining anything."

She pulled her hands from the keyboard and pushed her chair away just a little bit, but the move did nothing to diminish the impact of his nearness. She could smell his expensive aftershave, the crisp clean scent of his designer T-shirt and signature black jeans, even the faint fragrance of boot leather so close to her. He was surrounding her with his presence as effectively as if he'd touched her and her heart wasn't going to bear the strain. Neither were other, more demanding parts of her body.

She took a deep breath and nearly cried out at how dumb that had been as every sense went up a notch in awareness of his masculine appeal. "Even if you aren't, and I'm not conceding anything, it's none of your business."

She was really proud of how calm and firm she sounded.

But he looked totally unmoved by her declaration. "Maybe, but I'm curious. And when I'm curious, I always find out what I want to know."

"Curiosity killed the cat."

"Not any cats I've known. You can tell me, or I can find it out for myself. I'm good at that sort of thing, baby."

He'd never called her baby before and he said it so seductively that the word went through her like a five-alarm fire, sending every nerve ending clamoring for things she could never allow. How she maintained her composure, she had no idea, but she managed it. Years as the daughter of a mostly absentee father and mother who made Machiavelli look like a political novice had been good for something, she guessed. She'd learned to hide her emotions early and had to draw on every scrap of that ability now.

"I don't know why you'd waste the time bothering, but

whatever floats your boat. Be my guest." She waved her hand in the air as if it didn't matter to her one way or another.

It did though. She didn't need her public humiliation re-hashed around the water cooler. But she wasn't all that worried, even though she knew Ethan was an extraordinary agent. He could only find out her past from two people and she didn't think either of them was going to talk. At least they'd better not.

He reached out and touched her. Just a light brush with the back of his fingers along her jawline, but it sent the desires inside her careening out of control. "Don't worry, little Beth, I intend to."

"Why?" she asked, meaning more than his determination to know her past. But why had he decided to start treating her like a flesh and blood woman now? Why did he care about her past? Why had he touched her?

He shrugged. "Like I said. I'm curious."

The words hit her like a smack in the forehead. Curiosity. Nothing else. He wasn't touching her sexually. He didn't feel the sensual pull toward her she felt toward him. If she wasn't careful, she was going to make an idiot of herself.

She surged up from her chair, stepping toward her filing cabinet as if there was something in it she wanted. "You said you needed something."

"Yes, Beth, I need something all right."

The words were like dark sorcery, filtering through her mind and wreaking havoc with all sorts of connotations she knew he didn't mean. But with a superhuman effort, she managed to maintain her professional façade and answer the question that had him so impatient to begin with.

Chapter 2

Ethan saved what he was working on and closed down his computer system, his movement precise and controlled. Frustrations rode him hard though.

He'd come back from his last assignment with a name. Arthur Prescott. An information broker and the man responsible for the deaths of two foreign agents Ethan had considered his friends. The information broker was American and working out of a small town on the Oregon coast. His home was like a fortress overlooking the ocean, but he managed to keep his thumb on the pulse of high-tech discoveries nationwide.

That wasn't so surprising, considering many of the nation's top minds in the computer industry could be found in Oregon, Washington, and California. But the man did not limit himself to brokering deals on pirated computer technology. He had his fingers in pies all over the country and Ethan was determined to see that those fingers got burned. Badly.

But he couldn't find any way into the bastard's house or network of contacts. External attempts to crack Prescott's computer system by TGP's best hackers had proven fruitless, and for a rich man, the guy hired few employees, even domestics. There should be openings in his organization. There always were with men like this, but nothing was showing up. Anwhere.

Prescott was one careful SOB, but Ethan was determined to find a way in and when he did, he was going to shut the man's operation down. Completely. Ethan had no tolerance for people with no loyalty but to their own desires. Even mobsters could be patriotic but not this guy. He was in it for Number One and to hell with his own country and everyone else in it.

He wasn't even a spy for the opposition. Hell no, he sold information to anyone with enough money to pay for it. Prescott showed no favoritism and he had few friends, but then men like him rarely did. He didn't have a lot of enemies either, though. He was a broker and the people who bought his information knew that he brokered deals with their enemies and they didn't care. There weren't a lot of scruples in the world of espionage.

And this man had even fewer than most. Ethan was damn sure he was responsible for the deaths of more than just the foreign agents. Which gave him all the more reason to want to take Prescott down, but for right now he was hitting one brick wall after another.

Time to go home and let his subconscious work on it while he focused on something else. Maybe he could set up a jump. Isaac had said he wanted to go skydiving. Maybe they could even invite the new guy. Get to know him a little better, find out how much metal he was made of.

Ethan finished buttoning up his office before he stepped into the corridor.

Beth was still at her desk, her curly brown hair falling out of its clip, her lower lip caught between her teeth while she closed her system down. Her movements were hurried and her expression almost furtive.

"Got a hot date tonight?" he asked as he reached her. The possibility that she was going out with the new agent dispelled all thoughts about his current case from Ethan's mind more effectively than if he'd taken a bungee leap into a three-hundred-foot ravine.

Her slender shoulders jerked like he'd surprised her and

she looked up, her soft brown eyes not focusing on him immediately. It was the kind of look a woman gave a man after they'd made love and she was still off in the never-never land of satisfaction. His gut tightened with something he'd worked very hard to sublimate for going on two years.

It shouldn't be so difficult. She was not his type. He went for sophisticated and usually glamorous . . . the type of woman who knew the score and didn't mind the tally.

With doe-brown eyes that sparkled behind glasses she was forever fiddling with, gentle features, and a figure that landed somewhere between Uma Thurman thin and Mae West curves, Beth looked and acted more like the girl next door. She was friendly and warm to everybody, a little stubborn, and a lot innocent. She was the kind of woman who expected marriage and a white picket fence on the other side of hot and sweaty sex, if she imagined getting down and dirty like that at all.

He gave an internal shudder at the thought. Of the marriage . . . not the sex. His gut told him sex with her would be mind blowing, which made no sense. But he couldn't shake the feeling. Nevertheless, he wasn't even sort of ready to start settling down. Free climbing a sheer rock face didn't make him break out in a sweat, but the idea of getting married would have him breaking out in hives all over if he let it take root.

Beth was a committed kind of woman and he was a no-commitments-but-his-job kind of man.

She was also the boss's daughter and Whit could be a mean son when riled. He might be out of the field, but he still maintained an aura of hardness an agent of his caliber never really lost. Beth's refusal to date agents was a well-established fact as well, but that didn't stop Ethan's libido from surging in her presence. It was getting damn annoying . . . not to mention physically uncomfortable.

She had this way of looking incredibly innocent and enticingly sexy at the same time. All the internal reminders in the world that she was not an Ethan Crane type of woman were about as helpful as a taser against an automatic weapon.

"Oh, it's you." She adjusted her glasses and made an obvious effort to focus on him. "Hi, Ethan. No hot date . . . just dinner with my folks."

If he knew the old man, dinner wasn't for another couple of hours. "You're leaving early tonight."

She sent a furtive glance to the corridor behind him. "Quitting time is five o'clock."

Was she hoping Hyatt was going to show?

"Not for you. Not usually." He'd teased her about it a few times, saying she couldn't have much of a social life if she spent all of her time at work.

She'd always replied that there was plenty of time for socializing after seven o'clock. His lips quirked now at the memory. That was one of the things he liked about her. She might not be sexy in the conventional way. She didn't exude confidence like a lot of the female agents, or even what he might expect for the daughter of the old man and his politically well-connected wife, but Beth always gave as good as she got.

And watching her with her dad was like seeing two peas in a pod, though he didn't think either one of them noticed the resemblance.

"Even I like to get home on time once in a while." She was grabbing her purse and locking her desk as she spoke. As if she was in a real hurry to leave.

Like he'd told her earlier, the one bane of his existence was his curiosity and this woman, as much as she was so not his type, sparked more curiosity in him than most. She was too private. Which he should understand, being the same way . . . but it made him want to peel away the layers.

He'd refrained up to now because he knew it was dangerous to get to know her better. With some women, familiarity bred contempt, but he had a feeling that learning more about Beth would just lure him in further. It didn't make a lick of sense, but then hormones and the male psyche rarely did.

Hadn't his mother and older sister always said so?

He leaned against her desk, blocking her exit. "You meeting someone before dinner?"

She stared at him like she couldn't comprehend what he was asking. Then, her dark eyes narrowed. "I am not, not unless you count my two new kittens." She bit her lip, frowning. "But if I were, that would not be any of your business."

He shrugged.

"Do I ask you about your personal life?"

"You don't need to. You have access to my voicemail and e-mail and take a lot of my messages." She probably knew more about his social life than he did.

"That is not the point. The point is, I'm not nosy and I don't ask. I would appreciate the same level of courtesy."

"I wouldn't mind if you asked."

"That's not the . . ." Her voice trailed off when she realized she was repeating herself and she glared at him like it was his fault. "Well, I do mind. Can we just leave it at that?"

"You sure are prickly for a woman who doesn't have plans later."

She made a sound like steam escaping a safety valve. "I am not prickly."

"Of course not. In fact, she's rather sweet," Hyatt said from behind Ethan.

Beth tensed and the glare she'd been giving Ethan turned hotter than molten metal. Curiouser and curiouser.

He turned slowly to face the newcomer, making it possible for Beth to come out from behind her desk. "Is she?"

Hyatt smiled toward Beth. "Yes."

"You would know?"

"Yes."

Now why that one bitty word should rub Ethan so wrong, he didn't know. But it did. It also increased his already dangerous level of interest in Beth's secrets to extreme risk levels. Which was probably why he found her so interesting. He liked risk. Thrived on it.

Yes, that made sense.

"Past history is not something we are going to discuss," Beth said with an expression that was no doubt meant to intimidate, but in Ethan's mind made her cute as hell.

She was too darn innocent and free from violence to truly intimidate a man who was neither.

"We aren't?" he asked mildly.

But she looked at Hyatt, not him, her dark eyes flashing a warning, before answering. "No, we are not."

"No, we are not," Hyatt parroted with an irritating smile.

"*At all or ever*," she emphasized, "with this annoyance that calls himself an agent."

Didn't she realize the more she fought him knowing what she sought to hide the more his predator's instincts would be aroused? She spent enough time around agents that she should realize they weren't tame or easily led.

Hyatt measured Ethan up and down and then nodded. "Our past is a closed book as far as he's concerned."

"As far as anyone is concerned."

Hyatt merely shrugged and if Beth missed the significance of that, Ethan didn't. The other man wasn't about to drop the issue of their shared past and that made Ethan even more determined to find out what it was.

Beth grimaced, but nodded. "I'm off."

"I'll walk you to your car." Hyatt smiled, his expression reminding Ethan of a saying his grandmother used to utter.

The man looked as happy as a donkey eating saw briars and Ethan just naturally resisted letting another man be that smug in his presence. "I'm leaving, too; may as well walk with you both."

Beth walked out of the building flanked by two of the sexiest and most dangerous men she'd ever known. For a woman who did not exactly command legions of male admirers, it was a heady if strange sensation. And being seriously annoyed with both of them did not diminish that feeling one iota.

She thought she might know what was motivating Alan,

despite his agreement to be nothing more than friends, but she didn't get Ethan at all. She knew he had a bone-deep curiosity that made him a really good agent because he was so observant, but why be curious about her?

Her past held pain and embarrassment for her, but certainly nothing that would or could interest a man like Ethan.

He was the one who opened her car door for her, though, after she pressed the unlock button. The look he gave a clearly disgruntled Alan was pure one-upmanship and she couldn't help laughing. She wasn't exactly either of their types.

Despite the fact that Alan had once claimed to love her, Beth had long since figured out her main attraction for him had been the fact that she was so serene and cozily domestic. He liked the contrast of coming home to her to the high-adrenaline life in the field as an agent. He'd even said as much once and she had been foolish enough to think that meant he was getting ready to truly settle down. That maybe the stress of fieldwork had started to get to him.

She'd been spectacularly wrong and his signing on with TGP proved it.

But both men were acting like a couple of alpha wolves marking territory. She supposed that was only natural when a new agent came on staff, for him to settle his boundaries, but she'd never had one use her to do it with before. And she found the whole experience downright hilarious.

"When she laughs like that, you can't help feeling she's laughing at you, not with you," Alan said with resignation.

Ethan's left brow rose in a gesture she'd never been able to perfect. "Are you laughing at us, Beth?"

She grinned, tugging on her door. "Yes."

"Why is that, I wonder?"

"Why are you holding my door?" she countered.

"I'd say that was obvious. I'm not ready for you to leave yet."

"I'd say why I'm laughing is obvious, too."

"Maybe you'd better explain it anyway. I'm just a simple

Texas boy. We don't always get the subtle nuances in a situa-tion," he drawled, his accent exaggerated.

If anything, her mirth doubled. The man was as far from simple as an expert-level Sudoku puzzle. "There's nothing simple about you, Agent Crane, which is why I'm sure you'll get the concept that if you don't let go of my door, important messages might start getting mislaid. Messages from friends wanting to go skydiving, women hoping to see you again . . . that sort of thing."

"Never piss off the secretary," Alan intoned with mock solemnity.

"Central Administrative Agent," Ethan corrected, looking far from worried.

Beth tugged on her door again, but it didn't move. She gave Ethan a pointed glance.

"Tell me why you are laughing at us."

She shook her head at him, humor tinged with exaspera-tion. "You're both so intent on marking territory, you haven't even stopped to consider that neither of you wants the thing you're working so hard to pee a circle around."

"Are you sure about that?" Ethan asked.

Her heart skipped a beat at the implication of his words be-fore reason kicked in. She could so not afford to let her imag-ination go there. Alan was going through some sort of nostalgic feelings for her and apparently Ethan, swift observer that he was, had latched onto that fact. Like men the world over, he was getting entirely too much enjoyment out of pulling the other man's chain.

It was just another way to razz the new recruit.

"I'm sure I want to leave," she said in answer to his taunt. "I've got two kittens that are going to destroy another set of draperies I spent months trying to find if I don't get home and feed them soon."

He smiled at that. "Then I had better let you go. Drive safely, Beth."

"I always do."

"See you tomorrow," Alan added as Ethan gently closed her door for her and knocked on her window in salute.

Beth arrived at her parents' home bare minutes before she was supposed to sit down to dinner with them.

Mozart and Beethoven had knocked over one of her Chinese planter pots and she'd had that mess to clean up, two rambunctious kittens to scold, and then she'd had to change into an outfit her mother would approve of for dinner at home. Her work gear wouldn't cut it.

Mother expected her to look feminine after office hours. Even for a simple family dinner. Though, as Beth had expected, it was not a private family dinner. They rarely were. Though this once-a-week ritual was something her mother had instituted when Beth had moved into her own condo, there was no attempt to make it a cozy night of domesticity.

That was Beth's tendency . . . it had never been either of her parents'. Tonight, they were also entertaining a senator's aide and his new fiancée.

"I knew you wouldn't mind me inviting them to join us for dinner to celebrate the engagement," Lynn Whitney said with a charming smile that had done more for her than most lobbyists' arguments when influencing politicians.

Beth returned it. "Of course not."

But spending the evening discussing wedding plans after coming face-to-face with her own spectacular failure in that regard was not Beth's recipe for a relaxing evening.

And when her mother went so far as to give advice based on her own experience with Beth's "unfortunately aborted" wedding, Beth's patience ran out.

"You'll never guess who is working for Dad now," she said with a smile that would have done a crocodile proud.

"Who, dear?" her mother asked while her father went rigid in his chair.

Ah, so Mother hadn't known? Somehow, she'd suspected that.

"Alan Hyatt and he hasn't changed a bit. You could have turned the clock back three years and not even noticed the difference." Except that three years ago she'd been planning to marry him and now she was simply doing her best to deal with the revelation of having to work with him.

Her mother's eyes actually widened in shock while her mouth formed a perfect O of astonishment. "I thought he worked for the FBI."

"He did, but apparently Dad convinced him to take a chance on the State Department."

"You hired the man who stood your daughter up at the altar?" her mother demanded, for once her political mask stripped completely away.

"I hired a man who is very good at his job, Lynn. It's been three years."

"He stood you up at the altar?" the senator's aide's fiancée asked, her own eyes glittering with interest.

"Yes."

"You mean he just never showed?" the other young woman asked, agog.

"Never showed. Didn't call to explain why until three days later. By then I had already returned most of the wedding gifts. I'm very efficient."

"And he's still alive?" the senator's aide asked with a laugh.

"I practice a policy of nonaggression," Beth said, tongue in cheek.

"And you hired him?" the fiancée asked of Whit, her expression filled with appalled fascination.

"Yes."

Sensing that her small dinner party was traveling into dangerous waters, Beth's mother pulled herself together and changed the subject to one that had not a thing to do with weddings or jilted brides. And Beth breathed in relief.

After dinner, she managed to get her father alone briefly and demanded, "So, why didn't you warn me? It's pretty obvious you didn't tell Mom either."

"I have never shared my work with your mother. And you know that we don't make the names of new agents known to other staff until all paperwork has been signed," he said, making no pretense of not understanding exactly what Beth was talking about.

"I'm not *other employees*, I'm your daughter." Was it everyone in D.C., or just her parents who didn't understand the meaning of family loyalty? "You didn't even tell me we were getting a new recruit until this morning."

Unfortunately, she thought her parents fit the D.C. climate better than she did. There were a lot of politicians who talked great rhetoric about family values while spending almost no time with their own. Her mother worked with many of them and admired them, too. Sometimes Beth felt like she'd been born into the wrong world, but wasn't sure how to find another one to inhabit.

Were things different anywhere else?

"And you expected me to bend rules for you?"

"In this instance? Yes, I darn well did. The man stood me up at the altar. I had a right to know I was going to be working with him. That I would see him today."

"He had his reasons."

That wasn't the point, but she didn't expect her dad to get that. "So he said."

"And you refused to accept his explanation. So be it, but do not expect me to choose my agents based on personal considerations because that's not the way I work." It was the old party line for him . . . work came first, last, and always.

She didn't even try to argue that point.

"I didn't say anything about choosing your agents. I'm talking about the warning you owed me as your daughter that I would be in a potentially upsetting situation today."

"You told me you were over him. Were you upset?"

"I am over him, but that doesn't mean it wasn't startling and a little upsetting to come face-to-face with the man who jilted me at the altar."

Her dad's gaze was calculating. "You felt nothing for him?"

"If you brought him to work for you in an attempt at matchmaking, I guarantee you are going to be disappointed."

Something shifted in his expression. "I told you I don't make work choices based on personal considerations."

"*That* I believe."

Whit sighed. "I thought bringing you to work for me would help you to see why I made the choices I did when you were growing up."

"I always knew why. And that's not the issue here. You were wrong not to warn me you'd hired Alan. I'm your daughter and I deserved that little bit of consideration."

"He's a good agent. I like him. I always did," he said, once again skirting the real issue and focusing in on the job. "He can be relied on."

"He proved that without a shadow of a doubt on what would have been our wedding day, didn't he? Nothing, not even getting married, could get in the way of an assignment."

"You might not admire that kind of dedication, but I do."

"I know you do."

"And you never have."

"You're wrong. I do admire it, I just don't think it mixes with family."

"Your mother did."

"Yes. You two were well matched."

"You're our daughter."

"Are you absolutely sure I wasn't switched at birth?" she joked.

Instead of laughing, her dad looked pained. "Elizabeth . . ."

She sighed. "Just kidding, Dad. Look, believe it or not, I didn't intend to rehash old arguments."

"You're angry with me for not warning you of Alan's arrival," he said on a sigh, finally acknowledging the real issue.

"I always said you were a smart man."

"I didn't think giving you advance warning would improve the situation." Which was the truth, Whit thought.

He'd wanted his daughter's raw reaction to Alan to increase the probability factor of his own plans working out.

He'd lied when he said he never let his personal life impinge on his work decisions. This time, he was in up to his eyeballs on a personal basis. If Alan weren't an exemplary agent, it wouldn't have worked, but he was and Whit had no reason to doubt his choice.

His daughter had been running scared for too long. For a woman who wanted family more than he'd ever wanted the glory of thwarting enemies of his government, she was way too dedicated to her job. It was time she settled down.

He and Lynn wanted grandchildren. They'd talked about it, but they were never going to get them if Elizabeth expended all her maternal energy on those two kittens she'd just adopted when she'd started feeling like the condo was too empty. Why hadn't she thought of bringing another person into her home?

Lynn thought she was gun-shy about relationships and marriage. He agreed, but he wasn't willing to take his wife's approach of letting Time be the great healer. Trying to fix her up with eligible men didn't work either. His daughter was extremely strong minded when it came to some things and dating was one of them.

But Elizabeth had had three long years and instead of opening up, she'd grown more wary. Less willing to accommodate another person in her life.

She worked atrocious hours, but she dismissed his warnings in that regard as a joke. She could not take seriously that he of all people would really be telling her that she was too wrapped up in her job. But that was exactly what he thought.

His absentee parenting and Lynn's focus on her political causes instead of Elizabeth's emotional welfare had taken a toll neither of them had seen until too late. Then the wedding fiasco had happened with Alan Hyatt and Elizabeth had withdrawn completely from the risk of any sort of relationships.

She had few friends and held her coworkers at TGP at a

distance so she didn't make any more. He didn't know what made his daughter tick, but she was his only child and he loved her, even if she'd never accept how much.

But he had a plan to show her and that plan included getting himself some grandchildren. He'd always been one hell of a tactician and his daughter didn't know it, but she was his most important case.

He couldn't wait to see the look on her face when he instituted Step Two in the Plan.

Chapter 3

Beth walked into the briefing room, her mininotebook in one hand and a cup of mocha java light in the other. Six agents were in from the field, a pretty high number for their smallish agency, and she was prepared for a longer than normal briefing. Which meant being in close proximity to Ethan for longer than she'd like. Or rather longer than was good for her.

She *liked* being in the same room with him way too much.

She took her seat at one end of the long conference-style table and waited for the others to arrive. Ethan was the first one in. Of course. "Mornin', Sunshine."

"Good morning, Ethan." She kept her face averted, her attention ostensibly on her small computer monitor, but really she didn't want him to see the blush that his casual endearment caused.

He'd started calling her Sunshine soon after she began working for TGP. Other agents had picked it up, saying it fit her because of her sunny but shy smile. Only she never forgot that he was the first and, somehow, it always felt more personal coming from his mouth. It wasn't like yesterday's *baby*, but it was bad enough.

Especially after the dreams she'd had the night before. It was bad enough that she couldn't stop herself fantasizing about him, but now he'd taken over her subconscious, too. And her subconscious had no limits like her conscious mind. She'd woken up screaming from pleasure in the middle of the night and had to take a soothing shower before she could go back to sleep.

"Have a nice dinner with your folks last night?" he asked in that whiskey-smooth voice that made her inner thigh muscles clench tighter than her Thigh Master.

She squirmed inobtrusively, trying to ease the ache that never quite went away anymore. "Yes. Mother was entertaining a political protégé and his new fiancée."

"Sounds like fun."

She looked up then to find his green gaze fixed on her and she had to fight the fear that he knew just what kind of effect he had on her. "If you consider an evening spent discussing the best way to procure a caterer and how far in advance the right church has to be booked for a wedding, then it was fun."

"You don't like talking about that kind of stuff?"

"Not particularly. No."

"Why not? I always figured you for the orange blossom and white picket fence type of woman. I'd say that kind of talk was right up your alley."

If he knew the kind of fantasies she had about him, he wouldn't make such assumptions. The only kind of fences she thought about lately were the type she could tie him to and then have her wicked way with all that incredible male flesh. "I guess you don't know me very well, do you?"

"You saying I'm wrong?" He sounded truly shocked by the prospect . . . and intrigued.

She wondered why? She wasn't the intriguing type. "Dead wrong. Weddings and marriage are off my radar."

"Forever?" he asked disbelievingly.

She sighed. "For a long time."

The only man she was interested in at the moment was him, but she wanted his body not his heart. As candidates went for future husband of the year, he was everything she knew didn't apply.

"You surprise me, Sunshine."

"It's good to know that even a crack agent like yourself can't read me completely."

He looked at her and in that instant she felt like he was seeing inside her, that the fantasies she had were laid bare. Her mind told her it was impossible. The decadent fantasies she had could not be seen on her face, but it was all she could do to break eye contact with him.

It helped that two more of the agents had come into the room. Isaac, a big black man with bulging muscles that even a suit jacket could not hide, a smoothly shaven head, and a rich, deep voice that sounded like hot fudge pouring over ice cream, was talking to an older agent. Bennett looked like a mild-mannered accountant but had a black belt in judo and could kill with his bare hands. He was also a crack computer hacker.

They were discussing the newest covert camera developed in the technology lab and sat down still arguing its merits and shortcomings. It was a good thing Vannie wasn't there to hear them. She'd have broken something over Isaac's head for sure. He was of the opinion that a lady's compact with a camera was passé and that the lab shouldn't waste their time developing outmoded ideas.

Soon after Isaac and Bennett's arrival, one of the female agents came in. Elle had glossy black hair and was almost six feet tall. She was also gorgeous, but was more lethal than the older male agent who had come in before her. She could handle any weapon and throw a knife to kill a mosquito at a distance.

A second later, Jayne came in. She was one of their deepest cover operatives. The world knew her as a highly exclusive exotic dancer, but in reality, she was one of their best agents. Beth had always wondered why she and Ethan never hooked up, but in the two years she'd worked for the agency, she'd never seen Jayne give any man even a second blink, much less a look.

Alan sauntered in behind her, talking to Drew. Drew wasn't a regular field agent but was so conversant in the world of high-tech that he was invaluable to the agency in his role as information gatherer. He knew when things were going down and spent hours every day tracking the movement of technological information worldwide.

Alan was smart to be picking Drew's brain about his first case, as she was sure he was doing.

"What's that look for?" Ethan asked.

Her gaze skittered back to him. "Look?"

"The one you're giving the new guy. For someone who denies interest, you sure are watching him intently."

"I've been watching everyone as they come through the door. I'm taking notes. Would you like to see?" she asked as she spun her mininotebook for him to see where she was logging each agent's attendance on her spreadsheet. "It's my job."

"Well, you didn't look at the other agents the way you looked at Hyatt."

"If you must know, I was thinking he was smart to be picking Drew's brain. Not every field agent realizes how important Drew's knowledge is to the running of TGP."

"I do."

"I know you do." Was this conversation as bizarre as she thought it was, or was she overly sensitive?

Agents were a strange breed.

"Why don't you look at me like that?"

Because she was too busy trying not to look at him like she wanted to devour him, but she wasn't about to say so. "You're being annoying and I can't figure out why."

"Maybe the way you look at Hyatt bugs me."

This conversation was definitely entering the realm of the bizarre. "I don't look at him any special way, but if I did, I don't know why it would bother you."

"I didn't say it would." He frowned, as if he just realized how strange their conversation was. "The old man is late."

"He always comes in last."

"I swear he's got the room wired and an alarm goes off in his office once everyone else shows up."

She smiled. "No alarm. Just an IM. From me."

"So, that's how he does it. Sneaky."

"Efficient."

"You are that."

"Who says it was my idea?"

"I do."

"It just happens that you are right."

"I usually am."

She laughed. She couldn't help it. The man was too confident for his own good.

Her father walked in, talking on the Bluetooth headset attached to his glasses. The room went quiet. Her dad cut the connection to his cell phone and took his place at the other end of the conference table.

"Listen up, people, we've got a lot to go over."

The briefing went pretty much as she'd expected, right down to how hard it was to sit next to Ethan without ogling him. He kept invading her personal space, too. Using the pretext of reading her notes and then reaching across her to grab a mug and the coffee carafe from the center of the table and finally to point out that she'd missed something in her notes.

Which she never did, but her body was zinging with the electricity generated by his nearness to such an extent she felt like she needed a transformer before she blew a brain circuit.

"Okay, that's about it, except the Prescott case."

Ethan shifted beside her, his expression going cold. "I'm hitting a wall, but something is going to break soon."

"It already has." Her father tossed a newspaper on the table. A tiny ad in the employment section was circled.

Isaac pushed it down the table to Ethan, who read it. Beth peeked over his shoulder so she could, too. It read:

>*Eccentric millionaire seeks gofer to watch stock trends, oversee market investments, and keep employer apprised of personal stock movement as well as market trends. Position is part-time and in-house. Confidentiality a must as is experience in the field. Prefer applicants with quiet demeanor and ability to work without extensive supervision.*

"He's looking for a gofer?" Ethan asked.

"He calls it that, but the position sounds a little more specified."

"In the newspaper?"

"He wants someone to watch his stocks and investments."

"So why not go with an investment counselor?"

"It's not all that uncommon for the superwealthy to want a private party to take care of their investments. There is the belief that if you work for more than one client, your loyalty to their financial welfare could be compromised." Beth knew what she was talking about.

Prior to her father hiring her, she'd worked for one of the biggest stock brokerage agencies in the country. She'd hated her job and had jumped at the chance to work in a different environment. Even when her father had insisted she take basic agent training to work as TGP's central administrative agent.

"That doesn't make any sense."

"It does if you're investing millions of dollars rather than a few thousand. At that level, buying stock that earns an extra cent per share can mean huge income differentials."

"So why does he call himself an eccentric millionaire?" Bennett asked.

"Probably because his lifestyle would be questioned otherwise. We know Arthur Prescott is all about money. He wants lots of it, and investing his ill-gotten millions is just another way of guaranteeing that he makes more." When she was done speaking, Beth realized that she should probably have let Ethan answer that.

He was the agent assigned to the case after all.

He didn't look irritated, though. He was thinking. Silently.

"So he's looking for a glorified clerk?" Isaac asked.

"Not hardly. He's looking for his own private investment counselor. Someone who is willing to work part-time, move to the small coastal town he's living in, and work on-site."

"How do you know he expects someone to move?"

"Because he advertised in the major Portland and Seattle newspapers, not the tiny gazette that services the small town about ten miles from his cliff-top home," her dad answered this time.

"I can't believe he advertised at all." Ethan's brow was still furrowed in thought.

And privately Beth agreed, but she said, "He must be pretty arrogant."

"Or sure he can tell an agency plant from a real counselor."

"That's a difficult background to fake if he's got any experience in the area himself."

Her father nodded, his eyes glimmering with satisfaction. "Exactly. This kind of thing takes an expert."

Ethan said, "Agents are trained to simulate expertise."

"But there are some things that are harder to emulate than others and a genuine background in this field is one of them. In addition to that, the man wants someone who is non-threatening. The bookish type, for lack of a better term."

"You got all that from his request for applicants with a quiet manner?" Ethan asked.

"Yes. Didn't you?"

Ethan sighed. "Yes. Actually, I did. But I can do bookish."

James Bond? She didn't think so. Beth burst out laughing and a couple of the other agents snickered.

Her father sighed while Ethan glared at her.

"I'm a good agent."

"I never said you weren't, but playing the humble administrative role is one I would dearly love to see you acting out," Whit said. "Fortunately I have a better plan."

"You do?" Beth asked her father, feeling wary for no reason she could discern.

"Yes. We put you in as the mole and Ethan plays the part of your boyfriend, a much more suitable role to his personality. He's a writer who has been wanting to move to the West Coast for inspiration. You see this job offer as a godsend so you can stay with him."

It was a believable scenario and more tempting than she'd ever let on, but for one problem. "I'm not an agent."

"And I don't need you to be. It's Ethan's job to use the in you'll give him to take Prescott down."

"But this isn't how we do things," she said faintly.

Her dad knew she did not want to be an agent. He knew that fieldwork was the farthest thing from what she wanted to do. Especially a job that would require this kind of proximity to Ethan.

"We could use another agent, but we'd have to pull someone in from a different agency for the expertise. We don't have time for Ethan or anyone else to bone up enough on this. You have legitimate work experience to use for references and the mild-mannered personality he's looking for, Elizabeth. Not to mention that your background is going to be very tempting to Prescott."

"You mean he'll see her as a source of information?" Jayne asked.

"I believe so. Yes. Her mother has political connections and as far as anyone knows I work for the State Department."

"You don't think that will tip him off?" Ethan asked. "You want to use her real identity?"

"Beth's life is an open book except for her job here. The more real the person we plant as a mole is, the better chance we have of getting one on the inside. Arthur Prescott did not get where he is by being easily fooled."

"But she's not an agent," Ethan said, repeating her words. "It's too dangerous for her and the case to send her in."

Beth agreed, but didn't get a chance to say so.

"She trained, she just never used the training."

"Because I didn't want to."

Her dad's expression turned cold and stern. "I'm well aware you have no desire to be an agent, but TGP needs you, Elizabeth. Are you going to turn the assignment down?"

"Do I have a choice?"

"There are always choices, Elizabeth, but your interview is set up for the day after tomorrow at 9 A.M. Your letter of application is in this file, along with a brief detail on my recommendation for your cover with Ethan."

"I'm the agent in charge on this case, why wasn't I informed of this prior to these steps being taken?"

"The advertisement came out when you were finishing up your last case. You'd already started preliminaries on Prescott, but you had other fish to fry at the time."

Beth wanted to welcome Ethan to her world but managed to keep the flippant comment to herself.

Her dad turned to her. "You're a shoe in for the position, Elizabeth."

"Who will cover my duties while I am gone?"

"You've been asking for another admin, so I hired one. She'll cover for you while you are away."

"But she won't have any time to train."

"You'll be available via computer and phone and I will be here."

Her dad had no clue how key her role was in the agency, but he would learn and maybe in doing so . . . he would get a small lesson in not dictating other people's lives without giving them any input.

"If I'm working for Prescott, I won't be available all the time."

"We'll make do."

"Assuming she gets the job."

Now that nettled. "I assure you . . . the man would be a fool not to hire me. I'm exactly what he wants."

Ethan frowned. "You'll be working with me, Beth . . . as the subordinate agent. Remember that."

Something thrilled through her at his dominant tone, but she was careful to keep her expression cool. "Yes, sir."

"I'm still not comfortable with the level of risk for your daughter," Ethan said to her dad.

Whit frowned. "In this building, she's an employee, and right now she's the best chance we have of getting an in with Prescott. That's all that matters."

The words sliced through Beth, but she didn't let that show either. When had anything but the job mattered to her father?

"Besides, you'll watch out for her. You're too good at your job to let her get found out."

"You've got me slated as a writer? How is that more my speed than bookish?"

"Writers can be eccentric, brooding, whatever. And I never said you couldn't do bookish."

Personally, Beth thought Ethan could probably do brooding very well. Her dad dismissed the other agents, but he and Ethan stayed in the room to finish discussing the Prescott case.

"So a relationship between us is my cover," Ethan mused.

"Yes. Toward that end, you two need to spend some time together off hours. You know the drill. Your connection has to appear to have depth and as Elizabeth and you both pointed out, she's not an agent. She'll have a hard time faking it."

"You want us to have a relationship?" Ethan asked, sending Beth's pulse ricocheting toward the moon.

"I want you to be comfortable enough with each other for it to be believable."

Ethan nodded, while Beth got her breathing under control.

"So, we spend time together off hours."

"I'm not going skydiving as a form of togetherness."

"What would you rather do, meet at the library?" Ethan mocked.

What she'd rather do was get the guy naked, but that was taking the pseudorelationship a step too far. Make that several steps too far. "The library sounds like a good place for a writer to meet his girlfriend."

"A certain kind of writer, maybe, but not me, baby."

There was that *baby* word again. She squeezed her eyes shut, but that only made the images of what it might be like cuddled in this man's lap more vivid to her mind's eye.

"I'm sure you two can find a common ground."

She opened her eyes, doing her best not to hyperventilate. "Arthur Prescott is never going to believe I'm dating a man like Ethan. He's not my type."

"Aren't I?" Ethan asked, just as if he knew the kinds of fantasies that kept her awake at night.

"No one is your type at the moment, Elizabeth. And Ethan is a damn good agent. He'll have no trouble playing his role convincingly."

"What about me? I'm not an agent. . . . I don't play roles."

"Are you turning down the assignment?" her father asked in that no-nonsense voice that meant he wanted a straight answer. Now.

She looked at Ethan.

"I want the bastard, Beth. I'm not comfortable with you being the connection between us, but I'm damned if I can see another way in."

She'd taken the job with TGP because she wanted something different in her life, but she'd taken it for another reason, too. She believed in the work her dad and the other agents were doing. She really did. She might hate the toll it had taken on her life with her dad, but she admired and respected him for what he had done for his country. She couldn't help feeling that way.

And she couldn't help wanting to bring a lowlife like Arthur Prescott down, too. The man had no loyalty to his country, no consideration for the safety and welfare of others, and too much opportunity to wreak havoc in their technocentric world.

She sighed. "Maybe we could start with dinner?"

Her dad took it for the tacit agreement it was and nodded approvingly.

Ethan's eyes darkened with something she did not understand. "Dinner. Tonight."

"Tonight?" she squeaked, back to the verge of hyperventilation. "We don't even know if he'll hire me yet."

"He will," her father said with confidence.

"And we don't want to wait until we find out to start preparing the backstory. I'm not into sloppy agenting."

"I'm not sloppy." She also wasn't an agent, but no one seemed willing to give that bit of information the importance it was due.

And she might as well stop whining about it, even in her own head. She'd agreed after all. She had to make this thing work and her dad was right about one thing . . . the job was tailor-made for her.

"Maybe I should pick you up at your condo and find out, though I can't picture you having a messy place."

She hadn't meant that kind of sloppy and he knew it, but she didn't have a snappy comeback. She was too busy trying not to think about what she wanted for dessert.

Chapter 4

Beth was shaking with nerves by the time that Ethan buzzed her condo that night.

She'd told herself over and over again that this was not a real date. It was an opportunity to solidify their cover. Right. And the fact that they would be sitting across an intimate table for two should not be sending her libido into overdrive. She'd read somewhere that women were at their sexual peak in their thirties. Well, she was only twenty-nine and she'd been peaking for Ethan for almost two years.

Which meant it wasn't some kind of hormonal joke her body was playing on her. She wanted the man. So much that she'd stopped calling herself depraved and learned to deal with the urges. Only now she was faced with more temptation than she'd ever had where he was concerned. She didn't know if she could deal with that.

Darn him anyway for being the one man she was sure would not only not balk at her sexual fantasies, but who would know what to do with them.

She bit her lip as she took a final look in her full-length mirror. She had not morphed into a cover model for *Vogue* in the last ten seconds. More was the pity, because while she was sure Ethan would get her sexual fantasies, she was equally certain he would have no interest in sharing them. She was not his type.

At five-foot-six, she was at least three inches too short, a cup size too small in the curves department, and several lovers shy of the experience a man like him was no doubt used to.

None of that had stopped her from trying on six different outfits, doing her makeup three times, and trying her hair four different ways before settling for a sloppy topknot with tendrils framing her face that went well with the simple black dress she'd settled on. It left a good portion of her legs and back bare . . . all in the effort to look as sexy as she could for him. For this nondate. Sheesh.

She needed to get a life.

The problem was that she didn't want a life . . . she wanted him. Every sexy, tantalizing, irresistible inch of his six-foot-three frame.

The buzzer went again and she jumped, grimacing. Showtime.

She rushed to release the entrance lock for downstairs. Ethan was knocking on her door less than a minute later.

She opened it, keeping the kittens back with one wary foot. "Hi."

"Hi, Sunshine. Is there a reason you're blocking the door?"

"The kittens." She scooted back, keeping the cats away from the opening as she widened it to let him in. "Come on in and I'll get my jacket."

Ethan moved swiftly, grabbing Beethoven as the black-and-white kitten tried to make a break for the hall and shutting the door immediately upon stepping inside her apartment.

"Thanks. They want to go exploring, but with my luck they'd end up at the manager's apartment. She's allergic to feline fur and was very dubious about letting me get the cats."

Ethan grinned. "I can imagine." He whistled as he looked around. "Nice place. Exotic."

That's what she'd been going for. She'd decorated with Byzantine colors and rich textures like silks and velvets as well as faux fur throws on her sofa and chaise longue. It fit her, but usually surprised people that did not know her well. Even some who did.

Ethan didn't look surprised, only intrigued.

"The cats like it, too . . . too much sometimes," she said ruefully, looking at her gorgeous drapes, now shredded near the bottoms.

Ethan's gaze followed hers and he laughed as he scratched Beethoven's head before putting the kitten down. "There's a spray you can get that keeps the cats off your furniture and the like."

"Will it stop them shredding my curtains?"

"I don't know. My sister swears by it, though, and she's got four cats."

"Four?" Beth asked faintly. Two were enough to wreak more havoc than a marauding army in her opinion.

"She's got kids," he said with a shrug, as if that explained it.

Beth hadn't spent much time around children, but maybe it did. Maybe each child had insisted on having his or her own pet . . . or maybe his sister hadn't wanted any of the kids to feel left out and gotten them each a kitten. Being an only child, those kind of family dynamics were a mystery to her. But she found them interesting. She'd always wondered what family life was like in a "normal" household.

She used to dream of finding out. She didn't dream of that anymore. Mostly because she'd come to realize her dreams were more fairy tale than hopeful fantasy.

She grabbed her vintage velvet dress coat from the back of the chair where she'd left it in preparation. "I'm ready to go, if you are."

"Dinner's not for another hour." He took the coat and laid it back over the chair.

Then he shrugged off his own leather jacket and put it on top of hers. And she let him. Without a protest. Weird. This man brought out more than one unexpected reaction in her. Even odder . . . she then just stood there staring at him and trying really hard to remember . . . *this was not a real date.*

But his dark sweater clung to his muscular chest in a mouthwatering way. He looked so hot . . . in every way.

He cocked his brow at her and her stomach dipped. "Um . . . if not dinner yet, then what?"

"I thought we could have a drink and talk a while before we go." He looked around her living room again. "I want a chance to soak in who you are away from the office so I can relate to that person in front of Prescott."

It sounded reasonable, but Ethan Crane was the last person she wanted to invite into her life on a more personal basis. Why hadn't she given that thought more credence before agreeing to do this job? Probably because she hated making decisions based on weakness. And she definitely saw her feelings for Ethan as a major weakness.

She took a fortifying breath. "I keep the drinks in the kitchen. What will you have?"

"I'm partial to beer, but I don't suppose you keep that on hand." He managed to look sheepish and way too kissable all at the same time. "It's the Texas boy in me."

"Dark ale in a longneck bottle all right?"

His eyes narrowed. "Who do you keep that in the fridge for?"

"It's football season," she said with a shrug.

"So?"

"I like Sunday football, but don't tell my mother. It's not nearly as politically correct as baseball."

"Who do you watch it with? Hyatt?"

There had been a time, but Alan wasn't the football fan she was. He preferred participating in, not watching . . . any sport. She was sure Ethan would be the same way. "No. By myself."

"So, you drink the beer?"

"And eat peanut butter–filled pretzels? Yes. It's all part of the experience."

"Maybe I'll join you next Sunday."

"You like to watch football?"

"Sunshine, I'm from Texas. Of course I like to watch football."

"And drink beer."

"I'm not sure about the peanut butter in the pretzels, though."

"I suppose I could spring for a bag of regular ones . . . or some popcorn if you'd rather." What was she saying? Was she inviting him to invade her football season ritual?

"I could bring my own."

Somehow as they'd been talking, they had also been moving closer together and now their bodies were practically touching. She stared up into his face and forgot what she was about to say. How had he gotten so close? Had he been the one to move . . . or had she? Oh, gosh . . . she was not going to survive this assignment. She just knew she wasn't.

"Ethan?" Her voice came out a breathy whisper.

Not good. She sounded like she was issuing invitations, and she wasn't. Was she?

"Yes, *baby*?"

Oh, man. Warmth and moisture pooled between her legs. She needed to eradicate that particular word from his vocabulary, but she couldn't even get enough breath to protest it.

"What's happening?"

"Don't you know?"

She thought she did, but she couldn't believe it was happening between them. Sexual desire so strong it literally pulled their bodies closer. Or was it all coming from her? No. He didn't touch her, but he watched her lips, his eyes filled with predatory green lights. It excited her until her body shook with it.

A plaintive little wail and soft fur rubbing against her ankle snapped her attention back to some semblance of reality. What in the world had she been doing? She'd come this close to kissing the man and more than likely the whole moving near one another thing had been her doing. Even if it hadn't, it was sheer insanity to give in to her physical attraction for him at this stage.

Never mind letting someone else shred her heart for her, why not offer it on a silver platter and be done with it?

She jumped back and swooped down to pick up Mozart. "Are you hungry, sweetheart?"

The kitten meowed back and Ethan laughed. "I take it that was a yes."

"I think so." She smiled. "I'll just get your beer and feed the kittens before we go. I can't believe I almost forgot their dinner."

She'd been ready to leave the condo without feeding them. Guilt swamped her. Some pet owner she was.

"I have a feeling they wouldn't have let you forget."

"Um . . . look around like you said you wanted to, and I'll be right back."

"Sure."

She took her time feeding the cats and getting his beer, using the solitude to regain her equilibrium. That was the plan anyway; it wasn't working too well. Knowing he was in her living room, looking around with an eye to try to get to know her, did things to her body and her heart she didn't even want to think about.

She vacillated between getting a beer for herself in hopes of relaxing her rapidly frazzling nerves or forgoing it to keep her wits about her as best she could. Finally deciding to go for caution over optimism, she poured a glass of sparkling water for herself instead. Nothing was going to soothe her nerves and she could not afford to lower her inhibitions even marginally.

She walked back into the living room, wishing she'd had an hour rather than a few minutes to regroup and worrying that even that might not have been enough.

Ethan wasn't there. His coat was still draped across hers, but the living room was empty. From where she stood, she could see the door to the bathroom down the hall and it was open. The small room was dark. Besides her bedroom, the small condo had no other rooms. A small teak dining set served as her dining room at one end of the living room, and she'd just come from the small kitchen.

She turned in a full circle, somehow expecting him to magically appear, but he didn't. Where could he have gone? He would have said something if he'd needed to go back to the car for something. Not to mention, he would have donned his jacket again. Wouldn't he? Even Ethan wasn't immune to the cold and it was chilly for autumn.

A muffled sound came from her bedroom. What in the world was he doing in there?

She rushed down the hall and into her bedroom, stopping in mortified shock at what she saw.

He stood beside her bed, flipping through an erotic romance novel by one of her favorite authors.

"What are you doing?" she demanded in what should have been a shriek but that came out an embarrassing squeak.

"You read some pretty interesting stuff before going to sleep," was all he said before dropping the book back onto the table beside her bed, its blatantly sensual cover face up. He turned to face her. "If I read that kind of stuff before bedtime, I'd never sleep."

"It's a good thing you don't, then." Thankfully, her voice was stronger and she sounded almost like her normal self.

He didn't respond, but the look he was giving her spoke volumes. All of it hot, if she could believe the interpretation of her own eyes.

"What are you doing in my bedroom?"

"Getting to know you. It's this kind of thing that can make or break an assignment like ours." He indicated the book with a flick of his long, tapered fingers.

"My taste in reading material?"

"My knowledge of it."

"I can't imagine this sort of thing coming up with a prospective employer."

"You never know, Beth. And it's not just a cliché . . . it *is* better to be safe than sorry."

"Having you snooping around my apartment was one thing, but this is an invasion of my privacy."

"I'm not snooping . . . you gave me permission."

"To look around. I didn't think you'd come into my bedroom." Was that strangled voice hers? She sounded ready to kill somebody.

He didn't look worried. "We're supposed to be lovers, Beth. Of course I came into your bedroom and I've got to admit . . . I'm seeing a side of you I never expected to exist."

Had he looked in her drawers? Had he seen the dildo? Lots of women had them, or vibrators. She shouldn't be embarrassed. She was single, but that didn't mean she was sexless. She was also celibate . . . or had been for almost three years. A toy for self-pleasuring was practically a necessity for a woman in her position.

"Loved the hot-pink handcuffs."

Her cheeks burned. "I . . ."

"Who uses them? You, or him—or both of you?"

"Neither . . . no one. You had no business looking in my drawers."

"We've been over this. I need to know. It's easier to look than to ask and from the way you're reacting, I don't think you would have been honest if I had."

"You would have asked about my sex life?"

"Yes. This is a dangerous assignment and I'm not going to risk you getting hurt because I don't know the things I need to know to make our relationship look real."

"I'm not comfortable with you knowing this kind of intimate stuff about me."

"I'm sorry, but it's the way it has to be."

And she should have realized it. He didn't say so, but she knew he was thinking it. She had taken the training and she knew enough about their assignments to know what to expect. Or should have.

"Did you look through my other drawers?"

"I hadn't gotten to that yet."

"Don't."

"I need to, but look at it this way . . . you can come to my apartment tomorrow and do the same thing."

"It doesn't help."

He sighed. "Do you want me to wait to look at your clothes until we get back from dinner?"

"Yes." She didn't want to sit across the table from him right after he'd had a good peek at her lingerie drawer.

She liked sexy underthings and could only imagine how he would tease her after seeing them. He already thought the fact she liked to read erotic romance and use a dildo was shocking . . . what would he think of her black leather corselette or her selection of lacy demibras she only wore on the weekends when nip-ons were not an issue because no one else saw them?

He moved toward her, stopping a foot away. "The thing is, Beth, I can't get the image of you tied to the bed out of my head. And it's doing things I hadn't planned on."

Her gaze skimmed down his body, snagging on the rather large, rather long bulge in his jeans. Oh, my, yes . . . but the image of *her* tied to the bed? "Don't you mean you picture the cuffs on someone else?"

He laughed, shaking his head. "No, ma'am, I do not."

Oh, man . . . she was in trouble. She licked her lips.

He made a soft noise that was almost animalistic and stepped closer. "You've got kinky thoughts, baby. I like that."

"I don't picture myself tied to the bed," she blurted, stepping hastily back from him.

Instead of taking it for the denial she'd meant it to be, he saw below the surface. She just knew he did from the slow, easy smile that took over his hard features. "You picture tying your lover to the bed?"

"I'm not some kind of closet dominatrix."

"Not unless you're into pain, you aren't." He rubbed his chin, his green gaze too darned knowing. "Are you into pain, Beth?"

"No!"

"Not yours."

"Not anyone's!"

"But you like the idea of tying a man to the bed?"

Oh, they could not be having this conversation. "That is none of your business."

"I'll take that as a yes. Why do you want to tie your lover down, sweetheart?"

She shook her head, too choked to answer.

"Maybe we should talk about it over dinner."

"We aren't going to talk about it at all." But especially not over dinner. What kind of man thought sex talk at dinner was appropriate?

Ethan. Dangerous. Untamed. And too sexy for her health.

She shook her head emphatically. "N-no. No sex talk over dinner." She swung her hand up to emphasize her denial, only realizing she was still holding the glass of sparkling water when it sloshed over the sides.

Ethan grabbed his beer from her hand before it suffered a similar fate. He took a long swig. "Mmm. That's good, but I know something I'd like better."

"N-no . . ."

"I promise you, baby, I do . . . and you'll like it, too. But it will keep. Drink whatever that is you poured yourself and then let's go. If we don't leave soon, we aren't going to make it to the restaurant at all," he said in a dark voice.

She wanted to pour the sparkling water over herself rather than drink it. To cool off. He could not mean what she thought he meant. Could he?

That dangerous expression in his green eyes certainly implied he meant it.

He was right. It was time to go.

Ethan helped Beth into the passenger side of his low black Solstice. As she dipped down to settle against the leather seat, her skirt hiked up, showing him the top of honest to Hannah stockings. Did she wear them all the time? Or just for dates?

This wasn't exactly a date, but a get-to-know-you-better-for-the-sake-of-the-assignment dinner. She saw it that way, surely? But she looked sexier than he'd ever seen her.

The woman turned him on and in ways that other women had never touched. He'd dated women who dressed provocatively all the time, but the idea of Beth wearing stockings under her more conservative work gear made his cock lurch in response. Knowing she was wearing them instead of panty hose tonight had him hard and aching and he hadn't even touched her.

Was not going to touch her, no matter what he'd fantasized about when he'd seen those kinky pink handcuffs in her bedside drawer. He needed to know her better to pull this job off, but he didn't need to get involved with her.

That would be a bad idea.

He closed the door on temptation and sent a silent command to his hardened sex to settle down before going around to get into the driver's seat. Only her muttering something about two pairs of panties as he shut the door did not help. He did not want to think about her panties. He really didn't.

Did she wear a thong?

He wouldn't put it past her, not the Beth Whitney he was getting to know tonight. Just the thought of her butt bare against that little black dress was enough to undo any good his self-lecture might have done. What the hell was the matter with him? He'd been vamped by the best of them, but he did not lose control.

So, why did he have an almost irresistible urge to pull his powerful convertible to the shoulder of the road and find out if sex in a two-seater was really impossible?

He wasn't happy about using a nonagent as the contact with Prescott. The last thing he could afford to do was to mess up his own focus by getting involved with her. And he had a feeling that getting involved with Beth would be harder on his equilibrium than any other woman had been in a very long time.

She was just so surprising.

That book next to her bed . . . it had been hot. He wouldn't mind reading it himself and not just for the obviously intense sex in it, but the story had sounded pretty good, too. Damn it, he was losing his mind.

He pulled up in front of the small Italian restaurant where they had reservations, only now realizing he'd spent so much time thinking about her, he hadn't said a word to her for the whole drive.

She was busy looking out the window, but her hands were clenched in her lap and he wondered why. Was she still angry he'd invaded her bedroom? She was going to have a fit then, when they got back, because he had every intention of doing exactly what he'd said he wanted to. Go through her drawers. He needed to know her in a way only a lover would, or he would screw up his role in that capacity.

Failure wasn't an option for him, especially when her safety was at risk.

She said nothing as he came around to open her door and she avoided his eyes when she got out of the car, but she took his proffered hand. She moved away from him as soon as she got vertical and clear of the car though.

He frowned. "Are you mad at me, Sunshine?"

Her gaze snapped around. Sherry-brown eyes looked at him blankly for a second and then she shook her head. "No, of course not. Why would I be?"

"You didn't like me going through the stuff in your bedroom."

She moved toward the brick building that housed the restaurant. "No, but I understand you think it was necessary."

"It was."

"I'm not talking about my sexual fantasies over dinner," she blurted out, sounding pretty defensive.

Is that what had her avoiding his eyes? She was embarrassed by the prospect of talking about her sexual preferences? The woman was a mass of contradictions.

He couldn't help smiling. "Do you have sexual fantasies?"

"Doesn't everyone?" She stopped before the open door.

"I suppose . . . but I've always been more of an action man." Though he knew images of her and those hot-pink handcuffs were going to play a starring role in some heated fantasies for some time to come.

He'd like to take her home and play a few of them out. Right now.

Her small pink tongue darted out to lick her lips in a gesture that was both nervous and arousing. "Yes."

"Yes what?" He shook his head, clearing it. She hadn't meant yes to his thoughts, but his sex was acting like she had.

"You're an action man. I don't see you merely thinking about doing something . . . I think you'd do it."

His body thought so, too. "You're right. Usually. Are you saying you've never used the handcuffs?"

"I told you . . . I'm not having this discussion over dinner."

"We're not in the restaurant yet."

She took a hasty step over the threshold into the small restaurant. "Now we are."

He laughed and followed her inside. "Don't you know that denying my curiosity satisfaction just makes me more determined to know?"

"Don't you think it's time you learned to control that curiosity?"

"Now what would be the fun in that?"

She didn't get a chance to answer as the restaurant's owner, Vito, came forward with an effusive greeting before leading them to Ethan's favorite table in a quiet corner. The ambient lighting and brick walls on two sides of the table enhanced the feeling of intimacy while dining. And Vito's menu was superb.

Ethan's mouth watered as the scent of garlic and his favorite pasta dishes assailed his nostrils. He was hungry and food was going to have to do.

"You bring a beautiful woman this time, Ethan." Vito kissed his fingertips toward Beth. "*Bellisima.*"

She blushed a soft pink and Ethan smiled as he held her chair out for her, usurping Vito. "I agree, Vito. She is one-of-a-kind gorgeous."

"This is true."

That had Beth rolling her eyes at both of them.

"She no believe us. Why is this? You no tell her how beautiful she is before?"

"It's an oversight, I admit." Ethan took his own chair, letting one leg slide against Beth's.

She jumped and moved her leg away, giving him a chagrined look.

Vito shook his head. "I think you are smarter than this, Ethan my friend. Tonight I help you make up for your foolishness. I serve you a dinner that would make the angels weep, no? Good food, it is the way to a woman's heart."

"I always heard it was the way to a man's heart," Beth said with amusement lacing her voice.

"Ah . . . men are more simple than that, but that is no a discussion for ears such as yours. It is a woman that requires the wooing and I will help my friend tonight with this."

Beth laughed, shaking her head, and Ethan felt something tighten in his chest. He'd brought dates here before, but Vito did not act like this with them. He flirted, as all Italian males flirted, but he never made jokes about reaching the woman's heart. What was it about Beth that brought that out in the savvy restaurateur?

She'd said she wasn't into weddings, but even Vito saw the difference between her and the women Ethan usually dated.

"I go to order you dinner . . . you leave it up to me, no?"

The man had never made such an offer before, but Ethan trusted him. "That's fine by me. Beth?"

Her lush lips curved in a sweet smile. "I'd be honored."

Vito nodded, his expression filled with pleasure, and then turned to leave. A moment later, a waiter appeared with a carafe of red wine, which he poured before leaving them in solitude once again.

"Vito is a character."

"You bring out a different side to him."

"You mean he doesn't call all your women beautiful and promise them a dinner worthy of angels?"

"Now that you mention it . . ."

She laughed. "That's what I thought."

"But he has never offered to help me get to a woman's heart . . . or to select my dinner for me."

"He's probably wondering what in the world you are doing here with a woman like me."

She'd missed the point entirely, but he wasn't going to belabor it. "What do you mean, a woman like you?" he asked instead.

Chapter 5

She rolled her eyes again. "Come on, Stud, admit it. I'm not exactly your usual date."

He'd gotten the nickname at the agency long before Beth had come and it had never bothered him before. There was something about the way that she said it that made him feel as if she was mocking him though. The moniker *Stud* simply did not sound like a compliment when it rolled off of her acerbic little tongue.

"You're an unusual woman, period."

"I don't think so."

The waiter arrived again with a basket of fresh bread and the salad, then disappeared again just as quickly.

Ethan served her and then himself from the large bowl. "You're wrong, Sunshine. You are different than most women in this town and yet you were born and raised here."

Her eyes narrowed. "What do you mean?"

"You're fresh and sweet, and a man can't help wondering how you maintained such an aura of innocence in a city so filled with anything but."

"Are you saying I lack city sophistication?"

He looked her over, letting his gaze linger extra seconds on the parts his body craved to touch. Her little black dress was perfect and the last word in sophistication, not to mention

sexy as hell. The way she'd styled her hair was both tantalizing and chic . . . her makeup was neither too gaudy nor under-
done. Nothing about the individual elements lacked the polish
he would expect of her mother's daughter, but Beth still managed to project an innocence that challenged the predator in
him to teach her the depths of her own passion.

"No. You don't lack anything, but you don't fit this city either. Not like your mom does."

"Or the women you actually date."

He shrugged, not sure what to say. It occurred to him that
another woman might be justifiably offended by his comments, but Beth was only looking at him with curious specu-
lation.

She sighed. "If you want the truth, I've never felt like I fit.
Not my family. Not this city. Not any of it."

"So, why do you stay?"

"I love my parents even if I don't always get them and vice
versa. Besides, D.C. is all I know. I've thought of moving . . .
I just wonder if I'd fit in any better someplace else."

"So, why take a job with the agency?"

"There were a lot of reasons. It was time to make some
changes and that felt like the right one. I was also bored out
of my mind doing investment counseling."

"You got a degree in finance."

"And didn't realize until too late how much making money
bored me. I love what I do for the agency . . . the way I get to
be involved in so many different things and people's lives."
She buttered a piece of warm bread and put it on his plate.

"Thanks." He took a bite, his hunger warring with his need
to know more about this surprisingly enigmatic woman. "But
you don't live the adventure yourself."

"Until now."

But that hadn't been her idea and he was sure she would
have refused if she could see another way around the problem. "What are you afraid of?"

"Who said I was afraid of anything?" She ate a bite of

salad, her eyes closing in apparent bliss. She moaned. "This is good. The dressing is perfect."

"Everything here is perfect."

Her eyes opened and she smiled. "Good. I'm starving."

He was, too, but the food was not as alluring as the woman sitting across from him. Or her secrets. "You like touching the pulse of a project, but you've never wanted to be out there where the blood is really pounding. I'm wondering what about life scares you so much you don't want to live it."

Her brow furrowed. "I never said I didn't."

"You read about what you want to do sexually. You don't do it." She hadn't confirmed that, but he was almost positive it was the case. "You hide sexy lingerie beneath conservative business attire," he said, taking another guess.

Her hand stilled with a forkful of salad halfway to her mouth. "You said you hadn't gone through my drawers."

"I haven't . . . yet. I saw the top of your stockings when you got into the car."

"Oh." Her Madonna-like features blushed. "Conservative attire is appropriate for the office."

"Maybe . . . but the more I think about it, the more I realize you hide your natural sensuality."

"So, now you're a mind reader and a pop psychologist?"

"No, just a man who knows a lot about women."

"Now that I believe, but you don't know as much about this one as you think you do."

"I'm going to remedy that."

"So you say."

"It's necessary. For the case."

"What a convenient excuse to sate your overactive curiosity."

"Isn't it?"

She ignored that and tucked into her salad.

He let her eat in peace until she finished it and then said, "I still think you're afraid to live."

"Are you goading me for a reason?"

Was he? He guessed he was. He wanted to push her past her control and get to the real woman under the put-together, sunny exterior. "You don't date agents . . ."

"That merely shows my intelligence, not some deep-seated fear of really living."

"Why, Beth? What is so smart about refusing to date men who fascinate you?"

"You think agents fascinate me? Brother, you are so wrong."

"I don't think so."

Her dark eyes snapped with irritation. "Stop being a prick."

"Whoa . . . that's a pretty strong reaction for what is essentially a harmless conversation. I must have struck a nerve." And that interested him. A lot.

"Why don't we dissect you and see how much you like it?"

"Go ahead, Beth. What you see is what you get." He put his palms out in an open gesture. "I left my family behind in Texas when I realized I wanted more from life than I could find following in my daddy's footsteps as a cattleman. So, I left that for my sister and both she and Daddy are happier for it. I like to test my limits with extreme sports and my job, which makes me a little more primitive than your average Washington politician, but that's not something I'm ashamed of. I'm nowhere near ready to settle down, no matter what my mama might like, and I have very few sexual inhibitions."

He didn't know why he added that last bit—like a challenge—except he couldn't get the image of those hot-pink handcuffs out of his head.

"Which is exactly why I don't date agents."

"Because of the lack of sexual inhibitions? I'd say that would be a benefit considering your leanings in that direction."

"Because agents aren't good long-term relationship material."

"You said you weren't interested in getting married." And he'd about convinced himself to believe her because doing so would mean he could go after those pretty pink handcuffs with a clear conscience.

After the assignment.

If he made it that long.

"I'm not, but things happen. If you date a man, you can fall in love with him and end up married to him against your better judgment. My mother once told me never to date a man I wouldn't want to end up married to."

"That doesn't sound like your mother. She seems like the type that would encourage dating whoever got you the connections most beneficial to her."

"She's not that much of a barracuda. Now if it were my Aunt Connie . . ."

"Your mom's sister who is an actual politician, not someone who likes to play behind the scenes like your mom?"

"That's the one. She makes my mom seem positively June Cleaver maternal by comparison."

"So, your mom told you not to date agents," he said, going back to the topic that interested him.

"She told me not to date a man I wouldn't want to end up married to, and agents make lousy family men."

Considering the fact her dad had been one, that said a lot about how Beth felt about him as a parent. "You don't think agents should get married? At all? That's pretty extreme, don't you think?"

"I didn't say that. You're really into twisting my words tonight. I merely said that agents make lousy family men and that I have no desire to end up married to one. Ever."

"It's a good thing for you your mom didn't feel the same way, isn't it."

"I don't know. Is it?"

"Your dad is a good man."

"Yes, he is. I'm very proud of what he's accomplished with his life, but it came at a price." She sighed, her expression not so much sad as determined. "He wasn't the only one who paid it either. I know what it's like to grow up with a very absentee father. Lots of kids do, but that doesn't make it any easier to live with when you are one of them.

"Dad didn't settle for a desk job until I was in my teens. By that time, Mother had developed a whole life independent of his. So had I. That works for them, but it's not what I want for myself or for any children I might have. I'm not sure that what I *do* want is anything more than a pipe dream, but I'm not settling for something less. Which is why weddings and marriage are not high on my list of interesting conversational topics."

It was a hint to let the subject drop, but he didn't want to. He didn't want to settle down right now either, but someday he had every intention of getting married. Maybe even having kids. Family was a good thing. He was just too busy enjoying the single life at the moment to have one. But she sounded like she really never planned to go that route, and something told him that would be a real waste.

She was warm and sweet . . . the kind of woman that would thrive in a family like the one he'd grown up in.

"Okay, so your dad missed a few school plays, but think of all the good he did."

She laughed, her expression almost pitying. "It was a lot more than a few school plays and someone else could have done what he did in the field."

"He was a damn good agent."

"Yes, he was . . . but he wasn't the only agent, not even the only really good agent. And who is to say that him moving to a desk job earlier wouldn't have done the agency more good?"

"But he wouldn't have been happy." Didn't she see that?

"I know. But his happiness came at the cost of mine. I can understand that as an adult . . . that he had to do what he felt was right, but I can never condone subjecting any child of mine to a similar situation. It hurts too much. I didn't understand why he had to do what he did when I was little. All I knew was that my dad didn't love me enough to be there for me when I needed him. I love him, but I'll never allow a child of mine to go to sleep at night wondering what is wrong with her that she's so unimportant to her dad he's missed her birthday *again*, or her first date, or her high school graduation."

He opened his mouth to speak and then shut it again. He didn't know what that was like. Sure, things had come up when he was a kid that made his parents have to miss something here or there, but never one of his birthdays . . . or his graduation. It would be too easy for him to say it wouldn't have mattered, but he didn't know because he'd never had to face that.

"It sounds to me like you know exactly what you want—"

"Or don't want."

"Or don't want. You're definitely strong enough to turn down a guy if he wasn't offering you the kind of lifestyle commitment you're looking for."

"You'd think so, wouldn't you? Maybe I am now . . . but I wasn't always."

"What do you mean?"

"Just that I've made mistakes in the past I have no intention of repeating."

"You've never been married."

She winced. "No, I haven't."

Did she have any idea how her half answers were driving him nuts. The more he learned about her, the more he wanted to know until it was a burning thing inside him.

That was just his curiosity. Nothing special, but he hadn't been intrigued by something outside his job like this for a long time. Not since wanting to find out who had killed the uncle who had lived estranged from his family for decades.

He'd had to learn that info secondhand . . . another man had discovered the identity of the killer. But this time, Ethan was going to be the one to discover what made Beth tick.

"So, you'd be safe dating agents."

"And if I fell in love?"

"Love?" He didn't deny its existence, but he'd never felt it. Not for a woman. Sometimes he wondered if he just wasn't the type of man to fall in love.

"Yes, you know that pesky emotion that causes people to do lots of stuff they swear they'd never do."

"I don't see you letting it rule you."

"Don't you?"

"You're too stubborn."

"Stubborn . . . what kind of talk is this? You are supposed to be telling this one of her beauty . . . *ai, ai, ai* . . . you leave the talk of stubborn for after the marriage." Vito was shaking his head and staring at Ethan in horror.

Beth grinned. "You tell him, Vito. Besides, I'm not stubborn. I don't know where he gets the idea that I am." She batted her long dark lashes at him and the old Italian beamed, eating up this flirtatious side to the quiet little admin.

Who damn well *was* stubborn. Very. His mama would love her. So would his sister. His daddy would say to steer clear unless he wanted to end up roped and hog-tied. He frowned. Not bad advice.

"Now you glare at her? This sweet thing. What could she have done?"

"Nothing. Honest." Beth smiled coquettishly. "He's a little upset because I think he's a poor prospect for a long-term relationship like marriage. He thinks jumping out of airplanes and forgetting to pull the rip cord on his parachute until the last minute is entertainment. I have my own ideas about how to pass the time."

She said it so suggestively Ethan almost choked on his wine. This vixen was not the shy, but stubborn little secretary he was used to dealing with.

Vito was shaking his head again. "There is nothing romantic about jumping out of an airplane, but he did bring you here for dinner."

"That's true," Beth mused provocatively. "I suppose I'll have to give him marks for some level of romanticism."

"That is good, no?" Vito placed their dinners on the table before leaving to greet another obviously well-known customer at the door.

"I can be as romantic as the next man, but this is not a real date, or had you forgotten?"

"My memory is just fine, thanks."

"Then what was all that stuff you spouted at Vito? I never said I wanted to marry you." He realized how ridiculous he sounded only when the words were out of his mouth.

He was coming off like a defensive kid who was not confident of his ability with women so had to tell her what a great guy he was.

She laughed, the sound warm and filled with amusement. At his expense. "Would you prefer I told him that our get-to-know-you session for the sake of the case was getting too intense?"

"Of course not."

"He thinks we're on a date, so I acted like I was on a date."

"Then I pity the poor man you actually deign to allow yourself to go out with."

"Do you?"

Hell no. He envied him . . . the date and the pink handcuffs.

He was envying a lot more later that evening as he poked through Beth's closet and drawers. Okay, so he'd guessed she wore sexy undergarments, but damn . . . he hadn't expected anything this hot. She had lacy thongs and see-through bikini briefs and bras that were nothing more than a couple of bits of silk. The demibras killed him. He'd picked one up and his hand had actually shaken.

He had a real thing for that particular piece of lingerie . . . the way it held a woman's breasts up and left the nipples bare, as if they were waiting to be touched and played with. He couldn't help wondering what kind of breasts she had. Were they perky? Or a little heavy? Cone shaped or round? Did she have big nipples or small ones . . . dark or light?

Her skin was pale, but her hair and eyes were dark . . . it could go either way. Did she like having her breasts and her nipples touched, suckled . . . bitten? He was aching to find out.

Her clothes were a revelation, too. He'd seen the office gear she wore to work, but she had a rack of filmy, feminine dresses that made his mouth water. Thinking of her in them, worn over some of the more risqué lingerie, sent another surge of blood rushing to his groin. It was all he could do to stifle a groan of pure male hunger.

He'd never done this before, going through a woman's closet. He'd sure as heck never considered doing so could be such a turn-on, but picturing Beth in the clothes—or partway out of them—was making his dick hard as a rock and his brain short-circuit.

"Are you about done?"

He didn't have to look at her to know what he'd see. She'd taken off her heels but left her stockings on and was sitting on the edge of her bed. One leg swung gently while she had the other lifted so she could lean her head on her knee. Dark brown eyes watched him with mysterious thoughts that he'd give his spot on the next bungee jump for.

Despite the fact that her skirt was short and her leg was lifted, nothing showed. She'd made sure of that with a quick tug on the hem of her flowy skirt, but if she moved just a little bit, he would be able to see her panties. He was killing himself wondering what type she was wearing and how much else he would be able to see. If she moved her leg just a half an inch to the side.

Had she done so already? That was another thought that was tormenting him.

He turned to face her, to see. He made no effort to hide his erection. If she was looking below the waist, she was going to see the effect going through her closet and dresser had had on him.

But her doe-brown eyes were trained on his face and he wasn't sure if he felt relieved or disappointed by that fact.

"Yeah . . . I'm done. In here. I'd like to look over the rest of your apartment some more."

"Okay."

"Tomorrow night you can come to my place for dinner and do your own reconnaissance."

She bit her lip and damn if he didn't want to help her out with that little habit. "Do you really think that's necessary?"

"Yes."

She sighed . . . and shifted. And he got his wish. She was wearing black panties. Not a thong. They were sheer, but not at the crotch. There was a small dark splotch right in the center. She was wet. So wet that she'd soaked through her panties. His knees nearly buckled. His dick had been hard. Now it throbbed. He was not going to make it out of the apartment without at least kissing her.

But what he really wanted was to bury his face in that little bit of silk and take in her scent and her taste until he was drowning in both.

She gasped and he realized she'd just become aware of where he was looking.

She didn't move though. Or say anything.

"You're wet," he ground out.

"You're hard."

"I wondered if you'd notice."

"It would be impossible to miss."

Primitive male pride filled him. He was no monster, but he was big enough. And from the tone of her voice, she liked that . . . and was a little awed by it. Good. *He* liked *that.*

Their gazes met . . . locked.

"I would have expected you to be more sophisticated in your tastes." She was probably trying to sound caustic, but her voice was too breathy for that.

He smiled. "What do you mean?"

She licked her lips. Nervous . . . or excited? "I've never seen you as the type of man to get his jollies from looking at a woman's underwear."

"I didn't get my jollies, I got a hard-on, and it wasn't the little bits of fabric you call underwear that turned me on. It was the image of you in them."

"Oh." Her leg moved a little more and her skirt slipped, showing her stocking top, the smooth, pale skin of her thigh, and the dark curls of her mound through the sheer fabric of her panties.

He inhaled deeply, the scent of her arousal turning his up another notch. "What about you?"

"I haven't seen your underwear," she whispered.

And that added to his excitement. Hell . . . everything about her did that. "Want to?"

"Yes . . . no . . . this is a bad idea."

He didn't agree. He undid his pants and slid them down his thighs. His cock sprang free. The air brushed against him like a caress. It felt good, but not as good as she would feel.

This time she moaned . . . a tiny sound that nearly obliterated his control. "You aren't wearing any."

"I like commando."

"I can see that."

"Now, tell me why you're so wet you've soaked your panties."

"It's not a new thing around you," she admitted with a choked laugh.

They were looking into each other's eyes again and hers were glistening with need.

"You fantasize about me?"

"Yes."

"A lot?"

She blushed. "Yes."

"And the pink handcuffs."

The blush spread down her throat to cover the tops of her breasts revealed by her neckline. "Yes."

Hot damn. "I'm not looking for a long-term commitment right now."

He just could not get the image of her and orange blossoms out of his head. Most women he dated didn't need it spelled out for them, but she was special and he owed her honesty.

She didn't look hurt . . . or bothered even. "I'd never want that with you."

For some reason, despite his arousal and his brain telling him that was exactly the way he wanted it, her response made him mad. But he had enough intelligence not to tell her so. It was just his ego taking a hit and he wasn't going to let that get in the way, not of an attraction this strong.

"Do you want me?" he asked.

"You can see the effect you have on me."

"Wanting is more than a physical reaction, Sunshine. I need to know if your brain wants this too, because if it doesn't, I need to tuck my hard-on back in my pants and get out of here. Fast."

She was silent. A long time. Too long.

He might have pushed another woman, but probably not and definitely not her. He'd learned long ago that both the sex and the aftermath were better when a woman was absolutely sure of what she wanted. It was agony, but he started the painful process of tucking himself back into his slacks. His body protested, but his brain told him this was the right thing to do. He had few relationship rules, but this one was firm.

Her eyes widened. "I didn't say no."

He couldn't quite manage a smile, not when his cock was so hard it felt like it was going to shatter. "You were taking too long to say yes. If it's that hard to decide, you aren't ready for what I want from you."

She blinked in confusion. "Sex."

"Mind-blowing sex."

She stood up, her face flushed, her bottom lip caught in her teeth again. "I'm sorry," she whispered. "I thought I wanted it. . . . I *do* want it, it's just . . ."

"It's okay, baby."

"I teased you," she said in an agonized voice.

"I liked it."

"But I'm not ready to follow through," she admitted. "I don't know if I ever will be."

He had more confidence, but he knew she'd have to deal with whatever was holding her back.

"It's okay."

"It is?"

"Yes." She looked unhappy with his agreement, like it bothered her.

She should be grateful. A lot of men wouldn't have been as understanding, but he wasn't a kid. And he liked her. He wasn't pushing her into a sexual relationship she wasn't ready for. The things he wanted to do with and to her required a lack of inhibition that wasn't going to come if she was doubting the rightness of letting him touch her.

He crossed the room and brushed his thumb over her lip, disengaging it from her teeth. "If you don't stop doing that, you're going to end up bruised . . . or bleeding."

She looked up at him, the sensual longing in her eyes so strong he had to exert iron control to keep from stripping her naked and showing her how much she really did want him.

He kissed her, softly—almost chastely—on her lips, but his tongue took an irresistible swipe of her taste before he pulled away. "I'll see you tomorrow."

She nodded, following him silently to the door.

He stopped there. "Remember, dinner at my place. Right after work."

"I'll have to come home and feed the kittens first."

She was sugar sweet and that was another thing that was different from the women he usually dated. He liked it. "Okay, make it six-thirty."

"I'll be there." She didn't sound sure, but on this . . . he didn't have the luxury of waiting or being understanding.

She needed to come to his home and get an idea of who he was outside the office. "Take a taxi. I'll drive you home."

"Okay."

He almost told her to bring the pink handcuffs, but he wasn't into self-torture.

Chapter 6

Idiot. Imbecile. Ninny. Blockhead. Dimwit. Dope. Dumbbell. Dummy. Nitwit. Numskull. Pinhead. Birdbrain. How many words for stupid were there? Not enough.

Beth rolled in her bed, the silk sheets mocking her with their sensual feel, her body tense with unspent passion. She'd had the man who embodied her most intense fantasies in her bedroom . . . his hard penis jutting from his body in desire for her, and she'd sent him away. Okay, so she didn't want to get involved with him, not long term . . . but was she nuts?

He'd accused her at dinner of being afraid to live. He said she was a dreamer, not a doer. Or something close enough to it. Was he right? She thought maybe he was. What other explanation did she have for not jumping at the chance to make wild passionate love with him?

Well maybe it would be sex and not love, but wasn't that better than always dreaming and never doing? He'd asked why she'd never left D.C. since she felt like she didn't fit in here. The true answer was that she was afraid to try to make a life for herself somewhere else. But why? What could be worse than knowing her own parents thought she was an alien? Or as good as.

She could get a job somewhere else . . . live somewhere else. But she was afraid. Afraid to live in any real sense.

Why?

She couldn't think straight enough to answer her own inner demand. Her body was screaming with sexual hunger left unsatisfied. It was not a good feeling.

She looked at the clock and blinked, but the numbers stayed the same. It was nearly two A.M. and she was too excited to sleep. She could touch herself—would probably end up doing so—but right now she was so mad at herself for being such a wuss, she wouldn't give herself the relief.

Her eyes filmed with tears. It hurt to disappoint yourself.

The phone rang and she lurched up in bed to check the caller ID. Middle of the night calls usually meant trouble. Had something happened with her mom or dad? The digital readout on the back of the phone read *Crane, E.* It was Ethan!

She snatched it up on the second ring. "Hello?"

"You awake?" he asked in that low rumble she found so sexy.

"If I wasn't, I am now."

"Were you?" he pressed, giving her no out with flippancy.

She sighed. "Yes."

"Me, too."

"Why?"

"I got hot and bothered over a very sexy woman with surprisingly kinky tendencies and I can't get the image of her pretty little panties out of my brain."

"I'm sorry."

"I'm not."

"Oh . . . I'm not wearing any panties now." Somehow, she didn't think that would help the situation, but the words had just slipped out.

He groaned and she smiled, in spite of herself.

"I'm not wearing anything," he said in a dark voice that made her shiver.

"Um . . . " She swallowed. "Me either. Well, except a gold silk sheet." She hated any kind of restriction when she slept.

"You're killing me here, baby."

"I don't mean to."

"I know . . . you're just having a hard time deciding what you want."

"I know what I want."

"You didn't when I left your apartment."

"I wanted you then, but I was afraid."

"Of what?"

"Living." She sighed. "I guess you were right. I am more of a dreamer than a doer."

"What scares you so much about living?"

That was easy. "Getting hurt."

"Pain reminds us that we are alive."

"I suppose."

"It's also a good reminder not to take the times of pleasure for granted."

A man who practiced extreme sports in his free time and whose job routinely put his life on the line would think like that.

"I spent a lot of my childhood daydreaming. It was more fun than dwelling on real life." It had hurt less, too. "I guess I never got out of the habit."

"What did you fantasize about?"

"Having two parents who loved me, having a real family."

"Your parents do love you, Sunshine."

"Yes, but when I was little, I wasn't convinced of it."

"I'm sorry."

"I don't want pity, Ethan. They never abused me, or set out to hurt me."

"But they did hurt you, and now you find it easier to expect nothing from life but your fantasies."

He was right, but she'd admitted that once tonight. She wasn't going to say so again. Besides, he might not realize it, but for a woman who had prided herself on her honesty, realizing she'd lived most of her life in a dream world wasn't a happy thing.

"I tried once to live the dream, but it exploded in my

face." She wasn't sure if she was defending herself to herself or to him.

"What dream?"

"The get-married-and-have-a-real-family one."

"What happened?"

"He stood me up at the altar."

Ethan said a very bad word.

She winced . . . but not from his curse. She hadn't intended to tell him about her aborted engagement. In fact, she'd been firm in her desire to keep it all in the past where it belonged, but apparently late-night phone conversations weren't good for her resolve. Her room was dark around her. No one was there but her and the kittens sleeping in their cushy little bed on the other side of the room. The phone tucked next to her ear felt more like part of a dream than a reality . . . and therefore safe.

"I didn't date a lot in college," she admitted, not sure why the words were still spilling out. "I was shy."

"Afraid."

"That, too."

"How did you meet him?"

"I was the investment counselor assigned to his stock port-folio. I didn't find out he was an agent until we were on our fifth date. By then, I liked him. A lot. I didn't want to stop dating. He'd told me he worked for the government like half of D.C. and I even understood why he waited to tell me he was an agent. The fact he trusted me with the information that early made me feel special. We fell in love. Or I thought we did. But I don't think you can stand up your bride at the altar if you really love her. Do you?"

"Why did he stand you up?" Ethan asked instead of an-swering.

"He was on an assignment. He wasn't supposed to be, but a former case reopened and his role was key. He thought he'd be done before the wedding, but he didn't get back into the country until three days after. He didn't call either . . . he just didn't show up."

"Maybe he couldn't call."

"That's what he said, but it doesn't matter, does it? If our upcoming marriage had really mattered to him, he would have found a way."

"Maybe . . ."

She knew the maybes and she even understood them, but they didn't change anything. "It doesn't matter. Being stood up at the altar made me realize our relationship was never going to go where I needed it to."

"You gave up the dream because it wasn't perfect."

The tears that had filled her eyes spilled over, but she concentrated on keeping them from her voice. "You could put it that way but, Ethan . . . do you know what it's like to wonder if you matter at all to the people who are supposed to love you? I really didn't want that for any children I might have. I didn't want it for me any longer."

She hadn't been strong enough and she had to face that, not that it would change anything.

"Are you okay, Beth?"

"I'm fine."

"You sound like you're crying."

She took a deep breath and got her feelings under control before talking again. "I'm fine. Really. Just tired."

"And horny."

She laughed, the sound choked. "That, too."

"Between your ex-fiancé and your dad, they convinced you that agents make lousy long-term partners, didn't they?"

"I was convinced of it before Alan and I met, but I took a chance." Not that she'd had much choice. By the time she'd learned he was an agent, she was already on the way to being head over heels in love with him. Her mom's advice had been sound, but she'd had no opportunity in that relationship to apply it. "It didn't play out like I'd hoped."

"*Alan Hyatt is the man you almost married?*" Ethan demanded in a voice that was a cross between a growl and shouting.

His inexplicable anger traveled across the phone lines, perversely increasing her excitement. Was there something wrong with her that his darker emotions sparked sexual need in her? She wanted to tame the savage beast . . . with her body.

Talk about kinky.

"Yes, now you know what we share in our past." At least Ethan's curiosity should be satisfied. "I think that's why my dad hired him and didn't tell me beforehand. I'm just guessing, but I have a feeling Dad was hoping seeing Alan again would spark dormant feelings in me."

"Did it?" Definitely a growl.

Wow. "Do you think I would have flashed you with my panties tonight if it had?" she asked softly.

"Maybe."

"I'm not like that."

"So, you have no feelings for him."

"None."

"You're sure?"

"Yes."

"How many lovers have there been since him?"

"This is getting personal."

"It crossed that line when I dropped my pants and showed you my raging hard-on."

She gasped.

A dark chuckle sent tremors rippling through some very interesting places in her body.

"So, how many?"

"None."

"Why?"

"It was easier and safer to daydream." And she'd only wanted one man since her broken engagement. Ethan. Definitely safer to daydream about him.

But was safe all it was cracked up to be?

"What about before him?"

"What is this? Are you trying to decide if I have enough experience to be an eligible partner for the Stud?"

"No, I'm trying to get to know you better, baby. Now answer the question."

"How come your version of getting to know me has so much to do with sex?"

"What do you mean?"

"You went through my panties drawer."

"And your shoe rack . . . and your bookshelf."

Point taken. Maybe she was the one with sex on the brain. "I was a virgin before I met Alan."

"Isn't that a little archaic?"

"I don't know. It was right for me. I told you I didn't date much."

"So, you want to wait until you have another very committed relationship before having sex again?"

That had been her plan, but now she thought it could stand to be improved upon. After all, she was starting to doubt that a long-term very committed relationship was ever going to happen.

She took the plunge. "No. I want to have sex with you."

"And you don't want a commitment with me. Because I'm an agent."

"Even if you were an insurance adjuster, I think you'd scare me, Ethan. You're not the kind of guy who could stay with the same woman very long. Especially one like me."

"There's a first time for everything."

It was a throw-away remark and she refused to take it as anything else. She knew Ethan agreed with her. He'd already said he didn't want to get into a long-term relationship, but he did want her. He'd called her in the middle of the night because he couldn't sleep for wanting her.

Maybe she would get a chance to make those fantasies come true after all. This time, she wasn't looking for the perfect rendition of her dream either. She wasn't going to let the limits of their relationship hurt. Because she wasn't going to fall in love with him. She wasn't that stupid.

"I want you, Ethan."

"No doubts?"

"None." Well, mostly none. None that she was going to

share with him. None that were going to get in the way of her actually living, not just thinking about it, for a change.

"Damn, baby . . . we both have to work tomorrow, but it might be worth coming over. We could call in sick tomorrow."

"I can't. Neither can you. I've got to get things ready for when I'm gone and you've got a case to work on." She wasn't just looking for excuses either. Things were happening so fast, she really could not afford to call in sick. She'd end up letting people down and she hated that.

"You're a heavy task master, Sunshine."

"I don't mean to be." She wished she could dismiss her responsibilities, just this once.

Because her body was throbbing with needs she'd never felt, even when she'd been at her most involved with Alan. She moved restlessly in the bed and wondered how much courage she had. She wasn't a scaredy-cat . . . she really wasn't. But she was a dreamer and it was past time she became a doer.

"We could . . ."

"Yeah?" One word said in that deep Texas drawl and she shuddered.

She wanted this. She hoped he would, too. "We could talk to each other . . . dirty . . . on the phone."

"Are you propositioning me for phone sex, little Beth?" He didn't sound amused. He sounded aroused. Hot. Like he definitely liked the idea.

And that gave her the courage to whisper, "Yes," into the phone.

He choked out another curse. "Put the phone on speaker mode and get comfortable, baby."

Speaker mode? The idea shocked her, but then she laughed at her own embarrassment. Who was going to hear? The kittens? She did as he said, sliding against the cool silk sheets until she was lying on her back, her breasts rising and falling with each rapid breath.

"Are you comfortable, sweetheart?"

"Yes. What about you?"

His answer was to laugh. "Oh, yeah."

"Are you touching yourself?" she dared to ask.

"My hand is wrapped around my cock and I'm pretending it's your fingers making me ache like this."

"Oh . . ." Her hands clenched and unclenched as she wished she were the one touching his big erection. "Rub it up and down."

He moaned. "I keep doing that and I'm not going to last long. You'd better make it even."

"Touch myself?"

"Yes. Now, Beth." His voice resonated with command.

He couldn't see her, but she felt like she was doing something horribly intimate right in front of him. She'd asked for this though, and she wasn't going to back out. She wanted this intimacy, even if it felt strange and a little scary.

Shaking from a combination of desire and nerves, she slid her hand between her thighs and lightly brushed her pubic hair. Pleasure arced through her feminine center. She moaned.

"You touching yourself, baby?" His voice sounded hoarse.

"Yes."

"Where?"

He wanted specifics? "My hair . . . down there."

"Not your lips yet?"

"No." But she could feel her wetness on the short curls and knew she wouldn't last long before swirling a fingertip over her clitoris.

"Don't."

"Why not?"

"Because I told you not to."

While most of her fantasies had centered around him tied to her bed at her mercy, this dominance game excited her so much she could barely breathe. "What if I want to?"

"Do you? Are you hungry to slide one little finger between your swollen folds and check to see how wet you are? That's what I'd do right now if I was there. Then I'd taste it."

She gasped.

He laughed. Oh, gosh . . . how did a man's laugh carry such dark and sexy overtones?

"I'm not tasting myself."

"We'll leave that for a time when I can watch."

She wasn't sure about that, but she was too excited to argue. "What now?" she asked, giving him unspoken permission to be in charge. For now.

"I want you to touch your breasts so I can picture you doing it. And tell me what you are doing every single step of the way."

Heat surged between her legs as she complied. "I'm sliding both my hands up my body . . . slowly," she dared to tease and was rewarded by a masculine sound of approval. "Now, I'm cupping myself and squeezing. It feels good."

"Are you fantasizing it's my hands touching you?"

"Yes." She sighed out a moan. "But your hands are bigger."

"Yes, they are. And stronger . . . though I would never use that strength to hurt."

"I know." She kneaded her breasts, finding the stimulation twice as erotic because she knew he was thinking of her doing it.

"You have beautiful, soft breasts." His drawl was so enticing, hearing it was almost enough to make her climax. "But I've only seen them through clothes. Tell me what they look like."

"You want me to describe my breasts?"

"Yes." Absolutely certain. No hesitation. "Do it, baby."

She thought back to what she saw when she looked in the mirror after a shower. "They're round and the nipples tilt up, not straight out."

"More."

What more could she say? "They're breasts, Ethan. I don't have any distinguishing marks. No freckles, or anything."

"What color are your nipples?"

"Uh . . . brownish pink. They're dark."

"Are they that color right now?"

"I don't know. I don't have a light on."

"You're lying in the dark, talking to me on the phone and touching yourself?"

"Yes."

"I like knowing that."

"Do you have a light on?"

"No. I want to picture you, nothing else."

"Oh." Wow.

"Do they turn red when you get excited?"

"My nipples?"

"Yes."

She tried to think back to a time when she might have noticed and remembered something Alan had said once when they were making love. Something about how he knew she was getting close because her nipples were red like ripe raspberries. "Yes, they turn red like ripe berries."

"I bet they taste just as sweet."

"You're going to find out . . . tomorrow night." It was the first sexual promise she'd ever made.

Even when she'd been with Alan, she'd kept so much of her sensuality locked up. She'd been afraid to let him know her deepest desires and that somehow if she expressed too much of her desire, they would come popping out. With Ethan, she didn't care. Maybe because he'd played a starring role in those fantasies for so long.

And he already knew about the handcuffs.

"I can't wait, baby."

"You have to."

He laughed, the sound harsh. "You like to tease, don't you?"

"I think I do."

"I know it."

"I'm teasing myself right now." The way she was stimulating her breasts and nipples was increasing her excitement to the point where she could barely breathe. She needed more.

"Good. Are your nipples hard?"

"Very."

"And swollen?"

She rolled them between her thumbs and forefingers. Definitely engorged. "Yesss . . ."

"Do they hurt?"

"Do you want them to?"

"Only in a good way."

"What good way?"

"I want you to be in pain for my touch."

"I am."

"Damn . . . Beth . . . you slay me." His words came out between gasping breaths.

She wasn't the only one who needed more.

"Would your breasts fill my hands?"

"I don't think so . . . I'm only a C cup."

"And I have long fingers."

"Yes." Fingers she couldn't wait to have on her body.

"I can't wait to play . . ." His words trailed off in a masculine groan. "Don't stop, baby. Tell me what else you're doing. What you like."

She squeezed her thighs together and released in an instinctive rhythm that increased her desire, but could not sate it. "I'm kneading them . . . kind of hard now. I like it gentle at first and hard later."

The only sound on the other end of the line was his heavy breathing. It excited her to think she was affecting him so strongly.

"I'm brushing circles around my nipples now, but I'm not touching myself there anymore. I'm teasing myself, but I want it . . ." She moaned as she allowed one fingertip to brush across a turgid nipple. "They're hard and achy . . . they've been that way all night because of you."

"You're killing me." He sounded tortured all right.

It was one of her favorite fantasies.

She smiled. "I'm pinching my nipples now. Hard. And

playing with them . . . it feels so good. I wish you were here to suck on them. I'd want you to use your teeth."

"Not at first," he said in a charged voice. "At first you'd want that gentle, too, but the more excited you got the more you'd want me to do it hard and with my teeth."

"Yessss," she hissed again.

"Put one hand between your legs, baby. Touch your labia and your clitoris. Feel the silky wetness I'm craving right now."

"Are you sure you want me to?"

"Yes. Do it, Beth. I'm not going to last and I want to come together."

"You're a bossy lover."

"I can be."

"So can I." At least she wanted to. "Squeeze the base of your penis."

"It's not going to help."

"Do it anyway."

He growled. "Fine. I'm squeezing. Now, what about you? Are you touching yourself like I told you to?"

She slid her hand down her stomach until her middle finger slipped between the slippery folds of her labia. It was hot and wetter than she could ever remember being. "Yes."

"Tell me what it feels like."

She circled her clitoris, then rubbed lightly and moaned. "It's so soft . . . like satin, but hot and very wet. My lips are swollen . . . my clit feels hard, but it's not big."

She'd read about women who protruded, but she wasn't one of them . . . even at her most excited.

"You're delicate."

"If you say so." She could barely think. Couldn't really make sense of words at the moment. She was so close.

"Can you make yourself come without putting a finger inside?"

"Yes . . . but . . ."

"I want you to do that . . . I want you to feel empty and waiting for me to fill you up tomorrow night."

"Oh . . . Ethan . . . I want that, too."

"Good."

She found a rhythm she liked with her fingers. It was hard not to dip lower, but she loved that he'd told her not to. It added an edge to everything . . . made it more real, as if he were there with her.

The only sound in the room was that of their combined breathing until she gasped, "Ethan . . . I'm going to . . ."

"Come for me, baby. Come now."

And she did, crying out his name and listening to his groan of release over the phone close to her ear on the pillow. He said her name softly, almost reverently, then moaned again . . . and then nothing. Just breathing and silence.

She didn't know how long they were like that, but finally he asked, "Are you there?"

"Yes." The word was slurred.

"You tired, baby?"

"Um . . . mmm . . ."

"Turn off the phone and go to sleep. I'll see you tomorrow."

"Good night, Ethan."

"Good night, Sunshine."

She pressed the button on the phone to turn it off and then turned on her side, curling into her usual sleeping position without worrying about putting it back on the cradle.

Chapter 7

Something was digging into Beth's side when the alarm woke her. She sat up, feeling strangely good, a smile of forgotten, but delicious dreams playing at the corners of her lips. She rubbed the sore spot on her side absently and then felt around the slick surface of her sheets, searching for the culprit.

Her hand closed over the cordless phone.

And everything came flooding back. Her sense of well-being vanished to be replaced with horror.

She'd had phone sex. With Ethan Crane. She grabbed the sheet to her chin as if he were going to walk into the room from the bathroom at any second. Which he couldn't, of course. He was home . . . in his own bed. Or his shower.

The image of that perfect body showering was enough to make the still sensitive flesh between her legs throb. This was ridiculous. Totally out of hand. She reacted to him and thoughts of him like he was a walking aphrodisiac, but he was just a man.

A man who had managed to talk her through the most amazing orgasm of her life. Had it been as good for him? Phone sex. She still could not quite grasp that she'd done that with Ethan. Nice women didn't do that kind of thing, did they? But then she'd long since decided her sexual fantasies were anything but nice. Which was one reason it was so much safer to dream than to do.

So, why hadn't she thought of that last night when she was flashing him? She couldn't even use the excuse she'd been tipsy, because she hadn't. She didn't need alcohol to be so affected by Ethan that her finely honed inhibitions went flying to parts unknown. She only needed him . . . or thoughts of him.

It had never been like this with Alan. Sex with him had been good, but not mind-blowing, knock-your-socks-off, out-of-this-world incredible. And that had only been teleintimacy.

What would it be like tonight, when he was actually touching her? When she could touch him. When she could taste him. Her mouth watered and she groaned at her reaction. This was so not good. It was too much. Was she really going to his apartment for dinner . . . and sex?

Originally, she was supposed to be doing her own investigation of who he was, what he liked, what his home life was like . . . reconnaissance. Only they'd turned the evening into so much more. Or was it?

Was Ethan's sexual interest in her connected to the case? He said the relationship had to look real to fool the adversary. He knew she wasn't an agent. Was he doing what needed to be done to make sure his case was not compromised, even in a twisted way . . . protecting her from her own lack of experience in playing a role?

She wished she could dismiss the idea as paranoid, but not only was he a great agent, he was beyond dedicated. He would do whatever he had to make sure he successfully executed a mission. She was absolutely sure it would not be the first time he'd manufactured a relationship for the sake of his cause. Her dad had done the same thing. That's how her parents had met.

They had fallen in love. Which some might say was a happy ending, but Beth had always wondered how her mom had felt about being pursued initially as a means to an end. She'd never asked and her mom had never offered. They didn't have that kind of cozy girl-chat-type relationship. But Beth knew that her mom had fallen in love with her dad and they had married, despite the fact her dad had not been the politician her mom had always thought she would marry.

Her mom had modified her dreams for her dad. Beth had never seen the opposite in action, but it could have happened. Who knew what plans her dad had treasured in his heart before he met and married a woman wed to the lifestyle in D.C.? As Vannie from TGP was fond of saying, that was their lookout.

But did Beth want to risk a similar scenario? What if she fell in love with Ethan? What then? Every fear she'd ever had about getting involved with an agent came flooding back. She'd be stuck in the very sort of relationship she'd spent so many years avoiding.

Just as painful a prospect, what if she fell in love and he didn't? Which was all too likely. He could walk away with his life and heart in tact while she was left to bleed and hurt again. She wanted it to be simply sex, but the chemistry between them was so strong. Intimacy with him was bound to engage her emotions. Deeply.

She knew some people saw lust as a purely physical reaction and maybe it was . . . for them. But there was a reason she'd only ever had one lover. Sexual desire went hand-in-hand with an emotional connection for her. And the way she'd felt last night—talking to Ethan and touching herself— had almost been spiritual. Which was really silly.

How could something as earthy as phone sex be that affecting? Maybe she was imbuing it with more than what it really was. Was it possible that because she'd always connected emotions with sex that she was doing so again now, but it would be possible not to? She was twenty-nine years old, not a starry-eyed teen. Surely she should be able to control her emotions while having wild-monkey sex with Ethan.

If she was going to make love with him, she would have to. Not to do so would be to court disaster of a magnitude that could outstrip her aborted wedding three years ago. One dose of that kind of humiliation and pain in a lifetime was enough.

And unlike Alan, who had wanted her for herself, Ethan's motives were murky at best.

The more she thought about it, the more certain she became that he was pursuing her sexually for the sake of the case. He'd never made an overture before and now all of a sudden, he wanted her naked. She couldn't be sure that the attraction was even for her. It wasn't that she doubted her sexual desirability, only his timing in discovering it.

He said he got a hard-on from going through her sexy lingerie, but he could have been fantasizing about someone else. He was a professional . . . he'd know how to do whatever it took to get the job done. Including how to project a façade of sexual desire when he was actually indifferent. He'd as much as said so the night before.

Certainly, she'd always perceived his reaction to her as more indifference than attraction. Why after two years was he suddenly breaking thermometers in his sexual pursuit of her? The most logical answer was that he was using it as a way to guarantee the viability of his case.

If the sexual need on his side was manufactured for the sake of the case . . . did she want it?

Would that make it better or worse for her? Would she be less likely to fall in love with someone who she knew was using their intimacy as a way to do his job better? Or would it matter? Love wasn't exactly a rational emotion, but she was a rational being. For the most part.

Could her own innate streak of emotional realism protect her from making the same mistake with Ethan that she had made with Alan? Did she even want to take the risk?

One of the kittens meowed and she jumped. It was time to get ready for the day and feed her furry friends. Only with the plaintive quality of the mewling coming from the kitchen, she'd better reverse the order of those actions.

She padded naked into the kitchen to put out their food,

her mind twisting with thoughts she could not tame into any semblance of order.

She was no closer to a sense of certainty by the time she sat down at her desk at work an hour later and started going through her e-mail.

"Good morning, Beth."

Her head shot up and she gave Alan a weak smile. "Good morning. How is your first case coming along?"

"Fine. It's more research than anything else. No sweat. You look peaked this morning. Stressed about your upcoming assignment?"

"A little." Which was the truth, if not all of it.

His hair gleamed almost blue-black under the fluorescent lights, his gray eyes narrowed under dark brows. "I was surprised your dad pushed you into it. Are you sure it's something you should be doing?"

She manufactured a smile, not sure at all, but unwilling to back out of a commitment she'd made. Keeping her promises was one of the things that Beth insisted on for her personal sense of honor. She'd had too many promises broken to her as a child, and then later, to ever dismiss her responsibilities for the sake of even roiling emotions.

"I'll be fine. It's not like I'm pretending to be something I'm not. Only something I used to be."

"What about the relationship with Ethan? That's pretense . . . isn't it?"

She opened her mouth, but nothing came out. She wasn't sure how to answer. Did the visual intimacy they had shared in her apartment and the wild encounter on the phone later constitute a relationship, or mistake?

"Not anymore." The words were Ethan's and his voice carried a warning note that made Alan's expression tighten and Beth's heart rate increase.

Her gaze jerked to Ethan, who had approached silently from his office. He was dressed in his signature dark jeans and a body-hugging, ribbed knit silk T-shirt. His blond hair was in its usual sexy style and his features did not show any of the ravages of lack of sleep. His eyes were filled with the warning his voice had implied as he met Alan's gaze.

Ethan must have come in early because he had not walked by her desk since she'd arrived. She'd been so caught up in her thoughts, she hadn't done her usual check to see whose computers were active when she arrived. She clicked a short-cut to a macro she'd created to do just that, while her mind grappled with his presence and what his words and attitude implied.

Alan's frown was more thoughtful than accusatory. "If that's true, you move fast."

Ethan shrugged and Beth felt a betraying blush climb up her skin. There was such a thing as keeping a private encounter private. He was from Texas . . . didn't they teach gentlemanly discretion down there?

Alan's eyes assessed Ethan and his expression turned forbidding. "Or is it that you move with necessity?" he asked in a tone that could have stripped paint.

"Not your business, old son."

Which was practically an agreement in her opinion. And an unnecessary one at that.

Alan faced Ethan head-on, his entire manner aggressive and borderline threatening. "Beth is a friend. I don't want to see her hurt."

"Don't worry . . . I have no plans to leave her standing at the altar," Ethan said with derision.

Alan flashed a look of surprise at Beth and then looked back at Ethan. "You do move fast, but you're smart enough to know that the past is going to make me more protective of her, not less."

Ethan shrugged in acknowledgment of a fact that Beth found highly suspect herself. What gave Alan the right to play her protector? He'd abrogated all rights in her life the day he left her standing alone to face three hundred wedding guests and try to explain the inexplicable, all the while wondering if her groom had been killed in the field.

"I am a grown woman and I can make my own decisions and fight my own battles when the need arises," Beth said acerbically. "I don't need, or want, a protector."

Alan's eyes filled with concern that grated. "Honey, you don't have experience with men like Ethan. You're twenty-nine, but you're still so damn innocent. He's not above creating a sexual relationship to give a sense of reality to your role in the case."

"I'm aware of that and I'm not that innocent." Especially after last night.

"I repeat, this is not your business," Ethan said to Alan, his drawl pure ice.

But she could not miss that he had not bothered to deny the accusation.

"Patently, I don't agree."

Beth stood up and leaned forward so she could speak low enough her voice would not carry down the hall to any interested listeners. "I don't really care what either of you think. You will stop talking about me and any potential relationship between myself and Ethan publicly *and as if I'm not even here* right this second."

They both looked at her like she was speaking in ancient tongues.

She could feel her facial muscles stiffen as her glare went sulfuric. "I mean it."

"After last night, our relationship is not a potential. It's a done deal," Ethan bit out, sounding offended.

"You know I care about you," Alan added, managing to inject injury into his voice.

She wondered which neck she'd rather wring first.

"Was a conference called that I'm unaware of?" her dad asked from behind Ethan as he walked up.

Beth turned her ire on him. As far as she was concerned, his actions had spawned the whole sorry mess. "No conference, just a couple of your agents stepping out of line. Care to rein them in?"

Both Alan and Ethan stiffened in affront, but her dad's

eyes glittered with a suspicious triumph. "Is that right? What are they stepping out of line about?"

"My private life." This time her frown was mostly for Ethan. "Some men have not learned to adhere to the adage of kiss and don't tell."

"I didn't say a word about kissing," Ethan drawled.

Beth had never had homicidal tendencies. She only knew how to shoot a gun because it had been required in her training. But right now, she could cheerfully have shot him . . . or at least threatened to.

"Face it, Sunshine," Ethan went on, obviously ignorant of his bodily peril. "Right now . . . I am your private life."

"And if I shoot you? What are you then?" she asked sweetly.

"Was she always this bloodthirsty?" Ethan asked Alan.

"I don't remember that particular trait, but it could have been latent." Alan shrugged. "Maybe you bring it out in her."

"Maybe you both do," she inserted.

"So, this is a bad time to ask if you'll have lunch with me today . . . for old time's sake," Alan said.

"She's having lunch with me." Ethan's voice dared Beth and/or Alan to argue.

Which she promptly did. "I don't remember agreeing to lunch and I certainly have no intention of doing so now."

"You're not eating lunch with Hyatt."

"I'm not?" she asked neutrally.

"She's not?" her dad asked, his voice laced with amusement that scored her nerves like nails on a chalkboard.

"She's not?" Alan asked, his own voice dangerously soft.

Ethan crossed his arms, his stance one of absolute purpose. "We need to discuss the case."

Beth took perverse and delighted pleasure in thwarting him. "I need to get the new admin as up to speed as I'm able and according to my e-mail, she's going to arrive any minute. I plan to spend the lunch hour with her."

Her dad had been busy and she'd thought again that he could have warned her he'd been prepared to act quickly. Apparently, he'd already screened applicants for the job and the new hire had accepted sometime yesterday.

"Another time," Alan said.

Ethan's eyes narrowed to green slits. "She'll be busy on the case."

"The case won't last forever," Alan replied, his voice laced with meaning—the implication being that the relationship would last only as long as the case.

"What you two had is over. Accept it."

Beth could not believe Ethan had just said that.

Neither could her father, if his expression was anything to go by. "She told you about their past?"

"Yes," Ethan replied shortly to Whit and then focused on Alan again. "You blew it. It's over. Forget about rekindling old flames because I'm here to put them out."

"For how long?"

"That's between Beth and me. Whatever you two had in the past has no bearing on the present."

"And if I'm not willing to accept that?"

"I don't plan to give you a choice in the matter."

Okay. That was it. She was dreaming. Men like Ethan did not have these kinds of discussions. He wasn't the type to kiss and tell. Which made his comments all the more jarring to her. Nor was he the type to announce his most recent liaison to the office staff. He was too suave . . . not some primitive Neanderthal who warned other men off what he considered his woman.

Definitely a dream. Because even primitive men didn't have this sort of discussion over her. Not Beth Whitney, who would have made an ideal small-town librarian in another life.

The dream had started yesterday morning when her dad practically ordered her to take an agent's role in a case. That just wasn't normal either. No . . . maybe it had started when Alan showed up in front of her desk and her dad said he was the new hire. Yes, she liked that scenario better. She nodded to herself. That's definitely when she'd started dreaming.

So, he wasn't here. Neither was Ethan. It was all just a really involved, really long dream. And she should wake up any second now to two hungry furballs and an apartment that had never been invaded by Ethan Crane.

"Are you okay, Sunshine?" the dream Ethan asked.

The dream Alan's brows furrowed. "She looks odd."

"*Elizabeth*." That was not a tone she liked hearing in her dreams and she frowned her disapproval.

She let her gaze slide to her dad. "I'm dreaming and I want you all to disappear right now. There are other ways I prefer to spend my fantasy time."

The dream office environment did not dissolve to make way for a more pleasant subconscious exercise in imagination.

And all three men now looked at her with varying levels of concern.

Until Ethan's face creased with a slow, knowing smile, his green eyes lit with wicked lights. "This isn't a dream, Sunshine. Neither was last night. You're no longer fantasizing your way through life. You are living it."

"Last night?" her father asked in an ominous voice, as if he'd just gotten the implication of all that Ethan had been saying.

Ethan shrugged. "We're working together, Whit. Don't get in the way."

"She's my daughter."

"And you assigned her to my case. Live with it."

The outer office door opened and Bennett Vincent walked in, an older woman following him. "I've brought down the new hire like you said to, boss."

The lines on the woman's face declared she was easily in her sixties, but her fiery orange hair and lively expression said she was far from retirement. She gave the men a once-over, sizing each one up with keen blue eyes before nodding briskly toward Beth. "I'm Maude and I hear I've got two days to learn my job before you go gallivanting. My favorite kind of challenge, but we'd better get to it, missy."

Maude had the voice of a drill sergeant and for some reason, that struck Beth as hilariously funny. She burst into laughter. If the sound was a bit hysterical, she could be forgiven. No way was this a dream because this woman had too much presence not to be real. Which meant everything else was real too. Darn.

She'd almost convinced herself otherwise.

Maude nodded approvingly, her head moving in a single bob of military precision. "I like to work with a woman who has a sense of humor."

Beth got her mirth under control and stuck her hand out, relieved her unrestrained humor had not offended her new assistant. "Beth Whitney. It's a pleasure to meet you. As you said, we've got a lot to do . . ."

She turned to the men standing around her desk. "If you will excuse us, gentlemen." Then without waiting to see if they took the hint, she dismissed them by turning toward Maude. "We'll start by familiarizing you with my setup. We'll train you on my computer system and then set you up with your own when I get back from my upcoming assignment."

"Sounds efficient."

And Beth got the distinct impression that to Maude, that was high praise. Beth launched into an explanation of her early morning routine to which the older woman listened to avidly. However, part of Beth was attuned and waiting for the men to leave. She didn't know when her dad and Alan left, but she could tell when Ethan did. The air around her stopped crackling.

"Well done," Maude said.

Beth looked up. "Excuse me?"

"You handled the testosterone brigade with just the right amount of authority. An admin has to establish her boundaries and let the suits know where she stands from the get-go."

"I agree," Beth said, certain that Maude would have no issues with that aspect of her job.

By the end of the day, she was confident the older woman wouldn't have any problems, period. She was an absolute dynamo and Beth felt better about leaving than she had since agreeing to the assignment. Maude even finalized her travel arrangements to Portland International Airport. She booked a seat for Ethan on her father's instructions as well, though Beth didn't understand why he was accompanying her to the interview.

She asked about it immediately after arriving at his apartment that night. It was actually the entire ground floor of a three-story brick house on the outskirts of the city on a street lined with trees and pristine sidewalks, though the neighborhood was older. He had chosen a similar color scheme to hers, but with a very different overriding theme. The influence of his home state was subtle, but unmistakable. His dark chocolate leather furniture and solid wood tables had a western feel that was both stylish and comfortable.

He had few knickknacks and almost no artwork on the walls, and yet the living area did not feel sanitized, simply uncluttered.

He hung her jacket in his entry closet as he answered her question. "Your dad and I decided I would play the possessive boyfriend."

He came back into the living room, where she sat at one end of the long sofa. He was wearing the same dark jeans he'd had on earlier, but he'd put on a snug-fitting Henley with them and taken off his boots and socks. His feet were very masculine. And dark. Like he'd been barefoot in the sun a lot. He hadn't gotten that way in D.C. But she knew his extreme sports took him south frequently.

He poured her a glass of wine from the bottle chilling in a bucket on his big, square coffee table. "I'll call you several times a day, show up to take you to lunch almost every day, drive you to work, and pick you up. That sort of thing. It will give me a chance to be on-site more than I would otherwise and will establish a precedent for you staying in pretty constant contact with me."

She took a sip of the wine. It was a Riesling and the tangy sweetness slid over her tongue with familiar pleasure. "Mmm. This is my favorite kind of wine."

"I know."

"You do?" She didn't remember telling him. "I didn't think we'd discussed culinary preferences last night. Though we probably should have."

"We've known each other for two years, Beth. My knowledge of you is not limited to what we discussed yesterday."

"Of course." She just thought he hadn't noticed. "Do you think Prescott will buy the overly possessive boyfriend bit?"

Ethan shook his head, his expression remonstrative. "I'm good at my job, Beth. I'll be very convincing as the jealous, possessive boyfriend. Trust me."

Suddenly the events of the morning started to make more sense. "You and Dad talked about this yesterday, didn't you?"

"Yes, why?"

"You were getting into character," she mused, both relieved and somewhat deflated at the same time.

"What are you talking about?"

"This morning. When you were going all macho primitive with Alan. That was all about you being in character." She took another sip of wine and tried to squelch even the tiniest niggle of disappointment at the realization.

Ethan leaned back on the sofa and put his bare feet up on the coffee table. "You don't see me as the macho, primitive type?"

"Macho yes, primitive no."

He did that thing with his eyebrow, lifting one in silent inquiry. "Hmmm . . ."

She couldn't tell what he was thinking. He shifted a little and her gaze traveled down his body involuntarily. Muscles bulged against the black denim on his thighs, but those bare feet snagged her attention and held on. It felt intimate, sitting there like that. Was that because of last night, or because there was something personal about seeing a man's feet? Maybe if they lived in Hawaii, or even Southern California, it wouldn't feel like this. But D.C. was not a barefoot town. Far from it. Which made this little scenario feel intimate . . . just like the night before.

Had she really flashed him with her panties?

She'd lost her mind, but that was better than losing her heart. And she wasn't convinced that organ was invulnerable.

"And if I told you that I don't consider it primitive to tell the man who stood you up at the altar three years ago to mind his own business?"

Chapter 8

She licked her lips and forced herself to meet his eyes again. He was watching her with another indecipherable look.

Still, whatever he said, she knew that wasn't Ethan's normal modus operandi. She just shook her head in answer and said, "I'm a little worried about this whole playacting thing."

"It's not all an act *now* is it?"

She didn't want to talk about that at this particular moment. "I mean this new thing . . . I don't think I'm going to be able to respond naturally to the possessive boyfriend type. It's likely to embarrass and maybe even annoy me and I don't know if I can hide that."

"Don't bother trying. Both reactions will just make you appear more real to the perp."

"I don't know . . ."

"Trust me, Sunshine. I know what I'm talking about. The possessive boyfriend bit is going to explain your job changes, too . . . all of them."

"How?"

"We've been together for two years—the closer we stick to the truth, the easier the deception will be to carry out—and you quit your job investment counseling to take a position that gave you more time with me. Now I want you to move across country with me, so I can explore my artistic muse on

the West Coast. In this scenario, I like the idea of you working part-time because it makes you even more accessible."

Turning to face Ethan, she slipped off her shoes and then
curled her feet under her on the sofa. "Any woman who puts
up with that sort of possessiveness needs a lesson in assertiveness."

"Are you saying you'd never compromise your lifestyle for
someone you love?"

"Would you?"

"Yes." He shrugged. "I plan to play the annoying, in your
face, needy boyfriend who hides that need behind arrogance.
And no, I wouldn't normally be that way. But I believe that
there are a lot of relationships that would do better if one or
both people learned to compromise."

"Did your parents . . . for each other?"

"All the time. They still do. And they taught us all to compromise for the family. It isn't always easy, but it works and
we may live several states apart, but we're still close."

"I like that." In fact, to her way of thinking, it sounded
like Heaven.

"They'd like you, too, Beth. Mama especially. She likes a
feisty woman."

"You think I'm feisty?"

"A total firecracker. You try to hide it with your quiet ways,
but you're damn good at getting your way and you don't play
emotionally manipulative games to do it either."

"How do you know?"

"I've known you for two years."

"You've worked with me, that's not the same as knowing
me."

"I've watched you, baby. I know you."

He was starting with the "baby" thing again. She wasn't
going to survive it. Or at least, her good intentions weren't.
"If you knew me so well, why didn't you know it was going
to seriously peeve me if you made allusions to last night in
front of Alan and my dad?"

"You want to hide our relationship while you keep Alan dangling?" he asked instead of answering.

"No. I want my private life to stay that way *and* we don't have a relationship."

"You can say that after last night?" He hadn't moved a muscle and yet she felt not exactly threatened . . . but sort of intimidated. How did he do that?

She wasn't backing down though. "It was phone sex." Even if she couldn't believe she'd done that with him and had never, ever, ever, *ever* considered doing anything like that with another man. "It wasn't the bonding moment of the twenty-first century."

He sat up and put his wineglass down on the table in one fluid movement, his green eyes hot with purpose. "It was incredible and tonight is going to be mind blowing."

He wasn't leaning forward, but he felt entirely too close.

She leaned back, into the sofa, with no noticeable improvement and took a hasty sip of wine. "I'm not so sure about tonight."

He removed her wineglass from her hand with deliberate movements. "You said you were. The time for waffling is over, baby."

"You said you wouldn't push me," she said in a breathy voice she barely recognized. She was not a breathy-type person. She was practical. Certain. Responsible. But he made her feel breathless, undecided, and reckless.

Not good.

"I didn't push you, Beth. You're the one that suggested we make love last night, not me." He was leaning forward now, his solid pecs too close to her chest.

If she breathed in too deeply her nipples would brush against him. The temptation to do so was almost too strong to deny. "We didn't make love. You've never even kissed me."

"We definitely did make love and I can take care of the kissing thing right now."

She jumped backward and toppled off the couch before he

could pull her into his arms. Scrambling to her feet, she demanded, "Answer a question for me first."

He stood and came around the table, giving no regard whatsoever to her obvious bid to increase her personal space. Gently curling his fingers around her upper arms, he held her in front of him. And the worst part was she didn't mind. At least her body didn't. It craved the physical closeness.

"What is it?" he asked.

"Are you trying to establish a sexual relationship with me for the sake of the case?"

"That damn Hyatt. He planted the idea in your head, didn't he?"

"Actually, no. I may be inexperienced compared to your other women, but I'm not naïve, nor am I stupid. It occurred to me this morning. You've known me for two years and never so much as asked me to coffee and then all of the sudden, you want access to my panties."

"I like your panties," he said with a feral grin.

"Ethan! Be serious." Even though said undergarments were safely hidden behind a pair of black slacks, she was acutely aware of their skimpy nature all of a sudden. "I . . . um . . . I asked you a question and I'd appreciate an honest answer."

He drew her in, just like a fish on a line, and she let him until their bodies were just touching. Electric jolts surged through her body until it was all she could do not to rub herself all over him like a feline looking for comfort.

"And if I was doing it just for the sake of the case, could you turn me down?" he asked softly, his lips a breath from hers, but not quite touching.

She wanted that touch. She wanted the kiss he'd offered. And she wanted it more than she'd ever wanted anything. Considering the kind of desires she'd known since meeting him, that was saying a lot.

He'd said a lot, too . . . in the way he'd worded his question. Not *would* you, but *could* you. He knew how much she wanted him and was not above capitalizing on the fact because he had taken her words and their encounter on the phone last night very seriously.

In many ways, that was a good thing . . . it made a strong statement about his own integrity, but she wanted to take back last night and the commitment she'd made to share her body with him. Didn't she?

"I don't know if I could say no," she admitted. "I doubt I could have turned you down last night, even if you'd pushed it. But I do know that whatever happens between us, I'd rather go forward without a blindfold."

"We can have a lot of fun with blindfolds."

She rolled her eyes, while her body throbbed in reaction to his words. "No doubt."

He sighed and stepped back, letting go of her arms. "I won't deny that the timing has something to do with the case, but I've always wanted you, Sunshine."

"Always? I don't think so."

"You think I can fake the kind of hard-ons you gave me last night?"

"You're a professional. I'd say you know how to fake sexual interest, yes."

He ran his fingers through his sandy hair. "You're right. I do, but damn it . . . that kind of thing doesn't give me erections hard enough to drill through rock. Only you do that."

She didn't know if she could believe him. "Would you lie for a case?"

"If it was necessary. Yes. But it isn't in this instance. I don't need to lie because the truth serves me better. I want you and I always have. The case will be easier in some ways because of that, but harder in others."

"Why harder?"

"When I'm with you, my libido tends to take over, but when I'm on a case, I need to have my brain engaged at all times. It worries me, but there's not a hell of a lot I can do about it."

"Really?"

"Really. I thought about talking to Whit about getting another agent to take your place, but frankly . . . with the way I feel about you right now, I don't think I could successfully manufacture the relationship with another woman." And he didn't sound happy about it.

"I'm sorry."

"Don't be." He smiled, the look so sexy, her insides were melting in little puddles. "I'm not."

"How do you feel about me?"

"I just told you. I want you so much I'm ready to explode just thinking about sinking my cock inside you."

That wasn't what she meant, but the fact that he answered that way made it clear his interest in her was purely sexual. His emotions weren't involved. "You can be incredibly crude."

"Call it a gift. And blame yourself . . . I don't get this basic with other women. Something in you brings it out."

"The same something that brings out Alan's protective instincts?" He'd certainly been overzealous in that department earlier.

"I don't think so," he said, as if the idea that he and Alan were affected by her in the same way was an anathema. "Though I feel a mite protective of you myself."

"Do you?"

"Couldn't you tell this morning?"

"No, I was too busy fantasizing about shooting your knee-cap."

"You would maim me for life for warning off your ex-fiancé?" he asked, askance.

"No, for embarrassing me."

"You're ashamed to be dating me?"

"Wanting to maintain a certain level of privacy in the workplace has nothing to do with being ashamed of who I'm dating, but we aren't dating. Not really."

"Last night sure felt like a date to me. It ended better than a lot of them do."

"With me sending you home?" she couldn't help teasing.

"With the image of the hungry look in your sweet brown

eyes as you stared at my hard dick. And the date didn't end there . . . did it?" As he'd been speaking, he'd been moving closer until she was against the wall and once again his body was just touching hers.

"No." She licked her lips, while staring at his. "I guess not."

He groaned. "Beth, baby, you are killing me again."

"I don't mean to."

"Huh." It was definitely a sound of disbelief. "So, do you acknowledge last night was a date?"

There was no hope denying it and she wasn't sure she wanted to. "Vito certainly thought so."

"He's a flirt."

"He's a sweetheart."

"He's an Italian lothario who is going to lose his charming accent along with his voice if he doesn't stop flirting with my woman."

Ethan was playing his role again, but she couldn't help the thrill of dark pleasure that raced down her spine at his words.

He nuzzled her neck, sending chills of pleasure down her spine. "So . . . you hungry?"

She let her head hit the wall as she leaned against it. "A little . . ."

It was a lie. She was starving . . . both for him and for the delicious food smells coming from the kitchen. The question was, which hunger was going to get to her first?

"If you're only a little hungry, then maybe you'd be okay with dessert first." His lips played along her jaw.

Oh, yes . . . dessert. Yum. "What's for dessert?" she asked in a whisper that sounded a lot more come-hither than she'd intended.

He kissed the corner of her mouth, but not full on her lips. "What do you think?"

"I don't know if I'm ready for that." What was her sanity doing asserting itself now? Didn't it know when to keep a low profile?

"Trust me, you are."

She was . . . but she wasn't. And the conflicting feelings only fed the overwhelming desire coursing through her. Shouldn't her ambivalence at least give her a little respite? And yet despite how her body buzzed with electric need, her mind and fears would not shut off. Had she gotten so used to dreaming about life rather than living it, she'd lost the ability to just exist in the moment?

It was not a comfortable thought . . . but none of them were right now. "You said you wouldn't push me."

He cupped her face and leaned his forehead against hers while his body pressed closer. "I want you to the point of madness, Beth. And as fantastic as it was, I don't want another session of lovemaking via the phone. I need the real thing. I think you do, too."

Her body certainly agreed with him. It ached to press closer to his heat, but part of her was more than willing to try the phone sex thing again. It had been incredible. What if the real thing was a disappointment? Not that she was expecting it to be. She liked making love. A lot. It had been good with Alan and she thought it would probably be spectacular with Ethan. Would she survive it though?

"I'd never done that before. The phone sex thing," she clarified as if he wouldn't know just what she was talking about.

He nuzzled her. "I figured that. Neither had I."

"N-never?" She shivered as his nuzzling affected her in ways she wished she could better control.

"No. Now that you've taken my virginity, do you feel obligated to marry me?" he asked in a deep voice that masked the humor she knew had to be lying under the surface.

But even knowing it was a joke, the words caused everything inside her to freeze in shock. "Uh . . . no."

"Too bad, but maybe I can change your mind."

"Don't joke about that."

"Why not? Are you worried your certainty I'd make a bad long-term prospect is in jeopardy?"

"No. You're the one who said you were looking for sex without commitments."

But that didn't mean she wouldn't end up wanting one. And that would be a disaster on so many levels, she didn't even want to consider the possibility.

"More like sex without long-term commitments. I expect you to be very committed to me and only me while we're having sex and vice versa of course."

How could he talk so intelligently while she felt like her muscles and her will were turning to jelly? "I think maybe I should come back another night to do the get-to-know-you thing."

He leaned back so their eyes met. His were assessing and hungry . . . very, very hungry. "What are you so afraid of, Beth?"

"You."

He shook his head. "Don't you know . . . you've got nothing to fear with me, darlin'? Nothing at all."

He was wrong. She had no doubt he knew exactly how to give her more pleasure than she'd ever known. It wasn't her body she was worried about. It was her heart, but she wasn't about to admit her biggest fear was that she was falling in love with him. He knew too much about her desire for him already.

Besides hearts did not belong in discussions about sex without long-term commitments. Hearts and the feelings they held were very long term. She'd learned that with Alan. Walking away from him had hurt more than the humiliation of calling off the wedding. Way more. Only the certainty that a lifetime of the same was staring her down had given her the strength to end the relationship when he got home repentant and still wanting to marry her.

She hadn't dated for the first year after the breakup simply because she'd still been hurting too much to risk her heart. Then she'd met Ethan and every other man had eventually faded into the background. If he had that kind of power over her when she didn't love him, how much worse would it be if she did when he walked away?

Even more terrifying was the prospect that he might change his mind and not want to. She didn't think she'd have the strength to do it herself.

"What is the matter, Beth? You look like you're watching a horror movie and it's reached the really gory part."

Now that was apt, but she attempted a shrug. It didn't work very well considering how close they were. "Nothing."

He looked at her like he was trying to read her mind, but for all his super spy abilities, he couldn't do that. Thank goodness. She looked back, blanking her expression so she would not expose her churning emotions any further. She had a lot of experience with that particular feat.

His green gaze narrowed like he wasn't buying the suddenly peaceful façade. Her dad used to look at her like that, but if he hadn't been able to break through the barriers she'd learned to erect around her emotions, Ethan sure wasn't going to.

He shook his head. "You are going to learn to trust me."

Not likely, but she was smart enough to keep that thought to herself. An alpha male like him would see it as a challenge and he was determined enough where she was concerned.

"I want to kiss you." He massaged her jaw with his thumbs like he was getting her ready, his expression still probing. "I need to taste your lips. So, if you're saying no for real, you'd better say it now. Once my mouth takes yours, my body isn't going to be long in following."

The proof of that statement pressed hard against her tummy.

An atavistic part of her suspected that if she said no, he would just look for another way to convince her. One thing was for sure. She wasn't going anywhere. She didn't want to, not really. Even though she should. And he wasn't about to release her without an argument. One she knew she was destined to lose because too much of her was on his side.

The man looking at her so intently right now had no intention of being thwarted and yet she knew with just as primitive a certainty that he would never actually force her to do anything, nor would he ever physically hurt her. The truth was . . . he would never have to. She was a hair's breath from kissing him herself.

"Dinner first," she forced herself to say. "And then I look over your apartment."

"And then I strip you naked and keep you that way for the rest of the night."

"We'll see."

"Yeah, baby, we will." It was as much threat as promise and she shivered in spite of her certainty he would never push her beyond what she could deal with.

He sighed and shook his head. "Dinner? You want dinner?"

The level of disgust in his voice made her smile. "It smells good." And it did. Some kind of pungent barbecue and cornbread. It had been making her mouth water since he opened the door. "You've been tantalizing me with it since I got here."

"I'd like to tantalize you," he said suggestively.

With a man like Ethan, a woman had to take charge, or she'd find herself doing nothing but reacting. She didn't want it to be that way . . . in or out of bed.

She pushed against his chest. "Feed me."

He stepped back, albeit with obvious reluctance. "All right, but I'm warning you . . . dessert is going to last a long time."

She said nothing and followed him into the kitchen, where he had set the table to eat. She liked that they weren't using the formal dining room. It felt warm and homey. He'd made BBQ ribs and all the trimmings and served them up, refusing her offer to help.

"How did you find time to make all this?" she asked.

"I did the ribs in the slow cooker . . . one of my mama's recipes. I threw the cornbread in as soon as I got home and everything else was pretty simple. Don't tell Mama, but the beans are canned."

"I promise to keep your secret." She crossed her heart.

He grinned. "Good. I'd hate to have to silence you."

"Would you?" she teased.

His gaze settled on her lips with tactile intensity. "Maybe not."

Oh, my. Time to deflect. If she wanted to get anything done tonight, she had to get their attention on something besides sex.

She indicated their full plates and tall glasses of sweetened iced tea beside them. "A lesson in getting to know you?"

"You could call it that."

They ate in silence for a little while until she felt the need to say, "It's delicious."

"I think so. Mama's recipes are foolproof."

"Do you cook this kind of thing often?"

"At least a couple of times a week. It reminds me of home."

"I'm surprised you chose to leave Texas."

"I couldn't have the life I wanted there."

"Why not?" There were plenty of opportunities to be some kind of government agent in Texas.

"TGP is here."

"And you wanted to work with high-tech?"

"It's where I'm needed the most."

"Even so . . . you could work remotely. You don't have to live in D.C., at least not anymore." Her father allowed certain agents to operate from bases in other locales and she knew he'd give the option to Ethan over losing him.

"I like being in the center of the action."

"You take the hardest assignments and usually the most dangerous."

"It seems that way sometimes."

"This one isn't."

"It's personal though."

"But if it wasn't, the assignment would be too tame for you, wouldn't it?"

"I like a challenge."

"You like danger," she clarified. "You live for it."

He thought about that for a second. "Living on the edge can be addictive."

"I know."

"Not from experience."

"No, but I've seen it enough and not just in my dad."

"Alan's addicted to the danger lifestyle," he guessed.

She didn't argue, though why he kept harping back to Alan and decidedly old news, she didn't know. "So are most of our agents. Men and women alike."

He nodded, smiling. "I think Elle and Jayne have it the worst, if you want the truth."

She thought about the cases the two female agents gravitated toward and had to agree. "They're good at what they do and aren't afraid to tackle anything. They're true professionals."

"My favorite kind of agent."

"Is it going to be a major problem for you working with me on this case?"

"Have I implied that it would be?"

"I'm no Elle or Jayne. I've got rudimentary training in procedure and the fact is, we both know I'm doing this out of necessity."

"I don't expect you to be an experienced field agent. Just do what you do best . . . be yourself and leave the supersleuthing up to me."

"But you'd probably rather be doing this with Elle." That woman was truly scary and Beth wouldn't want to face her in even an exercise-sparring session.

"No, I wouldn't. And you know why. We don't have a choice on this assignment. For a lot of reasons."

"I suppose." But she still had her doubts.

He squeezed her shoulder. "I think you've got depths you never realized, Sunshine. You're going to be great in your role. Trust me."

She grimaced. "You'll make sure of it, right?"

"I am the senior agent on the case. Your success is my responsibility."

"Some might call you a control freak with an overdeveloped sense of responsibility."

"It all comes with the territory."

"I don't think so."

"You think I'm different from other agents?"

"You like being in control. A lot."

"Usually."

She actually snorted at that. "When don't you?"

He leaned back in his chair in a way that would have given her mother conniptions. "You told me you fantasized about tying your lover to the bed and having your way with him."

She tried to maintain a casual attitude, but heat bloomed in her cheeks and she wanted to strangle him. "That's me, the closet dominatrix."

"You're not a dom, baby. We talked about this. You aren't into pain. You don't secretly want to dress in a black leather corset and wield a whip."

Maybe a velvet whip, but he was right. She didn't find pain a turn-on . . . though she wasn't sure about a sexy spanking. She shook her head. "I think I must be depraved. I fantasize about handcuffing you to my bed and doing all sorts of sexy things to you. What does that make me?"

"Adventurous. And it makes me horny as hell."

"So, you would let me?"

"Hell, yes."

Chapter 9

Very definite. Maybe he played those kind of sexy games a lot. As soon as she thought the question, she blurted it out.

"Actually, I've never let a woman handcuff me or tie me up, but there's a first time for most things, Sunshine. When you've got the courage to try them."

"I'm surprised you want me to do that . . . considering how much you like being in control."

"Me, too." But he didn't sound bothered by the fact.

"I want to torture you with pleasure," she admitted and then covered her mouth with her hand as if she couldn't believe she'd said the words.

The sane part of her mind couldn't.

"As long as you're the one doing it, that sounds damn fine to this ole boy."

She loved it when he went all Texan on her and she was guessing he knew that because his drawl definitely got stronger when he was getting sexy with her.

"You're not scared of giving up control?" she asked.

"Who says I'll give up control? I've been bound in far more dire circumstances and not lost control." Oh, he was arrogant.

"Maybe I'll take it from you."

He leaned forward, pushing his plate out of the way so he was practically sharing breath with her. "I'm counting on you trying."

"You don't think I can?" she asked in a voice that was a little too hesitant for her liking.

"We won't know until you try." But he didn't believe she could do it. That much was obvious.

Instead of making her feel underconfident, his lack of belief in the more rampant side of her sensuality only made her more determined to prove him wrong. Which probably made her crazy, but there it was.

She leaned back in her own chair, ignoring the way she cringed at doing so. She needed the distance. Crossing her arms over her chest, she said, "Tell me about your uncle . . . the one who was an assassin."

Ethan's look was knowing. He definitely believed he'd won that little difference of opinion. He'd learn better . . . later. But she'd always believed that actions spoke louder than words and she planned for hers to be in magnified stereo.

"Your uncle . . ." she prompted.

"Uncle Lester was a soldier in WWII. He came home and went into the business because he'd learned more about killing than a man should know if he wants to be something besides a killer. He went by the name of Arwan. He did freelance, but a lot of his work was for the government. He was in his eighties when he died. He had a girlfriend though. Queenie. I keep in touch. She's a firecracker."

"Why did he stay away from your family for so long?"

"For their safety."

"That must have been hard . . . for all of them."

"It was. My great- aunts and uncles missed him. We all did. In a family like ours, you can't have a member just walk away that everyone doesn't feel it, even the generations that come after."

"Is that why you looked him up when you grew up?"

"Yes. I'm glad I did. He was an interesting man."

"He killed people for a living . . . that's . . ."

"Hard. He paid for his career choice, but he had integrity. I wish I'd gotten to know him better, to tell you the truth."

"I'm sorry. I'm sure you're right about him paying a price for his choice. I'm glad you didn't decide to follow in his footsteps."

"Different experiences made up our lives. Besides, my job is more challenging." And that was the most important thing to Ethan. She thought it probably always would be.

"Yes, it is." She'd known trained assassins.

It was a whole different world, but finding a way to kill someone was often easier than finding a way to put them behind bars for a very long time.

"And I like saving the world from the bad guys."

"So does my dad. It's one of the things I admire most about him."

"Even though it took him away from you?"

"Yes. I may not want the same for my own children—if I have any—but I can really appreciate what a true hero he and men like him are. Like you."

"You think I'm a hero?"

"Yes."

"But lousy husband material." Like that really mattered to him.

"Don't sweat it. So was Superman."

"Spiderman got married."

"And look at what happened to Mary Jane. She was constantly getting kidnapped by evil villains. She was also smart enough not to have kids."

Ethan was shaking his head at her. "You would have gotten along well with my uncle. He never married. He refused to put any family at risk. Ever. He didn't even marry Queenie, though by the time they met, he was living as a senior citizen in retirement."

"His past came back to haunt him, though didn't it?"

"Yes."

"So, he made the right choice."

"You really don't think I should ever marry?"

"I didn't say that."

"But it's what you think."

It wasn't. Well, not exactly. And what she thought wasn't important anyway. "It's not my place to judge you, or anyone else, for your choices. What I think doesn't matter anyway, does it? We're faking a relationship for the sake of a case, not getting involved on a deeply emotional level."

"I told you . . . I don't just want you for the sake of the case."

"But you never would have pursued the desire you feel for me if not for the case."

"That's not true. The timing is affected by the case, but not the eventual outcome. It was getting harder and harder to ignore the need to strip your clothes off."

She laughed. "You have such a way with words."

"I've told you . . . at heart, I'm just a Texas boy raised on a cattle ranch."

"One of the richest ranches in the state."

"You do some background research on me, Sunshine?"

"Don't tell me you haven't read my personnel file and grilled Whit."

"Guilty on both counts. I wasn't complaining about your initiative, if anything, I'm impressed. What else did you learn that I haven't told you?"

"You dated a lot in both high school and college, but you didn't have a steady girlfriend for longer than a couple of months. Ever. You go home for Christmas and Easter, even when you're on a case. You call your parents and your sister on their birthdays, no matter where you are in the world. You don't have pets, but you had a dog growing up and you both got into enough mischief for ten boys and their crazy hounds. You learned to shoot before you started school and you can handle any gun made today, but your weapon of choice is a Beretta PX4 Storm. Which, along with your favorite designers and Extreme Sports destinations, goes to show that you have a definite preference for things Italian. You love your home state so much, you've bought land there to build on. Though you'll probably be an old man before you get around to doing it."

"You have learned a lot, but you're wrong. I plan to build in the next few years."

"Uh-huh."

"You're a skeptical woman."

"And a dreamer . . . but I don't think I'm the only one."

"We all need our dreams. I just believe you should spend more time living them than thinking about them."

"No one would ever accuse you of not living by that maxim."

"I am also not shy."

"I've known that since the first day I met you."

"Are you going to gift me with your body tonight, baby? Or are you going to keep me waiting?"

"I still haven't looked through your apartment."

"Putting off the decision won't make it go away."

"I know."

"Where do you want to start?"

"In here. You did a fantastic job with dinner. I want to see if you're a once-in-a-while cook, or a regular."

"I could just tell you."

"I could have told you about my lingerie, but you insisted on seeing it."

"You wouldn't have told me about it . . . or the hot-pink handcuffs."

"I might have."

"Riiiiight . . ." He drawled the word out until it was practically a paragraph.

"Believe what you like, but I'm starting in your kitchen."

His cupboards were neat and orderly, which she would have expected from him. But fully stocked as well. His spices were obviously used frequently and his freezer had everything necessary to pull together a complete meal. He might not be home often, but when he was, he cooked.

"Did your mother teach you to cook?"

He leaned against the counter by the sink, his long legs crossed at the ankle. "Her and our housekeeper. Consuela was a hard taskmaster. She expected me to know how to fend for myself and I learned."

"I took cooking classes. After I left home. I started with the typical Cordon Bleu stuff, but then decided I wanted to learn basic cooking, too, and took a home economics course at the nearby community college."

"While you were going to college?"

"Yes."

"Let me guess. Your university was too high brow to offer that sort of thing."

"Apparently."

"Do you like to cook?"

"Sometimes. Sometimes I make myself do it because I like the normalcy of eating in my own home from my own preparations. It makes me feel like I'm part of a family, even though technically . . . I'm not."

Soon, she moved into the formal dining room. There wasn't much in there to reveal who he was, so she moved onto the spare room. It had a bed for guests, but the closet and shelves were dominated by his extreme sports gear. She spent as much time as possible in every room, digging even more minutely than Ethan had in her apartment.

"Avoiding something, Sunshine?" Ethan asked as he leaned over her to whisper the question in her ear.

She was kneeling on the floor, perusing the titles on the bottom shelf of his bookcase.

It didn't startle her to hear his voice so close. How could it? She'd developed some sort of sixth sense where he was concerned. She was supremely aware of his presence and knew when he came near without having to see, or even hear, him.

"I'm trying to be thorough." The fact that they had not yet

made it to the master bedroom might not be a coincidence, but she wasn't about to admit that. "You're the one who said this particular endeavor was so necessary."

Strong, masculine fingers brushed her nape under the fall of her long hair. "Tell me what you've learned so far."

"I already knew you were into extreme sports and I've seen more evidence of that. But I didn't know you competed in the X-Games." And he'd placed in two events. She'd shuddered thinking the risks he took to make that possible.

"Is that all?"

"No. You're fascinated by history." He had several books on the subject, but he also had some DVDs and subscribed to a magazine that frequently had articles on archeological digs. "You don't watch a lot of television, but you do like to see movies in the theater." She'd seen some stubs in the kitchen drawer. "You don't make a habit of bringing women home to your apartment." He had no extra toiletries on hand in the bathroom. "But I'm guessing various family members have come to stay more than once because the linens for the spare room smell fresh and you keep a full complement of them as well as the extra pillows necessary on hand."

His apartment was bigger than hers, but storage space was always a premium and he had dedicated some of his to being ready for out of town guests.

"I'm impressed." The whole time they'd been talking, his hand had been gently massaging her nape.

It felt good. Too good. She fought the urge to lean back into his touch. "We fly out early tomorrow afternoon for PDX."

"I know. We'll drive to the coast early the next morning, before the interview."

"Maude told me you wanted us to stay in a hotel in Portland, but wouldn't it make more sense for us to stay in a motel nearer Prescott's home?"

"I don't like the feel of that. He's too in control in his own environment. We can't be sure he doesn't have flunkies at a local motel."

"What difference does it make? We're going in under cover."

"I always stack the deck in my favor." And he always won.

She wouldn't argue with success like that. "You're the boss."

"I like the sound of that."

"Don't let it go to your head. I was talking about the case."

"So was I." But the hand on her nape felt anything but businesslike. "It pleases me to know that you don't question the chain of authority on this assignment."

"You're the agent in charge, not to mention the only agent with any experience, but I'm not an idiot." She didn't want him thinking she was going into this as some sort of brainless robot.

"I know that. I won't treat you like one either."

"No dictating without explaining yourself?"

"I'll try not to."

But he wasn't making any promises. That didn't surprise her. She'd have been more shocked if he had. The man was a natural leader and while he might respect her enough to explain himself and even sometimes seek her opinion, she wasn't naïve enough to believe it would be that way in every instance. Which was fine with her . . . for the most part.

She was smart enough to know the difference between a situation when she needed to assert autonomy and one in which she should follow orders blindly. Though she wasn't sure how good she was going to be at that particular endeavor. Blind obedience wasn't something she had a lot of experience with, but she was willing to try. In a limited capacity.

"You ready to move onto my bedroom, baby?"

The air around them shimmered with tension that had nothing to do with the case. Or at least not directly. The master bedroom was the final room she needed to see. It was also the room where he slept. She found that thought unbearably evocative and she knew he did, too.

"Yes."

He stood, his hand withdrawing from her neck. "All right then."

Cupping her elbows, he lifted her to her feet and her backside brushed against his thighs and a titillating bulge on the way up. He did not move away when she was fully upright, but pulled her close, his harsh breathing further evidence that their closeness had not left him unaffected.

"This is damn hard, baby."

"I can feel that it is."

He laughed, the sound strained. "That wasn't exactly what I meant, but it'll do."

"Yes, I think it will," she mimicked his drawl.

He growled, one hand slipping from her elbow to rub across her tummy. She'd never considered her stomach an erogenous zone, but his touch was sending messages all over her body and they were very explicit. "Be careful, Sunshine. You're playing with fire and I've a mind to burn you from the inside out."

He was patently ready to do so—both physically and mentally—but she'd discovered something about halfway through her exploration of his home. She was enjoying stretching this game out. She'd never been so aroused, nor had she ever felt such a deep connection to her own feminine sensuality.

She stepped away from him with deliberate movements. "Show me your bedroom."

"I'd rather show you my hard-on."

"Later."

His hand clamped onto her shoulder, his expression intense. "No more teasing. Do you mean that? You can only push a man so far, Beth."

"But you've got more control than most, don't you?"

His eyes darkened with anger-laced desire that turned her excitement up another notch. "I have a feeling we're both going to find out just how far that control reaches."

"I'm counting on it."

"Let's get this over with," he growled and nudged her toward the bedroom.

She laughed, the sound resonating through her and increasing her sense of female power. She liked this feeling. She liked it a lot. She wished she had her pink handcuffs with her, but she was willing to improvise.

His bed was huge. That was her first thought as she crossed the threshold, but her second was that this was where he had been last night during their hot phone call. On that bed. It had to be custom-made because she'd never seen one as big. A huge pair of horns graced the top of the thick headboard, a pair of black handcuffs hanging from the right horn and a black satin sleep mask hung from the left.

Everything inside her clenched at the sight and she had to remind herself to breathe.

Licking suddenly dry lips, she scanned the rest of the monster bed. A dark brown utrasuede duvet covered it and there was a massive pile of pillows ranging in color from dark chocolate to a golden tan stacked against the mahogany headboard.

A single, very solid-looking nightstand stood to the left of the bed and a saddle hung on the wall above it along with a rope. Other than that, there was no additional furniture or decoration in the room.

"What's the saddle for?" she asked.

"I rode it when I won the statewide teen bucking bronc competition."

"The rope?" she practically squeaked.

The man rode wild horses? Of course he did.

"Bullriding."

"You won?"

"Yep. I'm an expert rider."

"How good are you at being ridden?"

"You know the saying, save a horse . . . ride a cowboy."

"But you aren't a cowboy."

"Once a cowboy, always a cowboy."

"So, why did they nickname you Stud instead of Cowboy?"

"Do you really need me to answer that?"

No, she sure didn't. "So, extreme sports has been a way of life for you since you were a kid?"

"You could say that. My daddy considered bull- and bronc-riding part of my education."

"My dad made me take tae kwon do until I went away to college."

"That wasn't in your file."

"It was precollege, therefore pre-TGP."

"Your dad didn't mention it either."

"Probably because he considered it a washout. It did not spark some deep-seated desire inside me to pursue law enforcement as a way of life."

"What color was your belt when you stopped taking the classes?"

"Purple. It's black now," she admitted. That was probably a piece of information he should know going into a case together. "Please don't mention that fact to my dad."

"No problem, but why?"

"Why do I have a black belt, or why don't I want you to tell my dad?"

"Both."

"I started taking the classes again, for exercise, my sophomore year in college. I missed them, but not the pressure from Dad about what a natural I was and how I was wasting my life on finance. He was severely disappointed his only offspring wasn't pursuing criminal justice, or something equally useful. Mom felt the same. . . . she wanted me to get a degree in political science and follow it up with a law degree. I disappointed them both."

She shrugged, as if that didn't bother her. And for the most part, it didn't. "I've kept up with the tae kwon do ever since though. I teach classes occasionally in my dojo, but I've only entered the competitions necessary to earn my next belt. Once I got the black, I stopped competing completely."

She waited for him to make another comment about how she chose to observe rather than experience life, but none was forthcoming.

"I am a grand master in Kajukenbo."

"I know. You can kill with your bare hands."

"That's part of agent training."

"Not basic."

"No, not basic." He turned and indicated a door on the other side of his bed. "I keep my clothes in the closet, but there's no sexy underwear for you to look through."

"You were commando last night."

"It's my preference."

"I find that very sexy, but then I'm sure a lot of women do."

"I'm not interested in any other woman's reaction right now. I'm glad it turns you on, though."

Everything about him excited her. "You have a pair of handcuffs on the horns on your bed."

His smile was gentle, but his eyes burned with desire. "I wondered if you were going to pretend you didn't notice."

"Are they always there?"

"No. I bought them and the blindfold on the way home from work tonight."

"Why?"

"Because I was hoping you'd want to use them."

Chapter 10

Her knees almost buckled and she grabbed the door frame for balance. The time for teasing was over . . . at least about whether or not they were going to make love tonight. Her fears had not abated, but she was not letting them hold her back. Not tonight . . . hopefully, never again. "I want to."

"I'm glad to hear that, baby, because my balls are turning blue from need." He moved toward her, but she stepped away.

"The closet."

"You're teasing me."

"Think of it as heightening your anticipation."

"It can't get much higher. I told you . . . my balls are about blue."

"I thought that only happened when men got cold."

"Or when all my blood is raging through my penis. Have pity, Beth."

"In a minute." She crossed the room with quick steps and opened the closet door.

It was a walk-in. Not a huge one. The building was too old for that kind of decadence. It didn't take her long to mentally catalogue its contents, but she waited an extra minute before returning to the bedroom, just to tease him a little more. She planned on doing a lot of that tonight. She hoped his control was up to it.

Not really.

She wanted him to lose it, and she was going to try her darndest to make that happen.

She backed out of the closet and turned to the bed and stopped dead. The pillows were strewn all over the floor and Ethan was naked, lying on his side, facing her. He was everything she'd ever fantasized he would be and more. Her imagination could not have conjured such a look of hot desire in his eyes, particularly when directed at her.

She'd seen men who worked out, but she'd never seen a body as beautifully honed as Ethan's. Golden skin covered perfectly sculpted muscles on a frame that dominated even that monster bed. At six-foot-three, he wasn't the tallest agent at TGP. He wasn't even the one with the most bulging muscles. Isaac held that distinction, but Ethan's presence more than made up for it.

She could feel the tautness of his body from where she stood, not just see it. She could also feel the singeing temperature of his sexual need. She would have fanned herself, but she was frozen for that moment, her senses completely absorbed with the sight of his nakedness and the electricity crackling in the air between them.

He wanted her. He planned to have her. His green gaze and unself-conscious nudity exuded that certainty.

And she responded to it on a basic level that she had not even known existed inside of her. Her body called out to his in silent acknowledgment of his unspoken claim while something deep within her echoed the primal cry. Almost as if her soul recognized his and was reaching out to claim a connection.

Which was really silly because this was sex. Not love. Not even really lovemaking. Sex.

But the feelings were so intense, she could barely breathe. She could not move at all and her thoughts felt splintered like glass shards from a shattered mirror. She no longer looked inside herself and saw the old Beth Whitney, but broken reflections of a different woman emerging. A woman who was both sexual predator and supplicant. A woman who experienced life in the moment, not one who spent her time dreaming about the possible tomorrows to come.

A woman who could match the man lying on the bed with his big, hard penis jutting out from his body and no apology for it.

Pearly white moisture glistened on the mushroom-shaped head and she craved it. She wanted to taste that essence . . . to inhale his most private scent . . . to touch it and see if it was as silky as it looked.

"Like what you see, little Beth?"

She didn't answer. She couldn't. But she wasn't *little* Beth.

She started to undress. Slowly. Provocatively. As if stripping for a man was something she'd done many times before. When in fact she'd only done it once for Alan and had been so shy about it, he'd never asked her to do it again.

She didn't feel shy now. Her body shimmered with wanton delight, responding to the hungry gleam in Ethan's eyes in a way that was wholly new to her. She watched him watching her undress and reveled in the way his sculpted cheekbones turned dusky rose and his jawline hardened with desire.

Before, that kind of reaction would have paralyzed her. Frightened her, even. But she was not scared. Not of him. Not of herself.

Perhaps a little of that confidence came from knowing that establishing a sexual relationship for the sake of the case was important to Ethan. He wasn't going to reject her and that gave her a sense of self-assurance she wouldn't have had otherwise. Maybe it should bother her that she knew part of his wanting her was for the case, but it didn't.

The truth was . . . nothing bothered her right now.

She felt so different. Like a butterfly coming out of its chrysalis. Each article of clothing dropped was like the silken cocoon she had to shed in order to unfurl her wings and fly. She would fly in Ethan's arms. She had flown last night, just talking to him on the phone. Part of her was flying even now. Feeling a freedom she had never known, the energizing sensation of warm, rushing wind beneath her wings.

She was not herself, but more essentially herself than she'd ever been. She didn't care if that made sense or not. She didn't understand the transformation happening inside her and did not seek to. How and why did not matter in that moment.

What was happening inside of her was not intellectual. It was wholly primitive and as such could only be comprehended at the instinctual level. She knew it was *right*. She could feel how right this night was.

This moment was not about her yesterdays or her possible tomorrows. It was about now. Only now.

Her shirt fell away, whispering down her body like a lover's caress. Ethan's gaze caressed her bare flesh and goose bumps formed, though the apartment wasn't cold. She undid her pants and pushed them down her hips before stepping out of them. Her feet were bare from when, at Ethan's invitation, she'd slipped her shoes off on arrival.

Ethan sucked in a breath, his turgid penis bobbing. "Your panties aren't any more than a couple of ribbons and triangle of lace. A tiny triangle. I can see your pretty dark curls around the edges. I like that."

"I don't wax." She didn't say it apologetically, though she'd often wondered if she'd be sexier if she did.

"I wouldn't want you to."

"Some men would . . . they like smooth skin down there." At least she'd heard they did.

"Alan?" he asked, his voice almost a growl.

"Uh . . . he never said. I just heard it . . . from other women about other men."

"That's their fantasy."

"Not yours?"

"You're my fantasy, Beth." His voice throbbed with masculine want.

"And you're mine." She brushed her hands down her sides, her thighs clenching at how that made her feel. Decadent. Sexy. Wanton.

He put a hand out to her. "So, come and get me."

If she did, she knew the fledgling sexpot emerging inside her would surrender to his superior experience, to the need radiating from him. She couldn't do that. She wanted more.

"I have a particular fantasy."

His hand dropped to his front and he gripped the base of his shaft. "So you said."

It was so sexy to watch him hold himself that she did just that, for several seconds.

Then she licked her lips and forced out the words that inner woman demanded. "I want to handcuff you to the bed."

"You sure about that, Sunshine? I can give you a lot more pleasure with my hands free."

"A different kind of pleasure," she dared to say. "I'm sure, Stud. Absolutely positive, in fact."

"Sounds like you know what you want."

"I do."

"All right then." He flexed his shoulders, rolled onto his back and reached his arms above his head, stretching that magnificent body. "Go for it."

Her throat went dry. He was amazingly gorgeous, but it was more than his physical perfection that drew her to him. His humor, his intelligence, his dedication to his country—to his job even—his intensity, his ultramasculinity, they all made a potent package that was totally irresistible to her.

And his confidence astounded her. Because she could sense he still felt completely, one hundred percent in control. He wasn't in the least bit worried about being bound to the bed.

Her inner vixen cheered. She'd known instinctively he would be like this, that he would not feel vulnerable even in handcuffs. And that was what she wanted . . . what she needed. Not a man who sought to be dominated, or would even tolerate dominance, but one who would seek to retain control despite the handicap of captivity.

In order to let her own strength free without reservation, she had to face absolute strength. It was the only way.

She approached the bed, her heart beating so hard in her chest he should be able to hear it. It was no small thing to be living out the fantasies that had dominated her sensual thoughts for more than two years. Longer if she counted the fantasies she'd had before her dreamtime lover took on Ethan's face and body.

Part of her refused to believe this was really happening, that he was lying on that bed, willing to be bound . . . willing to be blindfolded if the sleep mask dangling off one horn meant anything. And she was sure it did. But she didn't want to blindfold him. Not tonight. Tonight she wanted the built-up anticipation that came from him seeing what she was going to do . . . or what she wasn't.

Climbing onto the bed on her knees, she leaned over him to snag the handcuffs from where they draped over the horn. They weren't actually handcuffs, but wrist restraints made of black fabric with sturdy Velcro fasteners. They were attached by an adjustable belt of tight black webbing. Perfect.

He lifted his head and kissed her chest, running his tongue along her cleavage. "You taste sweet like sugar and you're about falling out of that bra, baby. Why don't you just take it off?"

She forced herself to lean away from that wicked tongue and the pleasure it was giving her. "When I'm ready. For now, why don't you just enjoy the view?"

"Oh, I am. I surely am."

She adjusted the belt between the cuffs to the right length, so his arms could rest comfortably on the bed but not have a lot of play for movement. Then, she leaned over him again. There were spindles as thick as the massive headboard lining its bottom half. She hadn't seen them at first because of the pillows, but they were perfect for her needs.

She felt the heat of his breath against her breasts before the sensual slide of his tongue along the top of her bra cup.

She gasped, almost dropping the cuffs. "You're supposed to be admiring the view, not licking me."

"You said I could enjoy it. I'm enjoying this."

So was she. She fought the urge to move her breasts so that one of her nipples was in line with his lips while she tucked the velvet-lined restraints around the center spindle. Then she secured his hands with the Velcro fastenings, all the while growing more and more aroused—both by her own actions and the way he was exploring the sensitive skin of her breasts with his tongue.

When she was done, she couldn't make herself sit back, away from the temptation of his mouth. What he was doing felt too good, but this wasn't the way she'd planned her seduction. She needed to take control. And soon.

A hand on the headboard for balance, she peeled down one side of her bra so her nipple was exposed to the air. It was already beaded, but even the gentle room temperature of his bedroom made it peak further. Or maybe it was the knowledge of what she planned to do.

Without warning him, she shifted so her nipple was right against his mouth. He made a feral sound in his throat and swiped it with his tongue. She moaned, arching her head back and pressing her breast closer to his lips. He licked the turgid, swollen peak again, and again, and again. His tongue swirled all around it, playing with her, teasing her and pleasuring her at the same time.

"Suck it," she demanded, her need making her voice harsh.

He laughed darkly and did just that, taking her entire aureole into the heated wetness of his mouth with an instant fervent suction. She had never known anything so intense. Pulses of pleasure traveled straight from her nipple to her womb, growing stronger and stronger until she felt every draw against the hard nub duplicated by a sensual clenching inside her uterus and vaginal walls.

She cried out. She thought she said his name, but her mind was fogged with bliss. He stopped suckling to nibble her, then he sucked again . . . then he upbraided her tender nipple with his teeth. The varying stimulations continued until she was shaking and near orgasm. How had she come so far from so little?

He nipped at her breast and then laved the same spot with his tongue and her entire body went stiff with preorgasmic tension.

Oh, he was good . . . and before tonight, she would have let him keep going, would have given into the pleasure shattering her insides. Would have welcomed it. But tonight she was a new and stronger Beth. A woman in control of her sensual journey and she wasn't ready to climax.

She pulled her nipple free and her body screamed for her to put it right back where it had been having so much fun. In his mouth. She shook her head at herself and turned unfocused eyes to him when he chuckled.

But his expression was not filled with humor . . . only hunger. It took everything of the new Beth to force herself to tuck her breast back into her bra and settle back on her haunches beside him. His eyes filled with feral heat, and he leaned toward her.

Only he couldn't reach her because of the restraints. He could lift his head and move his arms a little, but not enough to touch her or stop her from touching him. Just exactly what she wanted, she reminded herself even as her body buzzed with the need for culmination.

"You were close," he gritted out. "Why stop, baby?"

"Because that's not the way I wanted it to happen."

"Isn't it?"

"No."

"What do you want?"

"You. Tied like this." She surveyed her handiwork and a smile of anticipation creased her lips. "I haven't even begun to have fun yet."

"Not even begun, huh?" he mocked.

She felt heat steal into her cheeks and down her breasts.

"Okay, maybe we started, or you did anyway. . . ." She sighed with delight and looked him over again, letting her body thrill with sexual pleasure at the sight of him bound to the bed. "But now it's my turn."

He laughed, the sound husky and deep. "You look like a sweet little cat who's found herself a bucketful of unattended cream."

"You think I look like a cat?" She put her hands on his chest, to test her freedom to touch. It felt good.

He liked it, too, if the rumble of approval in his chest was anything to go by.

"I think *you* sound like a purring lion."

"Do you think a sleek little housecat can tame a lion?" he asked musingly, his voice all innocence.

Her spine stiffened with challenge and she narrowed her eyes. "Why don't we find out?"

"Why don't we?"

And then she knew. As innocent as his voice had been, he had been challenging her. She would meet that challenge and she would show him that she was no tame housecat.

Without a word, she got off the bed and left the room. It was all she could do not to stomp in her bare feet. She would show him tame.

He didn't call out and ask where she was going or why she'd left, and his lack of curiosity came off as another challenge to her. He didn't believe she was leaving him permanently, which she wasn't. But he wasn't even worried enough to ask. Then she remembered her clothes were lying on the floor and she supposed he was smart enough to figure out she wasn't going anywhere without them.

But that didn't mean he knew where she was going or why she'd left. And he wasn't worried, but maybe he should be.

She went into the spare room and rummaged in his sports equipment until she found what she was looking for. When she came back into his room, he was watching the door with a curious frown and satisfaction filled her.

Not so unconcerned after all.

She held up her find and his eyes widened for just a second before he wiped the expression from his face. Oh . . . he had tough agent who could face anything down pat.

She licked her lips, seeking the courage to voice her desires. In her fantasies she was pure vixen, but in reality . . . even the newly emerging Beth had her shy moments and asking her soon-to-be lover for this final thing was turning into one of them.

Taking a deep breath, she forced it and the words out in a rush. "I want to tie your ankles, too. Will you let me?"

Several seconds of silence went by before he answered. "On one condition."

"Maybe I don't want to grant a condition."

He let his head fall back, as if he was totally relaxed, without a care in the world. Not even the raging hard-on still sticking up from his body in adamant statement of his desire for her. "Good luck tying my ankles without my cooperation."

There was that. She nibbled on her lower lip and decided she wanted his cooperation. "What is your condition?"

"That as soon as you're done, you kiss me."

For some reason, that surprised her. Probably because what they'd already done seemed beyond kissing. He was naked, she was almost there and she'd been so close to exploding, her body still buzzed with it. "You want me to kiss you? That's all?"

His head came up again, the expression in his eyes almost angry. "All? Woman, you have not got a clue. I've been craving your lips for two years. The little taste I got last night was not near enough."

She shrugged. "Okay."

He let his head fall back and spread his legs without having to be asked, but she still approached the bed with trepidation. Which made no sense, considering he was bound, but she thought he'd probably been in situations that looked a lot more one-sided and come out the winner. Tonight he was her sexual opponent and she was not about to underestimate him.

She relaxed a little though when he let her tie his first ankle to one of the spindles that matched the headboard. She moved to do the other, but stopped when his foot slid away from her. "You'll keep your promise about the kiss?"

"I don't break my promises."

"But you do get doubtful of your decisions."

She couldn't stifle the laugh of incredulity that bubbled up. "We're way past me changing my mind now."

His answer was to slide his foot back into reach. When she was done securing it, she surveyed her handiwork and something scary moved inside her heart. He'd let her do it. He hadn't made fun of her, or refused her fantasies. He hadn't tried to seduce her past them. He'd even bought the restraints. Just for her.

Oh, man. It was as if he understood the woman inside her, the fantasy vixen who needed to become real. And while her body vibrated with a sexual charge unlike any she'd ever known, unexpected emotion stirred inside her, too.

She reached out with a trembling hand and stroked his calf. It wasn't a sexual caress, though the feel of his hair-roughened leg under her hand was intensely alluring. She just wanted to touch him, to connect to this man who made himself so open to her. "I don't want to love you."

The words came out of nowhere. She wasn't thinking about love right then. Did not want to think about it with him *ever*.

"You're making love to me, baby. Not loving me. There's a difference," he rumbled in that seductive Texas drawl.

"Are you sure?" the old Beth/new Beth asked.

"Yes. This is sex. Incredible sex, but that's all."

He sounded so sure. And why shouldn't he? He had more experience with this sort of thing than she did. She'd never had sex with someone she didn't love, but she knew he had. Probably a lot of someones. He knew what he was talking about. And she wanted to believe, so she did.

She climbed onto the bed and then onto him and he growled as the damp silk of her panties rubbed against his washboard stomach.

He hissed like she'd burned him. "You're so hot, baby. Wet and hot like molten lava."

She carefully pressed her hands against his shoulders and leaned down until their lips almost touched. "You're hot, too, but you aren't liquid . . . more like solid rock."

"Something feels rock hard right now."

"Yes. All of you," she teased huskily and gently bit his chin. He tasted salty, but he must have shaved before she arrived because his skin was smooth and oh so tempting.

She nibbled along his jawline. Stopping when she reached his ear and tugging on the lobe with her teeth. Then she flicked her tongue out and tasted.

"*Beth* . . ."

"What?" she whispered against his ear.

"Kiss me."

"Yes."

She slid her open mouth along his cheek until her lips met his and fireworks exploded inside of her. It was perfect. Different than any kiss she'd ever known. He tasted utterly masculine and sinfully delicious. And his lips exerted just the right amount of pressure, molding hers with possessive intent.

It did not feel like he was responding to her kiss so much as marking her with his own. A kiss could not mark you, could it? But she felt marked. Claimed. And she moved her lips against his with voracious abandon, frantic to make him feel the same way. Even if it was just physical . . . it felt so profound that it affected her soul and that had to be mutual.

It didn't matter if he was doing this for the case, or for the raging erection brushing her back . . . *it had to be mutual*.

A tiny voice amidst her shattered sense of self tried to tell her that soul stirring might not be a good thing, but she closed her mind to it.

This felt too elemental to be anything but predestined.

And if it caused her pain later, that was part of tomorrow, not now and now was where she was existing.

She licked along the seam of his lips and his mouth opened under hers with a groan. She dove inside with her tongue, craving more of his taste, more of him. He arched under her, pressing his hard stomach against the apex of her thighs and sending stabs of sensation through her. She pushed down with her pelvis, increasing the friction, but it wasn't enough.

She wanted to rip her panties off and mount him, but that would defeat the whole purpose of tying him up. How could she be so close to losing control . . . again?

She broke her mouth from his, panting. "That's enough kissing for right now."

Chapter 11

Ethan licked his lips as if he was savoring her taste. "I don't agree."

"That's too bad because I'm the one in control."

"Are you? You might be in charge, baby, but unless this old boy's eyes deceive him, you are out of control."

She sat up, pretending not to notice the way he flexed his muscles under her highly sensitized flesh. "Maybe you need to get your eyes checked."

"My vision is twenty-ten, baby. Maybe you need to get a condom out of the drawer and get me ready."

"We're a long way from that."

He pushed up against her and she couldn't stifle a moan. His smile was pure predatory male. "Sweetheart, you need it as much as I do."

"Do I?" she asked breathlessly.

"Yeah." He rolled his eyes. "But this must be the place where you deny it."

"I'm not denying anything."

"Aren't you?"

"Maybe myself." But she wasn't denying she wanted him. Only that she would give in . . . for now.

"And me. That's two pretty big things."

She reached behind herself and gripped his hardness, or

tried to. She couldn't quite get her fingers around him and that knowledge sent shivers arcing through her.

"Yes, very big," she said in a throaty voice she'd never used before.

He laughed, but the sound choked off on a deep groan as she squeezed the pulsing flesh in her hand.

"Much more of that and I'll go off like a rocket."

"Would that bother you?"

"To come before you?"

"Yes."

"I'd rather be inside you, but, Beth . . . you've been teasing me with that sweet body for so long, there's no way one time is going to be enough. Or even two . . . I figure tomorrow morning we're both going to be a little sore."

"But sated," she said on an approving sigh.

"For a while at least."

She grinned, liking the sound of that, and let go. She wasn't ready for him to come yet. She pressed both hands against his chest again. "There are so many ways I've fantasized about touching you. I want to do them all."

"Go for it, baby. I'm all yours."

She cast a significant look to his bound hands. "I know." Rocking herself against him, she brushed her fingertips through the light dusting of hair on his chest. "Some extreme sports-men shave here."

"Some shave their whole bodies." He made a face that showed his distaste at the idea. "I don't."

"I could tell," she mocked.

"Smart aleck."

She circled his nipples with her fingertips. "Why?"

"Why what?"

"Why don't you shave? I thought it was supposed to make you faster . . . more competitive." She liked the hair on his chest. It excited her . . . it was so very male, but she knew he took his extreme sports seriously, too.

"Besides the fact there are very few sports that body hair

can make any real competitive difference to, baby, I'm from Texas."

"What does where you are from have to do with it?"

"You ever seen a cowboy with a shaved chest?"

"I've never seen a real-life cowboy, period." She looked around his room, then back at him and smiled. "Except you."

"Trust me, then. Cowboys don't shave their bodies."

"Or wax?"

He shuddered. "Or wax."

"Not manly enough?" she teased.

"Real men do not wax," he growled.

She kept tracing over his skin and he moved restlessly under her. "Do real men like having their nipples touched?"

"You can touch me anywhere you like and it will pleasure me."

"Good." But she didn't touch the hard little points. Not yet. She'd fantasized so many times about this that she wasn't going to let it go too fast. She brushed a jagged scar that looked like a starburst on his right shoulder. "Where did you get this?"

"On assignment."

"You can tell me details. I have clearance."

He shook his head, his stomach muscles bunching under her. "I don't talk about work when I'm in bed with a beautiful woman." His muscles moved again, caressing her.

He was so sneaky. He really did think he could keep control even bound. And she loved that.

"Is that a hard-and-fast rule?" she asked, running her hand over the scar, noticing how sensitive he was there.

"Yes," he ground out.

"Hmmm . . ." She went back to his nipples, lightly scraping them with her nails. "Maybe I can make you break it."

He groaned as she went back and forth, back and forth over the rigid little nubs. "Why would you want to?"

"Because I want to know."

"You curious about me, Beth?"

"You told me I was supposed to be. Remember?"

"Yeah." He thought for a second. "I'll tell you. For another kiss."

"Okay . . . first you tell and then I kiss."

"Deal."

So, he told her. He'd been shot when taking down the enemy. It had happened before she started working for TGP. She'd read numerous accounts with similar scenarios, but hearing it from his lips affected her emotions in a way they never had been reading over and filing reports for the other agents. When he was done, she leaned down and kissed the scar, running her lips and tongue along each jagged line until she'd bathed the old wound completely with her sensuality.

"I thought you were going to kiss my lips," he said on a ragged breath.

She smiled and met his hot green eyes. "Did I say I was going to kiss your lips?"

"No."

"Then I kept my side of the bargain."

"That you did. You're wily, Miss Whitney. You know that?"

"I'm horny, Mr. Crane. And that is entirely your fault."

"Do I look like I'm complaining?"

"You look edible." She sighed as her fingers kneaded his chest like a cat and then she traced another, smaller scar near his ribs. "What about this one?"

"Same deal?"

"Same deal."

"A knife wound from a bar fight."

The bar had been in France and the fight had been started by a perp trying to cover a deal gone bad.

And so it went. She asked about a mark and he told her the story. Some were from assignments. Some were from mishaps when he was doing his extreme sports. Some were from growing up on a ranch. She kissed each one after his explanation, sometimes spending a long time on the area around it. He muttered her name and a curse in a guttural voice more than once.

She even undid the restraints on one ankle so he could turn on his side and she could reach his back. He wasn't exactly riddled with scars, but he had a sexy mole, right on his left flank and she made him tell her it was a birthmark before kissing it, too. He let her put the restraints on him again when she was done and they were both shaking with arousal and need by the time she'd pointed to a small scar near his groin.

"I got that falling off a horse." His voice was low-pitched and filled with tension.

She brushed the almost faded scar. "I thought you could ride anything."

"I was ten at the time."

She leaned over until her hair brushed his thighs and balls. He hissed and bucked, causing the silky strands to caress his erection, too. She turned her head back and forth, to do it some more.

"You're torturing me, woman."

"That's the idea," she whispered against his groin.

He laughed, having heard her. "You're damn good at it."

"I'm happy to hear that." Her lips closed over the old scar and her tongue darted out to taste. She sucked, giving him a love bite right there.

His hips flexed upward. "Damn it, baby. Put your mouth on me."

"My mouth is on you." And he tasted so good, musky, male and hot.

"I need your mouth on my cock. Now, Beth."

She sat up, straddling one of his strong legs, her feminine flesh clenching at the sensation of his hairy thigh against the smooth skin of her inner thighs. His muscles flexed against her. He had incredible definition and control. No wonder he was so good at his extreme sports. She shuddered from the intense pleasure of the subtle caress and couldn't help rubbing herself against him, just a little.

A harsh sound came from his throat. "You are killing me."

"You've said that before, but you're still alive."

"Edging toward insanity."

She cupped his sac very gently. "I'm not trying to drive you crazy."

"Then Heaven help me if you ever did."

She laughed, her whole body awash with sensation, but her humor triggered by his obvious sexual frustration. She squeezed oh so carefully and caressed his length with her other hand. "You are so soft here."

"That's not the word I would use to describe it."

"Really?"

"Really," he said gutturally.

She moved her hand up and down the entire length of his shaft. Once. Twice. Three times. He bowed beneath her again, making his thigh grind against her tender flesh. She couldn't stand the restriction of her panties anymore and scrambled out of them before resuming her position.

"The bra, too," he demanded in a voice that made her insides quiver with sensual delight.

"And if I don't want to?"

"Do it anyway."

He was tied to the bed, at her mercy, and yet she felt an overwhelming urge to do as he said. Maybe because her breasts were aching and swollen and she wanted the sensation of his scorching gaze on them as much as he wanted to look. Or maybe because a primal part of her wanted to submit. Regardless of why, she undid her bra and peeled it from her body slowly while he watched in hungry fascination.

"You have a gorgeous rack, Beth."

Despite the level of her arousal, laughter burst out of her. *"Rack?"*

"Would you rather I said tits?" he asked, one corner of his mouth tipped in a sexy smile, but his voice was strained.

She thought about it. "Uh . . . no."

"Boobs? Hooters? Cans? Boobies? Melons? Gozangas?"

She shook her head, giggling. "They're my *breasts*."

"They're a work of art."

"I'm glad you approve."

"That's a mild word for my reaction to seeing them."

Looking at the way his penis bobbed in angry arousal, she had to agree.

"Touch your nipples . . . like you did when we were on the phone last night. I want to see you do it."

"You're getting awfully demanding. First you wanted me to go down on you, then take off my bra . . . and now you're demanding I touch myself." She hadn't taken him in her mouth, but she had taken off her bra.

"Do it."

Her inner walls spasmed at the command in his voice. "Choose."

"What?"

"Either I touch myself or I take you in my mouth."

"You'll do whichever one I want . . . to my specifications?"

That wasn't what she'd said, but it made her get wetter to think about, so she nodded.

"Touch yourself."

She jolted. She couldn't believe he hadn't asked her for the blow job. Maybe she wasn't affecting him as much as she thought. Only his hard flesh looked ready to explode, pre-cum glistening on his tip in enticing wetness. Could he really want to see her touch herself more than he wanted to be touched? Or was he trying to wrest control from her despite his bonds?

If that was the case, she was just going to have to make watching her as exciting as experiencing her mouth.

She cupped her breasts, lifting them and moaning softly as she did so. "Like this?"

"Yes. Knead that pretty flesh."

She kneaded, excitement spearing straight from her aching nipples to her throbbing clitoris. "Do you want me to touch my nipples?"

"Yes."

She did, playing with them like she had the night before, rolling them between her fingertips and pulling on them as she rode his thigh with increasingly urgent movements. He helped her, pressing upward and moving his leg side to side. She was losing the momentum of her seduction, but she couldn't make herself care.

"Now touch your clit, but don't stop playing with your breast with the other hand."

"I didn't say I would touch myself there," she panted.

"You didn't specify where—only that you would do it to my specifications and I just specified."

How could she not have noticed such a glaring omission? She shook her head, trying to clear it, but Ethan misunderstood and frowned.

"You a welsher, baby?"

"No."

"Then touch yourself."

She wanted to, so why deny him?

So, she did, sliding her hand into the nest of curls at the juncture of her thighs until one fingertip encountered her sweet spot. Pleasure pulsed at the touch.

"That looks so hot, baby . . . just like I pictured it last night on the phone."

And suddenly she needed the same thing. She didn't know why he wanted to see her as she'd been last night, but she needed to see him touch himself to complete what they'd done. To make it real and not just another fantasy that he'd cooperated with creating. The need was a driving compulsion she didn't even attempt to stem.

She leaned up and unlatched one of the wrist cuffs. "Show me, too."

He required no second urging, but wrapped his long fingers around his shaft and stroked himself. "You're going to make me come this way."

"Like you said earlier, we have all night for other stuff."

But she really didn't want their first climax to be this way . . . she just wanted to drive them both closer to the edge.

His hand came up and she saw that he was going to brush it over his head and she didn't want him to wipe away the moisture there. She wanted to taste it.

She swept down and took his head into her mouth without any warning.

He shouted while she swirled her tongue over his essence, reveling in the flavor that was unique to him alone. His hand clamped in her hair and he thrust upward. She let him press himself farther into her mouth, not caring when he hit the back of her throat. But he felt it and pulled back, muttering a desperate apology while his hand fell away to fist against the comforter.

He was out of control. If he wasn't restrained, he'd have her under him or pulled on top of him in a heartbeat. That certainty pushed her own arousal higher until she was teetering on the brink of orgasm. One touch, delivered right, and she would go over, but she was careful not to give herself the stimulation. She needed it to come from him.

She pulled her mouth away with a pop and scrambled across the bed to the nightstand. She yanked the drawer open and scrabbled for a condom before returning to him and ripping the packet open. She put it on him carefully, her hands shaking so much she was afraid she was going to tear it. But she didn't and he urged her on with guttural pleas and compliments.

When she was done, she straddled him, but held herself above his rock hard erection. "Do you want me?"

"Yes."

"Enough?"

His free hand clamped her thigh and he tugged, but she managed to stay up on her haunches.

"Enough?" she demanded again.

"Too much," he bit back.

Then she slid down onto him, pressing his head into her

opening and immediately rocking for deeper penetration. But he was big and she was swollen, more swollen than she'd ever been. It wasn't easy. She was wetter than she'd ever been, too, and that helped, but she felt stretched and filled and he wasn't even all the way inside yet.

"Oh, yeah. Oh, baby . . . that's so good." He thrust upward, pushing himself deeper inside and putting her so-called dominance into question.

And again . . . she loved it. She'd known it would be like this. He was everything she had wanted. A man who was strong enough to allow her to bind him, to touch him, to tease and torment him, but too strong to be dominated by her. No matter what the circumstances.

But she wasn't about to cede all control to him. She continued her rocking movements until he was seated fully inside her and then she stopped, adjusting to the fullness, to sensitive tissues stretched to capacity.

"Don't stop, baby," he pleaded.

"It's so much," she gasped.

"But not too much. You can handle me, Beth."

"Yes." She was determined to, but she felt like she was going to die from pleasure. Her body demanded more and she started to move, riding him, finding a rhythm and angle that maximized stimulation to her clitoris.

"That's right, Beth. Just like that. Ride me hard!" He bucked under her, forcing her to match their body movements to stay seated.

And she did ride him hard, letting his penis pound into her with passionate force.

His free hand was all over her, touching her, urging her on and she didn't mind because he made her feel so good. The pleasure was building inside, sharp and urgent. Their bodies were both covered by a sheen of sweat and both their breathing was labored.

"Come with me, Ethan," she demanded. "I want to feel you lose control. Come with me *now*!"

And he did. They climaxed together, his pulses feeding her convulsions and her inner muscles milking him to greater heights until they both cried out and collapsed from the surfeit of pleasure.

His chest moved with laborious breaths and she thought she must be heavy . . . should probably help him dispose of the condom . . . but she couldn't make herself move. His body stretched under hers and all she could think was that felt nice. Then both his hands were free to rub her back and cuddle her close.

"Should undo your ankles," she slurred against his chest.

"In a minute, Sunshine. For now . . . just let me bask."

"Bask?" she asked drowsily.

"In pleasure. It was so damn good."

"Yes."

Chapter 12

Ethan gently rolled Beth off of him, not sure if she was asleep or awake. Her body was draped over him in boneless abandon.

She blinked up at him, her sherry-brown eyes drowsy. "Going somewhere?"

"Condom."

"Oh." Her eyes slid shut and she curled onto her side, facing him, one arm under her head. "'skay."

He smiled and reached for his ankle. It wasn't easy to undo the tie from that angle, but he managed it. It was a lot simpler to do the other one once he had more freedom of mobility.

Had she gotten what she needed from tying him to the bed? He didn't figure she would have fantasized so much about him being her bound lover if she'd truly wanted to dominate. But even so, he'd pushed for her to lose her control. It wasn't hard, she responded to him more intensely than any lover he'd ever had.

He couldn't help wondering how deep the pleasure could go if he tied her to the bed. But she would be no more helpless than he. Because his body reacted to hers like a power supply to electricity. She turned him on with the first connection.

He took care of the condom and then eyed his big claw-footed tub with interest. They would both sleep better if they washed the sweat from their lovemaking off. Besides soaking in the porcelain monstrosity with Beth sounded like a heck of a lot more fun than going straight to sleep.

He ran the bath, dumping some stuff in the water that made it smell okay and feel silky. Women liked that kind of thing. His sister had given it to him as a gift and told him to use it when his muscles were aching from a tough workout or competition. It didn't smell girly, so he'd agreed, but he'd never actually used it. Until now.

It was just the kind of thing his Beth would appreciate. She was a very sensual woman. He wondered if she even realized how much. Her own sexuality seemed to surprise her sometimes.

He left the tub filling and went back into the bedroom to get Beth.

She was still curled up on her side, totally naked. He'd taken the bedding off before lying down and she didn't have so much as a sheet to cover her. She was gorgeous. Sweet, feminine curves that were different than his usual lover. Beth was neither an agent, nor an extreme sportswoman.

She worked out with her tae kwon do and her body was toned, but it wasn't reed thin or bulked out like some women who lifted weights. The curve of her tummy and breasts were intensely feminine and excited him in a way that the ultra-honed women who usually populated his world had not in a long time.

This woman was all that made the female of their species unique and damned if that didn't turn him on beyond reason.

He leaned one knee on the bed and reached for her.

Her eyes opened and surveyed him with curiosity. "All done?"

"Yeah, but I thought we could take a bath." He hooked one arm under her shoulders and the other under her knees. "All right?"

"Yes."

He liked that sweet acquiescence. Too much. He lifted her and carried her into the bathroom. The tub was as high as it needed to be, so he turned the water off and then stepped into blue tinted depths with her still in his arms.

She moaned as he settled her on his lap, the silky, hot water lapping around them. "This feels sooooo good."

"You like baths?"

"I love them, especially in really hot water." She leaned back against his chest, settling farther into the water. "I've never taken a bath with a man though."

"You never tied one up before either. I guess tonight is your night for firsts."

"Yes, it is." She paused for a second, scooping water and pouring it over her shoulders and chest. "Do you mind?"

"What exactly?"

"That I'm not very experienced," she said hesitantly, turning her head so she could meet his gaze, her dark eyes serious and concerned. "That I have slightly kinky tastes in sex."

He almost laughed, but he didn't want to hurt the little darling's feelings. Only how could she be uncertain after the sex they'd just had? "You are incredible in the sack, baby. I don't mind anything about you. I enjoyed your *slightly kinky* tastes, or didn't you notice?"

She blushed right down to her still-engorged nipples.

Then he did laugh. He couldn't hold it back.

Sitting up, she smacked his shoulder with her fist and pouted. "What do you think is so funny?"

It was the cutest pout he'd ever seen, her full lower lip protruding just enough to tempt him to bite it.

"You're blushing because I said you're good in the sack *after* tying me to the bed and shamelessly pleasuring yourself on my body. Would the real Beth Whitney please stand up?"

She pouted some more and his dick reacted like she'd offered him the blow job he'd demanded earlier . . . and had given up in favor of watching her touch herself. "I think she's emerging now, but I have no intention of standing up. This water feels too nice."

He gripped her hips and pulled her so that she was nestled right against his growing hard-on. "You feel nice."

Her eyes grew wide. "What are you, the Energizer Bunny?"

"A certain pouty woman has this effect on me."

"I do not pout."

He laughed and leaned forward to nip her protruding lower lip. "Don't you?"

She gasped and he kissed her, taking full advantage and sweeping her sweet interior with his tongue. She was still for a second and then responded with all the fire he'd learned she had locked inside of her. Tangling her tongue with his, she collapsed against him, her soft breasts pillowing against his chest. It felt great. Hell, everything with her felt too damned good.

She was straddling him and rubbing herself against his now straining erection before he realized what was happening.

"This is dangerous, baby," he said against her mouth.

"D-dangerous?" she asked in a dazed voice that hardened his cock further.

"I didn't bring a condom in here."

"Would it stay on . . . in the water?"

"Yeah, but I have to put it on when I'm dry."

"Oh." She kissed him and then sighed. "I guess we'd better get out."

He held her to him. "Or we could touch each other."

"In the water?" she asked, sounding both intrigued and slightly appalled. "Won't that be messy?"

"We can shower after."

She rubbed herself up and down his length. "Okay."

"Not like this." She was too close. For the first time in longer than he could remember, he seriously doubted his ability to control his urge to slip inside a woman if they kept doing what they were doing. "With our hands."

She stopped moving and sat up again, pressing her silky, swollen flesh against his erection and making him groan. "I want to touch you first."

"Okay."

She grinned. "I like it when you're so accommodating."

"You're going to love it when I really accommodate you."

She wrapped her fingers around him and his mind blanked. For a woman who didn't have a lot of experience, she certainly knew how to touch a man. She used both her hands and gave extra attention to the ultrasensitive skin on his head. It usually took him longer to come with a hand job, but it didn't feel like any time at all before he felt the pressure building at the base of his cock.

He rocked and urged her on with guttural demands she seemed only too happy to obey. His climax had him arching up and sloshing water out of the tub, while she caressed him until the pleasure was so intense, he couldn't stand it anymore.

He pushed her hands away with a jerky movement. "Too much."

"You're crying uncle?"

"If you don't stop touching me, I'll be crying, period."

"Wow."

That was not the word he had been thinking. This woman got to him in ways that made him uncomfortable. He had thought just touching each other would be less intense than actually making love. He'd been wrong. He felt like she'd turned him inside out and now he was about to return the favor.

He pulled her around so she was straddling his hips but facing away from him, his still sensitive and semierect flesh nestled against her backside. "Now, it's my turn."

"How do you have the energy?"

Had she thought he would let her get him off and then call it a night? That was not his way. When it came to sex, Ethan took the game of one-upmanship very seriously. He liked knowing he'd wowed his partner . . . and not with *his* response.

"When it comes to touching you, I'll always have it."

"That's sweet."

Ethan had been called many things by his lovers, but sweet wasn't one of them and he wasn't sure he liked it coming from Beth. It made him sound safe and he was not a safe man. She ought to know that. "I'll show you sweet."

He touched her all over in ways he knew would please her, reveling in the way her resilient curves felt against his exploring fingers. He played with her breasts and nipples until they were hard and so sensitive she jerked every time the pad of his thumb slid over one. Then he played with her belly, exploring her belly button and the soft flesh just above her mound. She moaned and moved against him, but while he touched her inner thighs and the area all around her sex, he kept back from touching her there.

She begged him to touch her intimately and he brushed his fingertips lightly over her hair, making her body spasm with need. He didn't delve between her lips though, but he kept her on the edge, building her excitement higher and higher. She grabbed his wrist and tried to force his hand closer, but he hadn't worked on resistance weights for nothing.

He refused to budge, using her momentum to move his hand to her inner thigh again where he drew circles and kneaded her flesh until she was moaning and thrashing in the water. It wasn't enough though. He wanted her to plead and she did.

"Please, Ethan, touch my clitoris. I'm so close!"

When his fingers finally dipped between her legs while his other hand tugged on an engorged nipple, he was fairly certain she wasn't thinking he was all that sweet anymore.

She gave a keening cry and bucked in his arms. He swirled his fingertip over and around her swollen clitoris, then slid down into her silky wetness. Her inner muscles clenched as tight as a vice on his fingers and he remembered how incredibly snug she'd felt around his dick. She moved on him, riding his fingers like they were something more and moaning out her pleasure.

"Come for me, Beth. Come for me, now." He pressed the heel of his hand to her sweet spot and brought her to orgasm.

She screamed out his name as she strained against him, but he didn't stop and she launched into another immediate climax as the first was still waning. This time she sat straight up, straining against his hold and sending more water cascading over the sides of the tub as she screamed out an animal-like cry that went on and on and on.

The woman was the sexiest thing he'd ever seen . . . or touched. Her cry finally settled to a whimper while she moved restlessly as if trying to minimize her sensitivity to his touch.

Finally, she collapsed back against him as her body went boneless and her breaths came in sobbing gasps. "Too good. Too much."

He immediately gentled his touch to a soothing motion, rather than one meant to incite more passion.

"You crying uncle?" he threw her words back at her, smiling at the way she rubbed her head against his chest as if seeking comfort from the cataclysm he'd put her through.

"Juss . . . cryin'," she slurred.

And with alarm, he realized she was. He turned her against him, tucking one arm around her the other rubbing frantically at her back. "It's okay, Sunshine. Hush. Don't cry."

"'sokay. I know, but too good." She hiccuped a little and rubbed her cheek against his chest. "Do it again later."

He said nothing, but something strange happened inside him in response to her crying after climaxing. He'd heard about that kind of thing, but he didn't get deeply emotional with his lovers and had never experienced it. He and Beth weren't into heavy emotion here either, but their sexual response to each other was out of this world.

And that's all it was. Too much pleasure and she'd reacted with tears. Nothing big or earth shaking in that.

Right. Now, they'd better shower so they could get to bed before they drowned.

She wasn't cooperative about taking a shower and groused when he made her stand up. Instead of annoying him, her crankiness charmed him and he shook his head at himself. Cranky women were not appealing, but Beth was different. She was just so darn cute, the way she grumbled and pouted and leaned against him like she couldn't be expected to stand on her own.

He managed to get the tub drained, their bodies washed and dried, her back in bed, and the water mess on the tile floor wiped up before falling in bed beside her, exhausted.

He didn't fall asleep right away though. He was totally wiped, but his mind could not let go of how out of control he'd felt with Beth in the bathtub. It should have been a pleasant way to end their lovemaking session, not something that had been close to soul shattering.

He was thirty-two years old. Beth was right when she said he had more sexual experience than her. A lot more. He wasn't suicidal, he didn't sleep with anything willing in a skirt, but he'd had sex partners who were more sophisticated, more knowledgeable about what turned a man on and willing to use that knowledge than his little Sunshine, but not one of those women seduced his senses the way that she did.

He had never even come close to losing his control with another woman. He'd never forgotten the condom or doubted his ability to withstand temptation, no matter how alluringly packaged. But he'd been positive that if she tried to get them off by rubbing herself along his cock that he'd end up inside her. The knowledge was far from pleasant.

What was so different about her?

It had to be her innocence . . . her emerging sensuality . . . the seductress that shone forth from her soft brown eyes. The sex had been so intense because they'd been living out her fantasies. Beth wasn't the first woman who had told him that he starred in her most private dreams, but she was the first one who had exploded all over him with an excess of passion that came from not living those fantasies out with anyone else. Ever.

She'd been engaged to Hyatt, but she'd never bound him to the bed. She'd been a sexual powder keg waiting for the right spark and Ethan had been more like an inferno. And that's what bothered him. His response had been over the top. He enjoyed mind-blowing sex as much as the next man, but he always stayed in control and he couldn't do his job while he was at the mercy of an overactive libido.

Sex was fine. Hell, sex was great . . . he'd had it with other women on the job. Sometimes for the job, but he had to turn the intensity down a notch with Beth. Or he wasn't going to be able to keep her safe. And that was not an acceptable scenario.

Definitely no more handcuffs.

And on that note, he finally fell asleep.

Beth slid another surreptitious glance at Ethan. Doing a great job of ignoring her and the interested looks he received from the other female passengers and their flight attendant, he was working on an expert-level Sudoku puzzle. The man did nothing in moderation. Not his job. Not his sports activities. Not his brain teasers. Not sex. Nothing.

So, why had she felt he was holding something back this morning when he woke her up for a quickie before they went to the office for a couple of hours prior to catching their flight? Her orgasm had been spectacular, though she hadn't cried afterward again. Thank goodness. His had seemed pretty darn good, too, but she couldn't shake the feeling that he'd stepped back from her.

The restraints had been nowhere in evidence when she woke up, not that she wanted to try that soul-shattering experiment again anytime soon, but he'd put them away. Why? And he'd barely talked while exciting her body to a fever pitch and then sending her over with him inside her.

He hadn't been cold, or anything. He'd smiled at her and insisted on making her breakfast. But he hadn't been warm either. Or maybe that wasn't the right word. Affectionate. He hadn't been *affectionate* and he'd neatly sidestepped any attempt she'd made in that direction.

He was so good, she hadn't realized at first that he didn't want her touching him outside of the bedroom. His subtle movements to avoid her had only registered as he'd taken her arm to lead her onto the plane and she realized it was the first time *he'd* touched *her* since they got out of bed that morning.

She'd stilled and almost pulled away in an instinctive shock, but he'd whispered for her ears only, "It starts now, Beth. I'm the possessive boyfriend, remember?"

And that's when she'd realized. He hadn't let her touch him at his apartment. He had avoided touching her in the office. He'd touched her on the plane, but that was because it was showtime. She didn't know who he thought was going to see her on the flight, but apparently, he'd decided that now was the time to start acting in character. Which only underlined his earlier behavior in bold black.

She turned to look out the window, her thoughts in turmoil.

Because along with the realization that Ethan did not want her touch outside of the bedroom was the disturbing revelation that she wanted to touch him with affection. She wanted to be touched. He'd told her what they had was only sex, but she hadn't let herself really think about what that meant. Now, she had no choice.

She'd thought it didn't matter that his primary reason for going to bed with her was the case, but now she knew it did. Ethan would do whatever it took to succeed in bringing down Prescott, but that didn't extend to pretending affection for her he did not feel. Because he didn't think he had to.

After all, hadn't she told him she didn't want love and happily ever after, or even a good run at it? Apparently, he'd taken that to mean she wanted nothing more than the overwhelming pleasure she found with his body. And really, that's almost basically what she'd told him, wasn't it?

Welcome to the real world of sex without commitment, Beth. It hurt. She didn't want to love him. Refused to consider even the possibility, but she hadn't expected this no touching outside of the bedroom except for the case thing. She'd had no idea what to expect, if she were honest.

Alan had loved her and she'd loved him and that had extended to all their time together. Ethan had none of those feelings for her. At best, he cared for her like a friend, but he was not a touchy-feely person. That meant he wasn't going to hug her shoulder, or brush her nape, or hold her hand—he wasn't going to offer or accept any of the casual touches of affection she craved. Except for the sake of the case.

Why did that hurt so much? Why did facing a reality she had known existed before she ever flashed him with her panties make her feel wounded and vulnerable? She wasn't vulnerable to him. She wouldn't let herself be. And she had no business feeling wounded by actions that were in keeping with everything he'd said to her, everything she knew about him.

But she felt cheap and that was an ugly feeling. She couldn't let herself feel used. It had been mutual. They had both derived pleasure out of the other's body. But he was more prepared to deal with commitment-free sex than she was and she was just waking up to that fact. Was she dumb, or just a little blind when it came to her own limitations?

He didn't need the trappings of a relationship to enjoy her body. And she was going to have to learn to deal with that reality because she didn't think she had the strength to turn him down for sex. Not now that she knew what happened when they touched. Fantasies were not enough anymore.

They picked up a car at the airport and then checked into a hotel on the western edge of the metropolitan area, so their drive to the coast the following morning would not be hampered by city traffic. There was only one bed in the hotel room and while it wasn't as big as Ethan's monster bed, it was king sized, dominating the room and Beth's thoughts with its presence.

"You ready for the interview tomorrow?" Ethan asked from behind her after engaging the safety double lock on the door.

She shrugged. "I'm not worried about that part."

"Not at all?"

"Why should I be? I'm perfect for the job and I just have to remember that." Funny how her preoccupation with her pseudorelationship with Ethan made everything else sort of pale in significance on her internal anxiety meter. She didn't feel even sort of nervous about tomorrow.

"Not worried about playing the role of a woman with an overly possessive boyfriend anymore?"

She turned to face him, hugging herself so she wouldn't reach out to touch him. They were alone now, no longer on the stage of their pretend life together. "No. I think we've got the act down."

He snorted at that. "We haven't even started."

"I'd say that after last night, we'd more than started."

"That wasn't part of the act."

"Whatever you say." She wasn't going to argue with him over it.

Maybe he didn't see it that way. Maybe for him, it was enough that he genuinely wanted her, so he didn't see the timing and the fact their relationship was bound to the case as actually being part of the act for the case. Whatever his reasoning, she wasn't about to get into a drawn-out discussion about it.

He tipped her face up with a fist under her chin, his green gaze penetrating hers. "Something bothering you, Sunshine?"

She moved away from his touch and headed for her suitcase. "Nothing you need to worry about."

"If it's going to affect your effectiveness on assignment, I do."

She shook her clothes out and hung them up, mentally noting she needed to spot iron the jacket she planned to wear to the interview tomorrow. "I'm good to go with the assignment."

"You tired?"

"Maybe a little."

"It would probably be best if we forgo sex tonight and you get some uninterrupted rest."

She paused in unpacking her case and then went back to what she'd been doing. "Whatever you think is best. You're the agent in charge."

He was silent for several seconds, but she just finished unpacking and then slid the small case in the bottom of the closet before turning to face him again.

He was watching her, an odd expression on his sculpted features. His eyes snapped to her face and he frowned. "I could use a run. I hate the enforced inactivity of being on a plane."

"You weren't exactly inactive. You did several sets of isometrics in your seat."

"It's not the same thing."

"No, I don't suppose it is." Was he asking for her permission? No. Not in character . . . for either the pretend or real Ethan.

"Besides, if I'm going to leave you alone, I need to work off some of this extra energy."

"That makes sense." Not that she really thought it would be all that difficult for him.

"You want to come?"

She shook her head. "I'm not a runner. I like my tae kwon do, but that's about it. I'll probably go to the exercise room and use their mats for a workout, or ride a stationary bike for a while."

"I'd prefer you not go by yourself."

"Why?"

"It's not in character for me to let you work out alone."

"I don't think we need to be fully in character right now."

"The sooner we start, the more natural the role will be for you to play."

"You aren't going to have any problem with the role. You said so."

"I'm not the only one playing a role here."

"My biggest responsibility is to react." He'd said that, too.

"To an extent, that's true, but you've also got to get in the mind-set of a woman who is used to asking her boyfriend about everything. We've been together two years . . . that would have affected your behavior some."

"Okay . . . here I am asking: Do you mind if I work out in the exercise room while you go running?"

He made a sound of frustration. "I already said I'd prefer you not."

"This is where I assert some of my dormant independence and say tough."

He laughed. "Fine. If you're sure you don't want to go running with me instead."

"You're kidding, right? Even if I was used to jogging, I wouldn't run with you. You'd leave me in the dust and the whole running together point would be defunct by the end of the first block."

"I'd match my stride to yours."

"And walk?"

He frowned, but didn't say anything before grabbing his jogging shorts and T-shirt from his carryall. He took them into the bathroom to change and that surprised her, but she wasn't going to say anything about it. When he came out, she tried not to look, but it was a lost cause.

The man had an incredible body. His long, muscular legs were exposed by his shorts and his tank top stretched snugly over his chest, making her mouth water.

"If you don't stop looking at me like that, I'm going to choose a different form of exercise."

"And that would be a bad thing?"

"I want you rested and relaxed at the interview tomorrow, not hungover from a surfeit of explosive sex."

She'd never had so much sex she got a hangover from it, but she'd heard of that happening. "Are you saying that if we start, you don't think we'll be able to stop?"

"It's a distinct possibility. You have a lot of years of fantasizing to make up for."

The words pierced her mind, but it took a second for her to accept their meaning. "You think I'm sex-starved?" she demanded, her voice going up an octave.

His eyes widened. "That's not what I said."

"You may as well have. Apparently, I've gone too long without real sex and therefore would make too many physical demands on you, so much so that I would not be in any shape to interview tomorrow morning."

"Settle down, little Beth, I—"

"Don't call me that! I'm not little. I'm not a child. *And I'm not sex-starved*," she finished from between gritted teeth.

Chapter 13

"I didn't say you were, but after last night . . . you've got to admit the sex between us can get out of hand pretty damn easily."

"I didn't notice it getting out of hand, but then I wasn't inside your brain, so maybe I just didn't see our time together the same way you did." He had seen that amazing experience as the result of a woman who had gone too long without sex?

Humiliated color scorched her cheeks. Because in one sense, he was right. She's spent so long fantasizing about him that when he'd touched her, when he'd let her touch him . . . she'd lost touch with reality and found a whole new one. Only, she'd thought he had, too, at least to an extent.

"All I'm saying is that tonight would be a bad time for a sexual marathon," he said with exaggerated patience.

She deliberately widened her eyes. "Did I offer to engage in one?"

He sighed, sounding exasperated. "No."

She hugged herself tighter, fighting to hold in the embarrassment and anger that he could see her in that light. "Go running."

"I don't think we are done talking."

"I get your message loud and clear. Don't worry. Beyond that, this conversation has no further productive value."

He looked like he might argue, but he didn't. He turned on his heel and left the hotel room with quick precision.

She stared at the closed door for a long time, trying to grapple with this newly recognized element to having sex with Ethan. He denied thinking she was sex-starved, but what else would he call it? She'd thought that the intensity at least had been mutual, but he made it sound like he'd been reacting to her neediness. That was just so mortifying.

She was not needy. She was horny for him. There was a difference, but apparently he didn't see it that way. She felt hollow inside, sick with embarrassment that he'd seen her acting out her fantasies with him in that light. She'd been so moved that he hadn't made fun of her desires, that he'd catered to them, but now that all felt tainted.

It was bad enough knowing she didn't have anywhere near the experience of his usual bedmates, but to discover he saw her as some sort of closet nymphomaniac was the absolute pits. How could she sleep in that bed with him knowing he thought that way about her? If she accidentally touched him in the night, he'd assume it was some kind of come-on.

The door slammed open and Ethan stormed back into the room, his expression stormy. She gasped, but didn't get a chance to say a word before his hands gripped her shoulders and his mouth slammed down on hers.

She started to shove him away, but he wrapped her up close and kissed her until they were both breathing hard.

He lifted his head, his green eyes fixed to hers. "I do not think you are sex-starved. Last night was intense. Too intense for the safety of our mission and that came from both of us. You turn me on, baby. In ways no other woman has in a long time. I can't afford to be sidetracked right now and neither can you."

"So, no more sex?"

"No more mind-blowing, soul-destroying sex. We've got to keep it light."

"Light. Right. Got it." But *no sex* sounded easier than keeping it light. She didn't know how to turn off her emotions, but she supposed he was an expert at it.

He shook his head and groaned. "You don't know what you do to me when you look at me like that, do you?"

"Like what?"

"Like you're trying to figure me out. That should make me want to turn and run, instead it turns me on."

"I'm not trying to see into your soul, just figure out this light sex thing. I'm not sure I know how to do it."

"We'll figure it out, but no more bondage."

"You didn't like it?"

"I liked it too much."

"Oh."

"Remember, we want light."

"Okay."

"Now, I've definitely got to go run."

"Because we can't have sex tonight."

"Right."

"Not even light sex?" Oh, man . . . did that make her sound needy and desperate?

Ethan frowned and stepped back. "I don't think I can keep it light right now. Sitting beside you on the plane for hours . . . being with you now, it's driving me crazy."

"I thought you didn't even notice me. You certainly had enough other female attention."

"I didn't notice."

"But you're saying you noticed me?"

"How could I not notice you? Your scent excites everything male and sexual inside me and having you close enough to touch is a major temptation."

"So, you're saying you're the sex-starved one?"

He barked out a laugh. "Maybe. It's been a while, that's for sure."

"How long?" she asked, helpless to hold the question back.

"Too long. Almost a year."

"That's unusual for you, isn't it?"

"Yes."

"But you've dated."

"Contrary to what you obviously believe about me, I don't do the nasty with every woman I take out."

"But a year . . ."

"Almost a year," he corrected.

"*Almost*. It's still a long time for you."

"I said it was."

"I'm just confirming I'm not the only person in this room with a lot of sexual energy to burn."

"Which is why I need to go for a run."

"Have fun."

He frowned at her, like a reprimand, but she just grinned back and shooed him out the door.

She felt tons better now that she knew he didn't see her as a desperate female, starving for sex. Or if he did, they were in the same boat. She was not going to let it bother her that he might have tipped in her direction because he'd been too long without a lover. The sex last night had not disappointed him. It had been too much for his peace of mind on a case. He'd as good as said so.

For some reason she could not fathom, that made her feel proud. Like she'd succeeded at something his other lovers hadn't. They would part ways after the case ended, but he wouldn't forget her. And that was only fair, because she'd never forget him.

But he wanted to keep things light and that was exactly what she wanted. Keep the intensity to a minimum and she wasn't going to start imagining herself in love with him. It was a good plan.

Declarations of intent were all well and good, but what was a man supposed to do when the woman whose body he craved was curled up beside him and making it impossible to sleep? What kind of damn fool told a woman he didn't want to have sex with her when he wanted nothing more?

A Texas-size fool, that's what kind.

She was sleeping like a baby, as if sharing a bed with a man was nothing new for her. It was, though, and she shouldn't be sleeping so damned peacefully. Well, okay . . . not peacefully. She hadn't been happy until she'd rolled across the wide expanse of the king-size bed and snuggled right up to his back. One of her small feet was tucked between his calves and the other pressed close to his bottom leg.

He'd been fighting the need to turn over and start touching her from the moment her warm little hand had landed against his shoulder blade. He'd worn a T-shirt and shorts to bed in some misguided belief that it might help fight the needs raging through him. All they did was make his erection more painful than it needed to be.

She'd donned a prim white cotton nightgown that looked brand new. He'd made the mistake of commenting on that and she'd admitted she normally slept in the buff. The way he wanted her right now. Not that the modest gown was really all that modest. It was thin cotton and the shadow of her nipples showed right through, as well as the dark ruff of hair between her legs. She wasn't wearing panties and one glance at the shadow crease of her backside through the thin cotton had been enough to confirm the suspicion.

His dick was so hard, it felt ready to split his skin. And he was the fool who had said no sex tonight. She needed her rest. Well, she was getting it . . . while he drove himself slowly insane.

Beth launched into wakefulness, her body throbbing with unrelenting sensual need. She gasped in shock, her eyes flying open, but the room was still cast in predawn shadows and she couldn't really see anything. All she could do was feel and what she felt was desire burning through her veins like lava.

"*Ethan.*" His name came out a long, low moan.

The lips nibbling at the ultrasensitive spot behind her ear paused in their ministrations to whisper, "Good morning,

Sunshine," then moved to cover her mouth with hungry urgency.

It was a kiss unlike any they had shared. She'd never sensed such uncontrolled need emanating from him and his lips had never been quite so possessive. Had they?

He cradled her head in the crook of his arm and his hand massaged her breast and teased her nipple while the other one played a tempting sonata between her legs. She could feel herself wet and swollen there, his fingers sliding easily between her slick folds. He swirled his thumb over her clitoris and something inside her shattered.

There was no time for her to think. Her body was on fire. She moaned against his devouring lips and arched into the pleasure exploding between her legs. She didn't know how long he'd been touching her to bring her toward wakefulness, but her body shimmered on the edge of orgasm and then went over in a shower of sparks and convulsions.

He rolled on top of her, never breaking their kiss, and speared inside her still-contracting sheath. His thrusts were hard and deep, driving her to a second climax with dismaying speed. This time they came together, his body rigid above hers, her insides going supernova until her mind went black.

She awoke a second time to gentle hands smoothing her hair from her face and lips pressing tender kisses to her temple.

She was still panting from the shocking pleasure despite the respite of her temporary blackout. "That was incredible."

"You are incredible, Beth." White teeth flashed in the dimness of the room, the expression in his eyes cast in mysterious shadow.

"Please tell me you remembered the condom."

"I did."

"So, you planned this?"

"I woke up touching you and had enough foresight to realize I'd best be prepared for when you woke up, too."

"You could have stopped touching me."

"No. I could not."

"I thought you said no sex."

"That was last night."

Funny, she'd been pretty sure he meant until after the interview. "What time is it?"

"Almost dawn. We have plenty of time to get ready and eat breakfast before we have to drive to the coast."

She snuggled into his chest, reveling in their closeness, even if it was nothing more than postcoitus tenderness. "Mmmm . . . hmmm . . ."

"You fainted. Only for a few seconds, but you were definitely out." He sounded bothered by that fact, almost accusing.

But wouldn't a man feel smug that he'd had such an impact on his lover? She would have thought so, but then she wasn't him and he obviously saw the world through a different set of binoculars.

"It was intense," she ventured.

"Too intense." He pulled away and stood up, his frown readable even in the thin light starting to fill the room from the crack in the curtains.

Then she remembered. That was his whole problem. He wanted to keep sex between them light. He'd made his feelings clear the night before and ultimately she'd agreed with him, but she still felt bereft as he left the bed. On the edge of rejected, but not quite there. Like she had the morning before.

She didn't like the feeling, but wasn't sure what to do about it. Especially since she agreed with him in theory.

Feeling at a disadvantage still lying there with her nightgown hiked up to her waist and her most intimate flesh bare to him, she hastily pressed her legs together and sat up. Grabbing the sheet, she pulled it over her and drew her knees to her chest in a defensive posture under it. "What do you want to do about it?"

He ran his hand through his hair, his own nudity not seeming to bother him at all. "Abstaining definitely doesn't work."

Relief coursed through her, but she tried not to let it show. She'd been half-worried he was going to say no sex altogether and she hadn't known how she was going to keep her hands to herself. Though she still thought that abstaining would have been more doable than trying to keep a lid on the passion that roared between them when they started touching.

"So, what do you suggest?"

"We're obviously going to have to make love often, but keep the encounters from getting too intense." He sounded perfectly serious, like he really believed what he was saying.

She stared at him, choking back a snort of derision. Did he really think they could do that? She didn't think it would matter how many times they had sex, her body was going to respond to him like it had never done to anyone else. Every single time. She knew it.

He had to know it, too, but the man really thought he could keep things light. He'd just given her a climax so intense, she'd fainted and yet somehow he believed he could pull back from that level of connection. Maybe he could, but it certainly seemed like he'd been with her all the way this morning.

And he was the one who said he couldn't stop touching her once he woke up and realized what he was doing. That did not sound like a response easily modified.

"We can try," she said doubtfully.

"It will work." He spoke with certainty that should have been comforting, but just made her feel funny in the region of her heart. He really didn't want deep involvement with her.

She just shrugged, unwilling to lie and say she agreed or argue with him and say she thought he was nuts. Which she did.

He nodded, as if it was all settled. "I'm going to take a shower. Why don't you go back to sleep for a while? You don't have to be up quite yet."

He was in the bathroom, the door firmly shut behind him, before she could even take a breath to respond.

Apparently, they weren't going to share a shower like they had the morning before. She grimaced and hugged her knees tightly to her chest. He probably considered doing so too intimate. Too intense. They'd gone from cuddling to no touching in a heartbeat and that sense of rejection was growing more solid.

There was a frozen lump inside her chest and it was spreading over all her feelings like an icy blanket. She didn't know why, but she couldn't push the pain away. It grew inside her until she was so cold she grabbed the blanket and huddled beneath it and the sheet, trying to understand why it hurt so much. Where the pain was coming from.

She didn't want involvement that would be too hard to walk away from. She knew she didn't. Just like she knew that eventually, she had to walk away from him. So why did his attitude bother her so much?

Why was it making her feel like she couldn't breathe?

She stared around the nice, but nondescript hotel room as a memory surfaced. She'd been about eight years old. Her dad had missed her school play. Again. So had her mom this time. Beth had been in her bedroom, huddled much like she was now under a purple princess comforter. She'd been crying like her heart was broken when her mom came in from one of her important meetings.

She'd laid her hand on Beth's back and tried to soothe her, but Lynn Whitney's words had left an indelible impression on Beth's heart. "You're so intense, Elizabeth. All of this emotion is exhausting . . . for both of us. You take everything far too much to heart."

Beth had turned tearstained eyes to her mom and flinched at the look of annoyance on the grown-up's features. "Your dad and I don't know what to do with you. This is not a tragedy, sweetie. You've got to learn to deal with disappointments without letting your emotions become so distraught. I swear sometimes, your father and I wonder if you are a changeling."

She'd laughed softly and ruffled Beth's hair, but the small girl had not shared her mom's humor. She already knew she wasn't like her parents. She'd never seen her mom cry, but Beth felt like crying a lot. Both her mom and dad acted like it shouldn't matter if Beth was the only girl in her class who didn't have any parents at the play.

She knew that if either of them had been little like her, they wouldn't have cared. Her mom was always telling her stories of what it was like growing up the daughter of a famous politician and the sacrifices that had to be made. Beth hated making those sacrifices, but often wondered why she had to care so much. At eight, she wasn't sure what a changeling was, but she thought it meant she didn't fit her family. As she'd grown older, she'd learned she was right.

Then she'd met Alan and assumed that finally, her intense emotions would have a safe outlet. It was okay to love him, to need him. He'd said so. Only she'd mistaken his sexual desire for her for a matching strength of emotion. When he talked about need, he didn't mean the soul-deep need she had to belong to someone else and have them belong to her.

He meant sex . . . and maybe the occasional moment of comfort. Not a daily living of two closely joined halves of the same whole. She'd discovered her error as their relationship progressed, but she'd hidden from the knowledge. He hadn't wanted her to make emotional demands on him any more than her parents had and the aborted wedding had been the ultimate object lesson in that regard.

She'd woken up in a pain-filled hurry on her wedding day and had refused to hide from the truth any longer. Once her eyes were open to reality, she'd realized immediately that she wasn't capable of settling for something less than her dream. It wouldn't have been fair to either of them and she'd stood beside her decision even when he pleaded with her to give them another chance.

But she'd recognized that what she needed might not be out there and rather than be hurt again, she'd pulled away from any male-female involvement at all. Her fantasies about Ethan had helped her to do that, but now he was telling her that even her sensuality was too intense and that made her angry.

What was so wrong with her that she had to withhold part of herself and disguise her needs from the important people in her life to be accepted by them? Even a casual lover wanted her to keep the sex low-key.

Part of her knew that was for the sake of the case, but her heart didn't seem to care about the reasoning behind it. It still felt like rejection. And she was so tired of being rejected for who and what she was.

When this case was over, she was going to stop trying to find a place for herself in her parents' world . . . in Ethan's world. Maybe there wasn't a white picket fence waiting for her in some small town in Iowa—and that wasn't exactly what she wanted anyway—but there had to be a place she fit better than the life she was living right now.

Ethan came out of the bathroom fully dressed. He hadn't wanted to risk the temptation of taking Beth back to bed. He'd kind of hoped she would be asleep, but she wasn't. She was ironing, a local newscast playing at low volume on the television behind her.

"The weather looks good for the drive."

She didn't look at him, but hung her blazer over the back of a chair. "Yes. I'll just take my shower."

He felt a wall between them as if it was made of solid brick. It felt so real, he was surprised he could see her through it.

She walked past him without looking up.

He put his hand on her arm. "Beth."

She looked at him then, but for once, he couldn't read a single thing in her normally expressive dark eyes. "What?"

"Are you okay?"

"Yes. Why shouldn't I be?"

"I don't know, but you seem . . ." He didn't know how to explain it. "Like you're separated from me."

A mocking smile curved her lips. "We are separate, Ethan. You are you and I am me and we are not a unit."

"We're a team on this mission."

"Yes."

Her agreement didn't alleviate his sense of separation at all. "We need to work together."

"I never said we didn't."

"Are you sure you are okay? Are you offended I touched you in your sleep?"

"No. I'm not offended. It was wild waking up that turned on, if you want the truth." Then she laughed. "You really should have been born to my parents and vice versa. I have a feeling the fit would have been perfect."

"I fit in just fine with the folks back home." It wasn't precisely true, but he wouldn't trade his family for the world.

Something moved in her dark eyes, but he couldn't read it either. "Maybe I'm just the one who doesn't have a place to fit."

"What brought this on, Sunshine? You fit this case so well that Whit assigned you as the contact even though you aren't a full-fledged agent."

She shook her head. "Don't worry about it, Ethan. Really. I'd really like to take a shower now though." She tugged on her arm, but he couldn't let go.

"You fit your life just fine."

"Whatever you say." She didn't roll her eyes, but it was there in her tone. "Can I go now?"

"Look, if something is bothering you, we need to talk about it."

She sighed, the sound pure feminine irritation.

And he found it adorable. What the heck was the matter with him? "Come on, Beth. Tell me what's bothering you."

She shrugged with one shoulder. "I've decided that after

this assignment, I'll be turning in my resignation and looking for a job outside of D.C., or any other big city for that matter. I'm ready to move on."

"Fainting from your orgasm made you decide that?"

She stared at him, her expression easily read this time. She looked like she thought he'd lost more than one of his marbles. "No. Having a climax that sent me into a dead faint is not what made me decide this." She laughed and he felt foolish. "Why I made the choice doesn't matter. Only that I made it. One thing you've taught me, Ethan, is that I need to live my life, not daydream about it anymore."

He liked hearing that, but not what it had led her to. Inexplicable panic welled inside of him and it was all he could do to hide it from her. "Living is good, but you don't have to move away from everyone who matters to you to start doing it."

"Yes, I do."

He didn't have an answer for the certainty in her tone. He didn't have any rights where she was concerned.

But something this morning had triggered her desire to build a new life. And if he was responsible in any way, he wanted to know. Or maybe, she'd just now realized it, but nothing this morning had actually prompted the revelation. He was being awfully conceited to assume anything she'd done with him had set off anything life changing for her.

All they'd done was had sex and while it had been a little too earth shaking for his comfort, he didn't think great sex was going to send her scurrying away to a new life. Unless she was worried she was starting to care for him.

He knew she didn't want that.

He didn't want it either. He wasn't ready to settle down and he doubted he'd ever be in a place to give Beth the kind of life she'd said she wanted. One that was safe and in which her husband was steady, dependable, and home every night.

He should leave well enough alone.

"Don't go making any decisions right now." He rubbed

the back of his neck, a gesture his dad used when trying to figure out his mom or sister—but not one Ethan had ever used much before. "It's a tense situation, you going into your first field case and all. Let yourself settle in. A lot of times, you'll end up seeing things differently later."

She shrugged again, her silky skin moving under his hand. "Whatever. Can I take my shower now?"

He didn't like it that she wouldn't agree with him or argue, that she simply wouldn't engage. He didn't figure he'd changed her mind, not one bit, but she didn't want to talk it through with him. Why not? He was a friend, wasn't he? "I'm here for you if you need to talk about it."

"There's nothing to talk out, but thank you for the offer." She sounded so distant.

Her years attending private school and living the life enmeshed in the world of politics certainly showed right then. Standing there with her hair around her face in a wild tangle, her nightgown hinting at a body that drove him crazy and the scent of their lovemaking still clinging to her, she still managed to exude an aura of superior formality.

"You fit your family just fine, Beth. Believe me."

She didn't answer, just tugged her arm free and went into the bathroom.

She hadn't taken her clothes with her and he wondered if she was going to come out in a towel, or maybe her bra and panties. She'd had something small clutched in one hand. He didn't think either was going to do his overactive libido any good. Maybe he should go down to the lobby and ask for a restaurant recommendation for breakfast at the front desk.

Chapter 14

Ethan pulled the rental car to a stop in front of the gate of Arthur Prescott's home. It was impressive. The stone wall was eight feet high with decorative wrought iron spikes at the top. Ethan was sure they were electrified and not for decorative purposes at all. They looked damn sharp.

The gatehouse was built into the wall and looked easily defensible, the gate itself was a huge double unit made of the same black wrought iron–looking material that topped the brick wall. A much smaller gate slid back into the wall and a guard in a smart black uniform stepped through the opening.

He stopped directly beside the driver's side of the car and just waited.

Ethan opened the window and met the guard's flat stare. "This is Beth Whitney. She's got an appointment to interview with Mr. Prescott."

The guard looked down at his clipboard and then up again. "Please step out of the car for a visual identification, Miss Whitney."

Beth went to pull the door handle, but Ethan stopped her. "Is that strictly necessary?"

"Yes, sir."

Ethan frowned, playing his role of overprotective boyfriend very well and nodded grudgingly. "Go ahead, sweetheart."

She climbed out of the car and came around to face the guard. Ethan was already standing in front of the driver's door, his expression brooding as he watched the guard.

The guard did a visual comparison to something on his clipboard and then smiled. "I'll escort you up to the house, Miss Whitney."

Ethan put a proprietary arm around her shoulder. "I'd rather drive her up, if it's all the same to you." His voice implied it had better be.

The guard's smile disappeared. "You are not on the appointment list, Mr. . . ."

"Ethan Grange," Ethan replied, giving an alias that Beth had learned was a well-established identity for him.

Apparently being a writer of rather depressing literary fiction was a good cover in the espionage world. He even had two books published by a small press that had been subsidized by TGP. It was a good cover, one Prescott could investigate if he wanted.

"Mr. Grange, I'm afraid you'll have to wait out here."

"No. I'm going in with Beth, or she doesn't go."

Beth gasped, but he squeezed her shoulder and she subsided.

The guard looked at her with something that might have been sympathy. "I'm afraid that isn't possible."

"Then, we're leaving." He started guiding Beth toward the car.

She couldn't believe he was doing this. "Ethan . . ."

He ignored her protest and kept walking. "If your boss doesn't understand my desire to see to your comfort, he wouldn't be a good employer. You can't even see the house from here, honey. You aren't walking all that way on a whim of some rich dude who thinks he can control you and the rest of the world. You know I'd rather you didn't work at all."

The guard was talking into his comm unit in low tones.

"But I wanted this job, Ethan. It's perfect for me and it's only part-time." If she sounded more irritated than cajoling, that couldn't be helped. She wasn't an actress and she didn't think the guard would notice the difference.

Ethan walked her around the car and tucked her into her seat before going back to the driver's side and climbing in.

"Wait. Mr. Grange . . . I've asked my employer to approve your entrance on the estate."

"I don't think—"

"Please, Ethan, don't be so difficult," Beth pleaded, impressed with Ethan's acting ability in spite of herself.

He smiled at Beth. "You really want this job, honey?"

"Yes," she gritted out, deciding right then that he could play the role of overprotective and possessive boyfriend, but she didn't necessarily have to accept the one of total doormat.

"All right." He turned to the guard. "Well, what did he say?"

The guard was listening to something in the comm unit. "Do you have proof of your identification?"

"Of course."

"Can I see it, please?"

Ethan leaned over and grabbed a book off the backseat. "Here's my picture."

The book was a hardback with a dustcover and on it Ethan Grange was emblazoned in bold letters under a pretentious title. He flipped the book open and a picture of him in a dark turtleneck and black-rimmed glasses was on the back inside flap of the dustcover. It was a totally supercilious move, and fit the persona of her pretend boyfriend to a T.

"I would prefer to see your driver's license, sir."

Beth's heart stuttered and then started beating again, but too fast. Of course Ethan would have a fake license to go with the identity, but she held her breath until he reached for his back pocket, grumbling the whole time. Adrenaline was surging through Beth in pulsing waves. This undercover stuff was stressful, but . . . weirdly fun.

The guard waved them through the gate and Beth breathed out a sigh of relief. "That was close."

"Don't say anything, Beth."

At first she thought he was staying true to his part, but then he shook his head imperceptibly.

And she remembered that he and her father had drilled into her that she needed to be circumspect about what she said while on Prescott's property or anywhere close to it. She hadn't realized they meant the car, too, but she should have. She knew as well as any agent that there were listening devices that could be targeted at her right now and relaying her conversation with Ethan to Prescott's security team.

"I wish you would have let me walk to the house with the guard. You almost cost me a chance at this job," she said, trying to play her role just in case.

It seemed like overkill, but then this man wouldn't be so hard to get to if he wasn't the ultracautious sort.

"I wasn't letting you walk anywhere with that guy. Did you see the way he smiled at you?"

"Oh, please . . ."

"He's interested, Beth. Stay away from him."

"Give it a rest, Ethan."

He winked at her, his approval of her playacting apparent and despite knowing that they were no better a fit than she and her parents, she felt warmth steal through her.

Another security guard met them at the front door and Ethan was shown to a room to wait while Beth was taken to Prescott for her interview.

According to their intel, Arthur Prescott was fifty-two years old, but with raven black hair, an unlined face, and the body of someone who obviously worked out, he looked much younger. Everywhere but his eyes. They were just flat, gray metal disks for irises, lacking all emotion and yet purveying the impression of a life that had seen things she never wanted to.

He asked the usual questions for a job of the nature he'd advertised and she answered them easily, confident in this aspect of the case. Though she felt like he watched her more closely than any other prospective employer had. There was a quality to his regard that she couldn't quite define, but she felt almost touched by his gaze.

It was not a nice feeling because despite his professional manner, she did not get the sense he was a nice man. She didn't think it was knowing he was one of the bad guys that was influencing her either. There was something about Arthur Prescott that gave her the chills.

Then he went silent and looked at her speculatively for several seconds. "I heard you had problems at the front gate."

"Not with your guard. He was only doing his job."

"But your boyfriend objected to leaving you."

"Ethan can be a little overprotective, but he didn't mean any offense by it."

Prescott frowned. "As a general rule, my employee's personal lives do not interest me, but I would have to be sure that your relationship with Ethan Grange would not impinge on your ability to do your job."

"It won't, I promise," she said earnestly.

Prescott smiled, his eyes assessing more than her value as an investment counselor. He was looking at all of her, his gaze lingering a tad too long on her breasts and she had to suppress a shiver. "You're a lovely woman, Miss Whitney. I understand your boyfriend's protectiveness, but I need your assurance he will not make trouble should I need you beyond the minimum hours for the job."

"I thought the job was part-time?"

"I may want to call on your expertise outside your usual hours and there are times I entertain business associates that I might find your presence invaluable."

"I'm sure that won't be a problem." But her shock at his request showed.

She didn't think it would be out of character for her to react this way, so she didn't berate herself. Besides, he'd said he was looking for the quiet sort. She did shy well, since it was a natural part of her personality.

Prescott smiled, his cold gray eyes going almost friendly. "Good. Do you have a number I can contact you at tonight to let you know my decision?"

She nodded and wrote down the number for the hotel. "We're checked in under Ethan's name."

"Very good. I'll call you and let you know my decision personally." He brushed her fingers with his and she had to fight to keep from yanking her hand away.

"Um . . . that's wonderful. Thanks." Her skin itched with discomfort as she unobtrusively slipped her hand back and stood up. "I'll just collect Ethan and go."

He stood and took her arm. "Let me walk you, Beth. I may call you Beth?"

"Yes, of course."

"Should you end up working for me, you will call me Arthur. I do not stand on formality with my closer advisors."

"Um . . . thank you."

He certainly stood on formality with his security team, but he was looking at her like a meal he'd like to devour. While it made her skin crawl, she couldn't help thinking it was a totally unexpected development. She couldn't wait to tell Ethan. Surely if Prescott was interested in her as a woman, she had a better chance of worming information out of him that could be useful.

They were thirty minutes from Prescott's estate back toward Portland before Beth felt comfortable bringing the subject up.

Ethan's reaction was explosive. "What the hell are you talking about? You are not the agent in charge of securing information. You are the conduit, Beth. You will not encourage Prescott in any way."

"Don't be ridiculous. With a little effort on my part, I'm sure I could end up at some of these business meetings he mentioned."

"It would be totally out of character for your role."

"Wrong. You're not looking at the big picture here, Ethan.

I'm a fairly intelligent woman. And no matter how shy I am, I'm bound to chafe at restrictions placed on me by an over-protective boyfriend. I can encourage the attraction under the cover of a minor rebellion on my part."

Ethan's jaw hardened and his hands tightened on the steering wheel. "You aren't encouraging anything. I mean it, Beth. This man is dangerous and you aren't trained to play that kind of role with him."

"I don't think it takes a lot of training to do the man-woman thing."

"That's where you are wrong."

"You seriously think I need agent training to engage in a light flirtation?"

"You are not engaging in anything with Arthur Prescott."

"You don't think I'm woman enough?" She crossed her arms and looked out the window. "I may not be gorgeous like Elle, but he's already interested, Ethan. All I have to do is encourage him a little."

"It has nothing to do with your feminine allure. I obviously think you have plenty of that."

She said nothing.

He frowned. "Believe me, Beth, this kind of thing requires proper training."

"I just don't see what kind of training I could possibly need just to flirt a little."

"You'd be surprised."

"Maybe I would."

He shot her a sideways look. "What's that supposed to mean?"

"Well, we've already agreed that you and I started this sex thing between us because it was good for the case and I'm just wondering if a big portion of your response isn't training."

"I never agreed to any such thing."

"You said the timing was because of the case."

"That's not the same thing as saying I'm taking you to bed for it."

"Whatever."

"I thought we already had this discussion."

"We did."

"But you came away with the wrong conclusion."

"I don't think so."

The noise he made was one hundred percent masculine irritation. "Do you honestly believe that if my response to you was nothing more than part of my training that I would be worried about the level of intensity? Believe it, or not, I'm more professional than that."

"You said it had been a while. You're reacting more strongly than you expected, but that doesn't mean it isn't part of some master plan."

"Seducing you was not part of my master plan for the case," he gritted.

"You didn't exactly seduce me."

"Damn right I didn't. It was entirely mutual."

"I never said it wasn't."

"You implied it was just part of the job on my side."

She was sure to an extent that was true, but he obviously felt there was more to it as well. The man was really worried about the intensity thing. "Maybe it would be less confusing if it was."

"Why? So you could compartmentalize me with your other fantasies?"

"It's more than a fantasy now."

"Yes, it is. It's a relationship."

"Not hardly."

"What the hell do you mean by that?"

"Do you notice how you swear a lot when you get irritated?"

"It only happens with you."

"I don't believe that."

"Ask my mama. She raised me not to curse in front of women, but you wind me up." And he sounded apologetic about that. Embarrassed even.

"I don't mean to."

"I don't believe that for a minute. You've got an ornery streak, Beth, about as wide and deep as a Texas gulley."

"Gullies aren't that wide . . . or deep."

"They are in Texas."

"According to Texans, everything is big there."

"It is," he said suggestively.

She laughed. "Well, I'd have to agree about some things anyway."

He smiled, but then went all serious again. "We have a relationship, Beth."

"We have sex. That you want to keep light."

"We're friends and we're lovers; that makes it more than just sex."

"If you say so."

"I do. And I also say that you are not going to encourage Prescott in his attraction to you."

"If I think otherwise?"

"I'll pull you from the case."

"You wouldn't. It took too long to get this in. You aren't giving it up on stubborn principle."

"No, I'm not. But I'll give it up to ensure your safety. You know he's dangerous."

"So you've said, but just because he sells information to the enemy doesn't mean he's going to hurt a woman."

"He's had women *and* men killed, Beth."

"Because he knew they were agents. He doesn't know about me and I'm not going to blow my cover."

"Are you attracted to him?" he asked through stiff lips.

"Are you kidding? He gives me the willies."

"And you think you can hide that?"

"I think if I can't, he'll like knowing. He's that kind of man."

"Which is all the more reason to keep your sweet behind out of his sights."

"I don't think it's my behind he's interested in."

"With a man like him, you never know."

"Now, you're just being an alarmist."

"No, dam—darn it, I'm not. Men like him eat women like you for dinner."

"Give it a break."

"I'm being serious here."

"You're being paranoid."

"We agreed I was the agent in charge."

"We also agreed that I'm not brain-dead."

"I never said you were."

"Then don't treat me like it."

"Disagreeing with you is not doubting your intelligence."

"Maybe not, but trying to lay down the law without talking about it is."

"We have been talking about it!"

"Don't yell at me. We started off with one of your unilateral commands if you'll recall."

"Which you didn't listen to."

"I listened, I didn't agree."

"I'm going crazy here, Beth. Stop arguing with me just for the sake of it."

"Is that what I'm doing?"

"It feels like it."

"As opposed to me simply disagreeing with your decision?"

"Yes."

She laughed. "But I do disagree."

"And when we disagree . . ."

She sighed, knowing what he wanted her to admit. "You get final say as agent in charge."

"Good answer."

"*After* due deliberation and discussion."

"Is there more you want to say on this?"

"Only that I think we should leave the option open."

"We aren't going to exercise it."

"I agree . . . for now."

*   *   *

Ethan questioned the sincerity of Beth's agreement that evening when Prescott called to tell her she got the job. She gushed and used a breathy voice Ethan considered strictly his . . . for those times when *he* made her breathless. He tackled her on it when she hung up the phone and she laughed.

"I was nervous. It showed." She didn't look nervous to him, sitting there in the chair by the desk. She looked excited, her dark eyes glowing with anticipation.

He'd taken off his boots and was lying on the bed going over the architectural plans for Prescott's house and grounds. The house was modeled after a large English manor, complete with a maze and rose garden. On the Oregon coast for crying out loud. The man was pretentious and rich enough to indulge his tastes.

"Sounded more to me like you were flirting. He probably thought so, too."

"I'm glad." And she had the temerity to look like she meant it. "I didn't realize I'd be so nervous when he called and I wouldn't want that to come through the phone lines."

He scowled. "We agreed you were not going to flirt."

"I didn't flirt, but I'd rather he thought I was doing that than that I was so nervous at a job offer I could barely speak."

"Try harder next time."

"Try harder to be nervous?" she asked, sounding confused.

Annoyance spun through him. "Not. To. Flirt."

She gave him that look, the one that said she thought he was being ridiculous. "Since I wasn't flirting, that should be no problem." She bit her lower lip and twisted a dark strand of her shoulder-length silky hair around her finger. "I hope I'm not a total basket case once I start working for him."

"You won't be. This job is going to be a piece of cake for you."

"Yes. Right." She looked like she was committing that fact to memory.

He bit back a smile. He wasn't sure why she was so concerned, but she had no reason to be and she'd realize that sooner or later. As long as she refrained from tempting the tiger to hunt with her flirtation.

At that moment, Ethan wasn't completely certain which man he considered the tiger she had to be wary of unleashing—himself or Prescott. "When do you start?"

"He would like me to start next Tuesday. He'll be out of town on Monday. I told him I could."

"No problem. We talked about this and we've already got accommodations."

"We do? Then why are we staying at a hotel?"

"Convenience. Another layer of safety. The team is still working on setting up security."

"When is move-in day?"

"Monday."

"That's good timing."

"Always."

"Are we staying here until then?"

"It makes the most sense. Did you pack before we left?"

"Maude has my suitcases she can ship tomorrow."

"Mine, too."

"I guess we were both pretty confident this was going to work." Beth was still twisting her curling hair around her finger, her expression uncertain.

"Yeah, we were. But you aren't sounding so confident now."

She took in a deep breath and let it out. "I guess it just became a lot more real for me when I got the job. How long do you think we'll be out here?"

"I don't know, baby. A job like this can last as little as a week with a lucky break and as long as a year if things get hard." Strangely, the thought of living a year in the same house, sharing a bed with Beth, did not bother him at all.

However, she blanched, looking almost sick at the prospect. "*A year* . . . I hope we get a lucky break."

Her reaction bothered him and he had to force himself to reassure her instead of demanding what her problem was. She probably wanted to get that new life of hers started right away and he didn't want to hear about it. "I've got a good feeling about this case. It won't last forever."

"You won't let it. You really want to nail Prescott."

"You know it."

"You really think he's responsible for the deaths of your friends?"

"I know he is, Beth. Don't ever underestimate the evil that lurks behind the charming exterior."

"He's not charming."

"You didn't sound like you didn't think he was charming on the phone." His voice sounded accusing and that bothered him.

He'd never been possessive like this with a woman before, but like he'd told her, she wasn't trained for that sort of undercover work. And he didn't want her hurt, or compromising the case. That's all it was.

"Are we back to that?"

"I'd rather be in bed."

Her eyes widened, and instead of interest he read panic in their dark depths. "We haven't had dinner yet."

"We can order room service. Later."

"But . . ."

"I told you . . . I think lots of sex is going to help us control the intensity."

Her face went blank and then she got that stubborn look. "About the *intensity*," she said the word like it was something sour she was trying to get off of her tongue. "I don't know how to do light sex."

"We'll work on it together."

"I don't think so."

"What do you mean, you don't think so?" His heartbeat was hammering inside his chest all of a sudden for no reason.

"I mean I think that no sex makes a lot more sense than

trying to keep intimacy between us low-key. I'm not like you. I haven't been trained how to divorce my emotions from physical pleasure with another person."

"I never said my emotions were divorced from you."

She stood up, slipping on her shoes. Not a good sign. "You said you need to keep your focus on the case and I agree. I don't want to do anything to put this assignment in jeopardy. I haven't had your training. I definitely don't have your experience with casual sexual encounters. The smartest thing for both of us to do is to pull back from any sort of physical intimacy."

"I'm not a damn gigolo."

"I never said you were."

"*Casual sexual encounters?*" he asked with a bite to his tone that would have made a rattler turn tail and run.

She just shrugged. "Call it whatever you want, but we just aren't in the same league. I knew that going in, but I didn't realize it would be so hard to hold back my emotions, or that you might have a problem with how good the sex was between us. I'm not like you, Ethan. I'm not like my parents. When I feel, I want the freedom to express those feelings and I'm not comfortable sharing my body or my bed with a man who has issues with intensity. I want you. You know that, but I'm asking you not to capitalize on it."

She didn't raise her voice, or get choked up, or any of the other feminine emotional weapons at her disposal. She spoke with quiet dignity, every word laced with conviction. She wasn't budging. Not for her own sex drive. Not for him. Not for anybody.

She picked up her purse. "I've come to realize I'm an intense person. And that's okay with me. You don't have to like it. My parents don't have to like it. Alan didn't have to accept it. But I do accept it and I'm through trying to fit in with people who don't. You said we were friends and I've always believed we are, but we're going to have to make this assignment work without the sex thing." She stepped toward the door. "I want to go to dinner. I'll wait for you to get ready if you want, but if you'd rather stay in and get room service, I'm fine going on my own."

"Just like that, no discussion?" He wasn't only talking about dinner and he knew she was smart enough to see that.

She nodded, a small but decisive jerk of her head. "It's the way it has to be. I need you to accept that."

"You think we can live together in the same hotel room and keep our hands off each other?"

"If we both try, yes."

"And you expect me to try?"

"I wouldn't respect you if you didn't."

"Only a woman would come back with an answer like that."

"If I were a man, we wouldn't be having this discussion."

"Damn right."

She laughed when all he wanted to do was howl at the moon in frustration.

He glared at her. "Let me get my boots on and we'll go."

Chapter 15

Dinner was quiet. Ethan refused to discuss the case, or anything else for that matter. He didn't pout—exactly—but she'd never seen him like this. He'd always been either teasing or professional, but right now, he reminded Beth of a wounded bear and she wasn't about to push him into lashing out.

She didn't know where the words she'd spoken before leaving the hotel room had come from. She hadn't made a conscious decision to pull away from intimacy with him. In fact, she'd realized on the drive back from the coast that as painful as his rejection of her intense nature was, their relationship was giving her an opportunity to get to know the woman who lived inside her skin in a way she'd shied away from doing before.

But his comment about trying to control the intensity in their sex had sparked something inside her. Not an explosion so much as a weary acceptance. She was not what he needed and he would never be what she needed. And she couldn't handle making love with him under those conditions. She was half in love with him already, wasn't even sure it wasn't a full-blown loss of insanity. Continued intimacy would tear her apart when she had to walk away, or watch him do so.

And if he wanted her, he had to want all of her . . . not just the parts he was comfortable with. He'd made it obvious he didn't and that left her no choice. No sex.

They were in the car, headed back to the hotel when she said, "Can we stop at a store that sells camping equipment?"

"Why?"

"I'd like to get a sleeping bag. I think it would be easier if we didn't share a bed, but I assume you'd have an issue with asking for another room or a rollaway."

"You'd assume right."

"That leaves a sleeping bag."

He nodded, but didn't say anything. When they reached the store, he left her in the car to go inside and buy it. He was so cold and uncommunicative, she didn't ask him to get her a pad for under it. She didn't want another one of those emotionless looks slicing her way.

When they got to the hotel, he made the pallet on the floor in silence. She noticed he'd gotten one of those extra long sleeping bags and a pad.

"Thank you."

He turned to face her, his green gaze flat. "For what?"

"The pad. It will make the floor a lot more comfortable."

"Will it?"

"I think so. I'll just go get ready for bed."

He nodded.

When she came out, he was in the sleeping bag, his back to the bed.

"I didn't mean for you to be the one to sleep on the floor."

Silence.

"Ethan?"

"Go to bed, Beth." He even sounded like a wounded bear.

"I really don't mind taking the floor."

"If you want me to ignore the way my body is aching for yours right now, I suggest you be quiet, get in bed, and go straight to sleep."

Even she wasn't going to argue with that tone and she did exactly as he suggested. Except going to sleep. She lay in the dark, thinking about Ethan, about her decision, and trying not to move so he wouldn't know she was still awake, long into the night.

* * *

Ethan got up a little after dawn. Beth was sleeping. Finally. She'd been awake most of the night. Like him.

She hadn't wanted him to know she was awake and he hadn't been sure of his self-control if he acknowledged it. It was that lack of self-control that had dumped him in his current predicament. The way he responded to Beth—the way she responded to him, the amount of pleasure they found in one another's bodies—had spooked him.

He'd thought he could control it, put some kind of barrier around it, but that hadn't worked. He'd hurt her in his attempt to regain a measure of his self-control. She'd lumped him in with her parents and Hyatt and that was not a place he wanted to be in Beth's brain. He knew she didn't consider any of them people she could truly rely on and he wanted her to rely on him.

Right now, she needed to rely on him for her safety and as much as he didn't like her "no sex" boundary, he had to wonder if it wasn't for the best. He didn't think straight around her and he couldn't afford to have his thinking and reactions clouded right now. Which he'd known all along, but Beth had been the one professional enough to take the stand that really needed taking.

And he was going to start acting like the professional he was. Starting today. The next two days would be best spent making themselves familiar with the area and getting a feel for the small towns closest to the north and south of Prescott's estate. It would also keep them out of the hotel room and away from the temptation of the bed that looked too big with Beth's small form curled in the middle of it.

They moved into a small cabin a few miles from the Prescott estate on Monday as Ethan had promised. The second bedroom had been rigged up as a home office for the pseudoauthor. The state-of-the-art computer and peripherals would serve two purposes. Ethan would use it to oversee their security and continue his research on Prescott. It would also perpetuate the cover of a writer seeking his muse in the coastal forests.

Beth noticed that a daybed graced the wall opposite the computer desk. She would insist on sleeping on it and this time Ethan would listen. He was much too tall for the twin bed, but she wasn't. And she didn't want to sleep in the middle of another king-size bed that only succeeded in making her wish she'd never made the no sex decree.

She didn't regret it. Not really. She had no choice if she wanted to maintain a shred of her emotions when the case was over, but she wanted Ethan. So much. He was no longer a fantasy, but a living, breathing man who she knew could give her more pleasure than she'd ever experienced—or probably ever would experience again.

But he didn't want that intense pleasure and she had to keep remembering that fact.

Despite its setting, the cabin wasn't at all rustic. The small kitchen was filled with ultramodern appliances and the television had satellite access. There was a whirlpool bath in the master suite and the furnishings were modern retro.

As she looked around, she realized it fit the image Ethan had chosen to portray of himself perfectly.

"Are we safe to talk here? Always?" Beth asked after discovering her clothes unpacked right along Ethan's in the master bedroom.

She supposed that made sense, but it felt funny in the pit of her stomach all the same. Did the special training Ethan had mentioned help a woman separate the fantasy from reality in situations like this?

Ethan was looking out the window with field glasses and jotting on his PDA. "Yes. We've got a signal jammer activated that mocks television satellite interference."

"Clever."

"We like to think so."

She swallowed, suddenly tired of the distance between

them but unsure how to bridge the gap without opening the sex issues. "I like the cabin."

"Good. It fits my image . . . our image."

"Yes, it does."

"I know you are going to want to sleep on the daybed in the office." His voice was devoid of emotion, but she sensed that offended him.

"Um . . . yes."

"Don't go in there dressed for bed at night until the privacy curtains are shut both there and in the master bedroom."

"You think Prescott is going to spy on his new employee?"

"He might. We don't make stupid mistakes counting on the opposite . . . ever."

"Got it, sir." She saluted smartly.

And he smiled. "Sassy, aren't you?"

"I've been accused of it a time or two."

"I bet."

At the return of his teasing demeanor, some of the tension that had clung to her since Friday evening dissipated. "I start work tomorrow," she offered for lack of anything better to say.

"I know." He turned to face her fully, putting the full weight of his attention directly on her.

For no reason she could fathom, her stomach dipped.

"Are you mentally prepared?" he asked.

"Yes."

"You were nervous before."

"I'm not any longer."

"Why?" he asked, disconcerting her.

She wasn't about to tell him that she'd realized the reality of working for Prescott wasn't going to be nearly as overwhelming as the reality of living with Ethan in the small cabin.

"I guess I just settled down. Like you said I would."

"Did it change how you feel about anything else?"

"You mean my decision to move away from D.C. or the sex thing?" she asked with more bravado than she felt.

"Either . . . both."

"No."

He nodded. "My car and your cats arrive in Portland on Thursday from the transportation company. We'll pick them up after you get off work."

"You could go in the morning, after you drop me off." She couldn't wait to see the kittens again and appreciated the fact that Ethan hadn't expected her to board them out for the duration of the assignment.

"No."

She frowned. "Why not?"

"I'm not leaving you alone at the estate."

"I'm going to be working there five days a week for who knows how long . . . it's not a problem."

"I will be here whenever you are there. Close enough to get to you if there's a need."

"That's ridiculous."

He just shrugged. The man and his protective attitude were going to drive her insane. But he'd figure out on his own that he had better things to do with his time than sit around the cabin and twiddle his thumbs while she worked.

He moved out of the room, going to the window in the kitchen to look out and take more notes on his PDA.

"What are you looking for?"

"It's just basic recon. I want to know what I can see of our environment from each vantage point in the cabin in case the information is necessary at some point in the future. I'll do outside recon in a little bit . . . checking to see what areas have a good vantage point for looking in through our windows."

"Can I go with you? I'd like to explore the woods a little."

"No problem." But a tightening around his mouth indicated a lack of enthusiasm for the idea.

"I can go for a walk on my own, if you'd rather."

"Not happening."

"Do you want me to stay here?"

"I said you could come with me."

"I sort of sensed you'd rather I not."

"Being around you without being able to touch you is a strain, Sunshine, but I'm not a hormonal kid. I can handle it."

"I'm sorry."

He shrugged. "You have nothing to apologize for."

His understanding made her feel guilty, which was really pathetic. But there it was. "It's not that I don't want you."

He turned to face her full on, his face cast in grim lines. "Hearing that is not helping. I respect your choice. Let's leave it at that, all right?"

She nodded. "I'll stay here."

"No. I'd rather you came."

"But—"

"You need to be familiar with our surroundings for your own safety. This is a job and we both have to remember that."

"How can I forget? We wouldn't be here otherwise."

"No, we wouldn't. Let me finish my interior recon and then we'll go."

"Okay."

The walk in the woods was a revelation. Ethan discreetly pointed out where they had motion sensors set up for the security system, he also showed her where a hidden assailant could see right in through the master bedroom window and the kitchen window. There was no such covered spot for spying on the living room or smaller front bedroom.

However, he still reiterated his desire she close curtains before getting ready for bed and going into the second bedroom to sleep.

"We'll have to do some cuddling on the couch watching television and light touching now and then in case we're watched."

"Why would he watch us?"

"He didn't get where he is in high-tech espionage by being careless with a new employee. We know he ran a background check on you. It would only make sense for him to follow it up with at least cursory surveillance in the beginning."

"So, we have to act like a couple when we are alone?" The thought made her stomach knot.

Not touching Ethan . . . not begging to be touched by him was growing more difficult with each passing hour. If they had to touch and pretend to be a couple when there was no one overtly around to help keep her urges under control, she was afraid she was going to lose the battle with herself.

"Don't worry, we can shut the drapes when it gets dark like any normal couple and hide our physical distance from prying eyes then."

"You really did think it would be easier to run this assignment if we were in a sexual relationship."

"I thought you'd already decided that."

"I just didn't realize all the ramifications of living together I guess. I thought we'd be off camera when we were alone at the cabin."

"Mistakes like that lead to blown covers."

"Sorry. I'm not an agent."

"I don't expect you to be. Follow my lead and we'll be fine." He slipped his arm around her shoulder, obviously taking his own advice to heart. "Okay?"

"Yes." Her voice was a mere squeak, but she was doing everything she could not to run a possessive hand over his chest.

She allowed herself to lean into him, telling herself she was trying to look natural, but underneath she knew she did it because she simply couldn't help herself.

Beth looked forward to going to work for Prescott as much because it would get her away from Ethan's presence as that she could start doing the job she'd been assigned. Ever since the walk, Ethan had continued the policy of "looking like lovers" whenever they were in a position to be observed. By the time they had closed the curtains the night before, she'd been a walking mass of oversensitive nerve endings.

And she'd missed his touches—the freedom to touch him— until it was a gaping ache inside her. On the other hand, besides a couple of speculative looks she could not read, Ethan acted as if he wasn't affected at all. He'd simply spent more time going over strategy and what they knew about Prescott.

She'd gone to bed determined to do a better job today of maintaining her emotional distance. So far, so good.

After being waved through the gate, Ethan pulled up in front of Prescott's house and stopped the car. He turned to Beth, reaching to cup her nape. She realized he was going to kiss her a scant second before he did so. His lips covered hers with possessive tenderness that felt all too real. He didn't linger, but he was thorough so that when he pulled away, she sat dazed for a couple of seconds.

"Be good today," he said.

She nodded and got out of the car, forcing herself not to feel her still-tingling lips. The man really knew how to kiss.

The job was very much as she expected and Beth actually found she liked the full-time secretary, Audrey Fisk, as well as the security guard assigned to the house.

"Mr. Prescott has a lot of security," she said to Audrey at one point.

The older woman shrugged pencil-thin shoulders. "He's a very wealthy man. In today's world, he needs it."

Prescott allowed his secretary to brief Beth on her job, but made a point of stopping by her desk to ask how things were going later that day.

"Great. I should have a preliminary analysis of your portfolio to you within a couple of days."

"Good."

He didn't linger, but he stopped by her desk twice more for small talk before she left for the day. The rest of the week fell into a similar pattern and Ethan made no bones about the fact that he didn't like how much personal attention Prescott was showing her. Since Beth wasn't encouraging the man, she didn't feel she was going against the agent in charge on the case.

But she thought that it was a good thing. Ethan would think so, too . . . if she'd been an actual agent. She was the conduit, though, and common sense dictated that the more personable her relationship with Prescott, the better chance she would have of opening doors for Ethan's investigation.

That Thursday, Prescott came in to see her and leaned against her desk. "How are things going? Do you like the job?"

"It's familiar . . . easy, if you don't mind my saying so."

"No. I'm glad to hear it." He smiled, the look not quite warming the depths of his eyes. "I'm impressed with your recommendations on diversification already."

She'd created a report for him the day before with some basic changes recommended to his investment plan. "I'll give you a more detailed analysis next week, but I need to re-search your investments and markets of interest more thoroughly before I do."

He leaned a little closer. "I knew you were the right woman for the job."

"I'm glad you think so." She scooted her chair back a lit-tle.

Where Ethan's sensuality could reach out and wrap around her like a blanket, this man's masculine presence choked her.

Mocking amusement filled his eyes at her movement. "You remember I told you about some possible after-hours work time?"

"Um . . . yes."

"I'm having a little get-together with some business associ-ates tomorrow night. I'd like you to be there to offer your ad-vice."

She bit her lip, having no problem manufacturing an

image of nervousness. "I don't suppose my boyfriend could come?"

Prescott's eyes narrowed, but he surprised her by nodding. "Certainly. An author might make an interesting addition to the gathering . . . keep things more social than business."

When she told Ethan on their way to Portland to pick up his car and the kittens, he frowned.

"I thought you'd be glad for the invite in."

"I am. I'm just wondering why he'd let me come."

"He said he wanted to keep the evening more social than business."

"But he invited you on the pretext of business."

"As to that, I'm not sure it was business he was thinking about."

"Was he coming on to you?"

"No, but—"

"What?"

"It was nothing, but he's not a man who respects the normal barriers of personal space. I shy away from him when he gets too close. It amuses him. I think he likes to play with people."

"I think you're right. That might be another reason he's letting me come. He sees me as the controlling boyfriend . . . he might get a perverse pleasure out of showing me that he has some control over you, too."

"I could see him doing exactly that. Lucky for us, we don't have a real relationship and his twisted games can't hurt us."

"I think they can hurt you."

"Not a chance. He gives me the willies, but I can handle it. You should have met some of the men my mom tried to hook me up with since the big wedding fiasco. There is a lobbyist or two and more than one aspiring politician who would make a great piranha fill-in on a nature special."

"But none of them would have physically hurt you given the chance. I'm not so sure about Prescott. There's too little information available on his sexual preferences for my comfort level."

"Maybe he's just discreet."

"Or his preferences make discretion to the point of cover-up a necessity."

"I'm not about to get involved that way with him."

"Stay out of situations where you might end up alone with him."

"We've had this discussion." Each day when she got off work, in fact.

Ethan sighed. "My gut is telling me the man is dangerous to certain types of women. The fact that he specifically advertised for the quiet type raises a red flag for me."

"I've thought about that, too," she admitted.

"Good instincts." He smiled at her, their eyes connecting for a millisecond before his went back to the road.

Warmth pervaded her whole being at his praise. "Thanks, but although I can be shy, I'm not weak."

"I know that, baby. But I don't think Prescott is as astute a judge of character. I'd hate for you to have to do him bodily harm because he's cocky. It could put a real crimp in our case."

She grinned, liking his assessment of the situation and agreeing. She'd never tolerate being manhandled, but if she got into a situation where she had to draw the line, Prescott wouldn't bat an eyelash at firing her. She was sure of it.

"Tomorrow night would be a good night to plant bugs," she ventured.

Ethan had refused to let her do it because he said if the bugs were discovered, they could be traced back to her since she was the only new person in the household. But after a party with several business associates, probably all of whom were as dirty as Prescott, they would fall under suspicion before her if the bugs were discovered.

"Yes, it would. The long-range listening devices don't work."

"He's jamming them like we are?"

"Only he makes no effort to mask his jamming device. It's

as if he's so arrogant he doesn't care who knows he's taken measures to keep his conversations private. He doesn't think anyone can touch him."

"He's wrong."

"Yes, he is."

Chapter 16

The small party of business associates turned out to be ten business associates to Prescott, many of differing nationalities, and their dates. Prescott had a woman at his side, too, but she had the hard stare of a professional bodyguard rather than a lover. Maybe she was both, but the way she kept distance from Prescott and yet maintained a position between him and the other guests said not.

She moved with the sinuous grace of an expert in martial arts, but Ethan would lay odds she was packing as well. She did not come off as the type of woman to rely solely on her prowess at hand-to-hand combat for protection. The security guard who normally patrolled inside Prescott's house was conspicuous by his absence from the large drawing room.

Though Ethan was sure he was in the house somewhere.

Prescott played the convivial host while Ethan played the part of possessive boyfriend and kept Beth locked to his side. The information broker was definitely giving her looks that spoke of too personal an interest in his new investment advisor. He was affable with Ethan on the surface, but made several adroit comments intended to irk Ethan Grange the author.

It was no more than he expected and Ethan enjoyed making it a point of not rising to the bait.

When it came time for dinner, he was not surprised to find

himself at the other end of the table while Beth was seated to the left of her host, breaking social custom. Prescott's "date" was seated to his right. Ethan could not hear their conversation, but he wasn't worried about Beth's part in it. She'd been attending political dinners every bit as dangerous in their own way since she was a child. He had complete faith in her, but that didn't mean he had to like the way Prescott touched her arm when he spoke to her or tried to tempt her to taste his appetizer of escargot when she declined her own.

For his part, Ethan listened to the discussions going on around him while appearing to be wholly engrossed in his flirtation with the woman on his left. Celine Fournier was companion to a middle-aged Frenchman who reeked of money and wore a wedding ring. She didn't. Not the wife. And not exactly enamored with her role as mistress either, if the amount of wine she imbibed as dinner progressed was any indication.

So far, the conversations around them were innocuous, but a man across the table made a comment about "the merchandise" to which the woman beside him said she hoped it was as impressive as Prescott had intimated it would be. Both hastily changed the subject after a cold-eyed glare from an Arab seated on the other side of the woman.

Between the salad and the main course, Ethan used the cover of dropping his napkin to place a microchip size bug under the table. For all its miniscule proportions, it had amazing range, but he still wanted to get listening devices closer to Prescott's office and at least one upstairs.

His flirtation with Celine continued after dinner while Prescott made a point of keeping Beth by his side, ostensibly discussing her investment strategy. When Prescott took Beth on a tour of the garden, along with the ever-present bodyguard and several of his other guests, Ethan allowed the now very tipsy brunette to lead him upstairs to a deserted bedroom.

She grabbed him and tumbled back toward the bed, her hands everywhere. His hand on her neck, he leaned down, pretending he was about to kiss her. Instead, he exerted pressure on a sensitive point and she lost consciousness almost instantly. He figured he had two minutes, five at the most, before she came to again. But he'd studied the house plans and architectural detail enough that he was confident he could achieve his objective before she woke.

Yanking on a spandex black ski mask and wafer-thin night goggles he had tucked in the inside pocket of his black blazer as he went, he climbed out the window onto the roof. He sprinted on catlike feet to the window for the master bedroom. It would have been quicker to use the interior hallway, but any movement within the house would be monitored by cameras. Those on the outside were unlikely to pick up Ethan's movements—even if they were directed at the roof as opposed to the grounds.

He'd dressed all in black for the evening in clothes that fit his literary author persona and made darn good camouflage in the dark. Black turtleneck, blazer, slacks, and what looked like designer men's dress shoes, but had soft soles for stealth.

He affixed the listening device in a mere second and ran back to the guest room, slipping in through the window with silent speed. He closed it as the sound of people coming up the stairs reached him. He had just stripped off the ski mask, tucking it and the goggles back into his jacket, and sat down on the bed beside Celine, when she woozily opened her eyes. She reached for him as the lights were turned on and a man's curse and woman's soft gasp could be heard from the doorway.

Ethan looked up and Beth was staring at him like he was a cockroach. She was with Celine's date; the Frenchman looked ready to kill.

Ethan smiled easily, used to this sort of "cover your ass" maneuvers in the field, but something inside him stuttered at the look of disgust in Beth's eyes before she masked it. "I was just helping Ms. Fournier. She was feeling faint and I carried her in here. I'm glad you've arrived to take over, Monsieur Bernard."

Ethan patted Celine's hand and stood up, careful not to adjust his clothing, or in any way make it appear they'd been doing exactly what Celine had intended for them to be doing.

She, obviously knowing a good cover-up when it presented itself, put her hand to her forehead and sighed dramatically. "It is true. Henri . . . you were too busy in your business discussions to notice my distress, but this gentleman cared for me."

Skin pale from the enforced blackout and her slightly slurred consonants from too much wine gave her performance realism, but her benefactor still looked suspicious. "The light was off when we arrived."

"It hurt my eyes." She shut them, allowing a single tear to escape and turned her head away. "Not that I expect you to notice, or care. Tonight was to be entertainment you said, but you have done nothing but talk business in whispers. You have ignored me."

The woman wasn't a bad actress; she played the part of neglected date very well.

Bernard looked at Ethan, as if asking for confirmation.

Ethan stifled a sigh of disgust. "Now that you are here, I will leave you to care for your date's discomfort."

Bernard nodded and rushed to Celine's side. Taking her into his arms, he whispered words of abject apology in French, all the while looking like a man who had to be wondering if having a young mistress was worth the trouble. Considering the fact that Celine made a good stab at being both a lush and unfaithful, Ethan would have said no.

But men who ignored the sanctity of their marriage vows got what they deserved, in his opinion. Dismissing the other couple from his mind, Ethan crossed the room to Beth. "I thought you'd gone into the garden with Prescott."

"I was going to, but I didn't realize you knew . . . so I came back to tell you where I'd gone." She bit her lip, looking vulnerable and her gaze slid to the beautiful brunette now clinging to her benefactor's Armani-clad shoulders.

Ethan took Beth's arm and led her from the room. "I'll come with you."

"If you're sure Miss Fournier doesn't need you." There was a bite in Beth's tone that made Ethan's smile genuine.

He liked thinking she could be jealous of him, especially considering she was smart enough to realize anything he did with Celine was for the sake of the case only. It made him feel less of a fool for his own reaction to the attention Prescott gave her.

Ethan tugged Beth out the door and down the stairs. "I'm where *I* need to be. Come on, Sunshine."

Beth let Ethan pull her along until they went out the French doors and met up with the group on the back patio. Like the rest of the house, it was slightly pretentious with huge cement lions guarding each of the far corners and the furniture wrought iron cast to look like a formal dining set complete with damask cushions and marble tabletop.

Prescott's ego reverberated in everything that represented him.

She pulled away from Ethan's hold just as her pseudoboss looked at them. Satisfaction flashed in his eyes and he beckoned her to him. She went, her mind whirling with the single question that she could not dismiss. Had Ethan been kissing the beautiful and exotic Celine Fournier?

Prescott smiled at her. "I was just explaining the difficulties my horticulturalist has faced in growing roses in the salty climate near the ocean."

"I'm afraid I'm not much of a gardener."

"Ah, but a lovely woman is not required to know how to grow flowers, only enjoy them when they are offered in homage."

"Are you going to offer my Beth some blooms from your garden?" Ethan asked, his tone deriding. "How very cliché."

Prescott's mouth tightened. "Alas, it is fall and the roses are not in bloom, but perhaps next summer she will enjoy that particular garden's delights. I have found that most women do not find flowers cliché at all."

"I love roses, especially long-stemmed ones," one of the women in the party offered.

"Don't I know it?" Her date's accent was Canadian. "It costs me a fortune to keep you supplied the way you like."

She wound her arm through his and smiled up at him. "I'm worth it though, aren't I?"

Beth didn't hear the man's reply because he whispered it, but whatever he said made the woman laugh.

One of the others, a dark, stocky man with an accent that could have been Russian or Ukrainian, she wasn't sure which, asked, "If the roses are not in bloom, what have you brought us out here to see?"

Once again, Prescott's mouth flattened into a thin line of annoyance, but he quickly smiled, and Beth thought he would have made a particularly adept politician. "The maze is always of interest to my first-time guests. Perhaps you will feel the same."

The stocky man shrugged. "Let us see."

Just then, Prescott's date for the evening came out of the house with the remaining guests, including Mr. Bernard and his girlfriend. "I've convinced the rest of the party to join us in the maze, Arthur. Isn't that lovely?"

"Yes. Quite lovely, my dear." Prescott led the entire group across the perfectly manicured lawn to a box hedge maze that easily stood eight feet high. "It is amusing to enter by twos at timed intervals. Everyone will be given twenty minutes to find the center, at which point the pathway that leads to the center will glow amber while the rest of the lighting within the maze will remain white. We shall all meet at the center and I will lead you out afterward."

A couple of the guests made faces at the proposal, but no one disagreed with the plan.

Ethan once again maneuvered himself beside Beth and took her hand. "This should be fun, honey."

"I thought we could trade partners for the exercise," Prescott said.

"Since you know the way to the center and your date probably does, what would be the point in that?"

"We will both refrain from giving hints. It will pit your wits against that of your girlfriend, Mr. Grange."

Ethan laughed and shook his head. "Not a chance. We both know Beth has a better sense of direction than I do. I'm relying on her to get me through the maze as it is."

"Beth, you must convince your boyfriend to agree." There was a core of steel in Prescott's tone, a subtle warning not lost on Beth.

Her boss was attempting to order her to do this. She wasn't sure if he wanted her to believe her job might be on the line if she refused, but he definitely wanted his way.

Before Beth could answer though, Ethan's arm settled around her, his hand curving to her waist and pulling her in tight against him. "I'm not a man who lets my woman tell me what to do, Mr. Prescott. Beth will be going in with me."

There wasn't anything subtle about the threat in Ethan's voice and it was directed right at Prescott. It fit his role well and Beth saw the wisdom her dad and Ethan had shown in creating this particular type of role for her partner. Prescott might get annoyed, but after the way Ethan had reacted to being told he could not escort her right to the door for her interview and the number of calls he made to her during work hours, his reaction now would not be suspect in the least.

They were the third couple into the maze. Ethan immediately started leading her away from the rustle of movement and low voices of the other guests.

Beth pulled on his arm. "I thought I was going to take the lead," she whispered.

He shook his head once, making no sound as he took turns as if he knew exactly where he was going. A minute later, he pulled her to a stop and just listened.

Two voices came from the other side of the hedge. Both spoke low, but the words were understandable.

"I do not know why you bothered to come. He's not going to sell the information to your people. His country is at war with yours." It was the stocky Russian/Ukrainian.

"Men like Prescott have no country. He cares only for the number of zeroes after the dollar sign and we are prepared to offer many." The man spoke with the cultured tones of the English, but Beth guessed he was the Arab who had sat near Ethan during dinner.

She'd spoken only briefly to him, an introduction from Prescott before dinner, but noticed the man's impeccable accent at the time.

"There are things besides money a man like Prescott craves." The dark promise in the Russian/Ukrainian's voice made Beth's stomach clench.

Somehow, she did not think the man was talking about power or prominence.

"There, too, you will fall short of what our people can offer," the Arab said, showing he knew exactly what the other man was referring to.

Or he was bluffing. It didn't matter which. Something about the conversation was making Beth nauseous.

"You would like to think so, I am sure."

"Rudi, will you stop talking business and help me find the center of the maze?" a feminine voice whined from farther away.

The Arab's companion was silent until the other couple moved on. "You risk a great deal talking with that man," she said in a voice both cold and hard.

"I risk nothing."

"You have no way of knowing which guests are buyers like we are and which are blinds he has planted to gain information, or play his little power games with."

"The stupid Russian spoke to me first."

"If he is here, he is not stupid and his speaking first is no guarantee he is not working for Prescott as a spy."

"Do not correct me."

"Do not be tedious. I give correction when it is needed. We both benefit if your people win the bid, but we both lose if you muck the deal." The woman's voice was definitely American and while she had seemed quiet during dinner and before, she was obviously no brainless bedmate brought along to even out numbers.

"You have no more loyalty to your country than Prescott."

"And you have a brain the size of a pea if you think you are safe in continuing to bait me, but I guess that means we both have our little deficiencies we must learn to live with."

Ethan stiffened beside Beth, but made no noise.

With a sound of disgust, the man moved off.

"*Pig*," the woman hissed under her breath before following him, her tread so quiet, Beth barely heard her move.

She looked up at Ethan. His brows were drawn together in a frown and he looked at the hedge almost as if he could see through it and was watching the two people move away.

"What is it?" she asked quietly.

He shook his head again, indicating silence. Beth obeyed. The other couples passed by on the other side of the hedge, some talking, some quiet, but none saying anything nearly as interesting as the original foursome.

Ethan looked down at his watch, looked up at Beth, and said, "Come here."

That was all the warning she got before he kissed her so expertly, her toes curled in her high-heeled sandals. He tunneled his fingers into her hair and devoured her with his mouth until she was panting and hot with arousal, rubbing her body against his and holding his head to her with desperate hands.

A chime sounded and he jerked away from her with a curse. "That damn near got out of hand."

She would have agreed if she could have breathed to do so.

He didn't say anything else and she had no idea why he had kissed her, only that it proved she was still dangerously susceptible to him. Something she had known, but would have been happy forgoing another object lesson on.

She figured out why he'd done it when they were the last couple to find the center. Prescott and several others looked at

Beth with knowing expressions and she realized she looked as disheveled as she felt. Ethan looked a little worse for the wear, too. She'd mussed his hair and he had a smear of her lipstick near his mouth.

She indicated it discreetly and he smiled that devil's smile he used sometimes, then pulled a white handkerchief from an interior pocket on his blazer and wiped the evidence from his face. Everyone would think they'd been lost to passion rather than lost in the maze.

No one would guess they were the last couple to find the center because they'd been busy spying on the others. It was smart, but Beth felt used. Her reaction to Ethan wasn't part of the case, but he wasn't above using it as a blind. She knew that made sense and told her susceptible heart to chill out, but there was an ache inside her that would not go away.

Prescott served champagne to his guests and congratulated the first couple to find the center before leading them out of the maze and back to the house, where dessert was being served.

The rest of the evening was uneventful and always mindful of Ethan's warning about talking in the car, Beth waited until they were back at the cabin with everything secure before bringing up the odd conversation they had overheard.

She slipped her shoes off and curled up on the sofa, her frothy cocktail dress flowing around her and sliding silkily against her stocking-clad thighs. For once, the kittens did not come to join her. They slept curled together in the center of the daybed in the spare room. They'd lifted their heads and blinked big kitty eyes at her when she'd gone in to check on them, but gone directly back to sleep.

She wished at least one of them had followed her into the living room. She could use a diversion from the tension that had nothing to do with the case shimmering around her and Ethan. "He's getting ready to auction something off."

Ethan stripped off his blazer and kicked off his shoes, his green eyes burning with something besides interest in the case. "Definitely, but we don't have a clue what. There's not even a whisper about it among my contacts."

She adjusted her skirt over her legs so nothing showed except her toes peeking from beneath the two layers of chiffon. "He's careful."

"Not careful enough." Ethan peeled off his turtleneck and tossed it on top of his blazer. It was quickly followed by his belt.

She didn't ask why, but did her best to ignore the expanse of chest rippling as he stretched before sinking to the couch beside her.

She kept her gaze locked to his face. "What did you think of the two men arguing over which one of them was going to win the bid?"

Ethan stretched his arm along the back of the couch, only an inch from where her bare shoulder leaned against it. "I think neither was as interesting as the American woman."

"In what way?"

"She's filled with rage and her partner has no clue."

"Rage?" Beth had heard disgust, even mockery, but not rage in the other woman's voice.

"She's good at hiding it, but it's there. If she's not a professional, she's next to it."

Her heart gave a funny twinge at Ethan's obvious admiration for the other woman. "A professional agent?"

"Yes."

"But that shouldn't come as a surprise. I'm sure a lot of Prescott's buyers are agents working for governments or dishonest organizations."

"But she's not the buyer. The Arab is. She's working with him, but I don't buy it's because their interests coincide. I think it's telling that she waited to give him her warning until after the man had talked to the Russian."

Beth pleated the fabric of her skirt between her fingers, trying not to reach out and touch the bare chest in front of her. "You think she wanted to hear what was said?"

"Yes."

"Then why point out the dangers of the conversation at all?"

"To keep the Arab off balance." Again that note of admiration in her voice.

"Do you think she's one of our own?"

Ethan's hand slid down so his thumb made contact with her shoulder. "We'd know if another agency was targeting Prescott. At least I think we would, but I've got a feeling about her."

He wasn't caressing her, it was a simple point of contact. A small point of contact. And yet her insides were liquefying and her breath was coming faster. She should pull away, but she didn't want to. Which was bad. Very, very bad.

She licked her suddenly dry lips. "You once told me that your instincts never mislead you."

His gaze was fixed on her mouth. "They don't."

"Then we've got to assume something is going on here that we don't know about."

His eyes moved to meet hers. "I've got a friend I can call and find out what he knows. He's got connections in Washington that run on a different path than mine."

"We can have Alan check with his sources at the FBI."

"Hotwire has sources in the Bureau. There's no need to bother Hyatt." The tone of his voice said he'd rather eat his boots than contact the other agent. Was he jealous?

"Is Hotwire a fellow Texan?"

"Actually, no. He's from Georgia. An ex–special forces, then ex-mercenary. He does some work for official channels in an unofficial capacity. He also runs a security company with his wife and a friend of his. I'll call him tomorrow and ask him to check into it for me."

"I don't think you got a lot of comments on your report cards in school that said things like, 'plays well with others.' "

His brows drew together in confusion. "Your point?"

She shrugged, rubbing her shoulder along his thumb and

dangerously multiplying her body's reaction to him. "I'm surprised you're going to an outsider for help."

"He's a friend."

"Wow, I didn't think you had friends."

He didn't look confused now. He looked offended. "What would you call my fellow agents?"

"Coworkers."

"They're my friends."

"If you say so."

"What are you trying to say here?"

She wasn't sure why she was saying anything at all, except maybe she wanted that label for herself and needed it to be real. "You don't run ops with the same partner twice in a row. You do your extreme sports with the others, but last year, not one of them commented when you came to work on your birthday."

He rolled his eyes, his expression saying her logic was not impressing him. "They don't know my birthday."

"Exactly. You aren't close with any of them. Does this other friend know your birthday?"

"His wife does." Ethan grimaced. "Queenie ratted me out."

"Your great-uncle's paramour?"

"Paramour, what kind of word is that?"

"One that seems to fit a woman who was dating your eighty-something-year-old uncle when he died."

"I see. And what do you call yourself in relation to me?" His hand turned and cupped her shoulder.

The movement should have been casual, but she felt branded. She sucked in air.

"I don't know." She was more than a coworker, but less than a lover. Especially since the no sex rule she'd instigated. "Your friend?"

"You said I don't have any."

"Maybe I was being harsh."

His brow rose. "You, harsh?"

"I'm not, usually."

"I know." The words felt like a caress. "I also know what I'd like to call you."

"What?"

"My woman."

"Your lover, you mean?"

"That, too."

"I thought the sex was too intense for you." She thought she'd been too intense for him.

"I'm going crazy not touching you."

"You touch me all the time."

"For the sake of possible watchers. I don't take advantage."

"Don't you?"

"No, damn it, Beth. I don't." He jerked his hand away and sat back. "I'm a good agent. The best. I cover every angle, but I don't take advantage of women. In any way."

Chapter 17

Beth felt bereft without the warmth of his hand connected to her, but there were unresolved things about the night roiling around inside her. She wanted him and the more they were together, the more the wanting grew until it was an aching need that reached more deeply than physical desire.

It clawed at her very soul.

But she had enough instincts of self-preservation left to know she couldn't give in to it if certain things were true.

"I have a very good sense of smell."

"What?" he asked.

"I grew up learning to judge a woman's place in the social strata by the perfume she wore."

"That's a handy trick. Your mom teach you?"

"Yes. My dad encouraged her. He was proud that I could tell so much about people by their scents."

"Not all women wear perfume and a lot of men don't wear cologne."

"I graduated to learning to recognize almost everything. Dad made a game out of it, teaching me to identify other types of scents and what they might mean as well. We used to call it the Sherlock Holmes game. The smell of mothballs on a designer suit that said it wasn't new or worn often. The fragrance of certain spices that linger after a meal on people can tell you where they've eaten, or even what they eat usually and can reveal a lot about their culture and background."

"That's very cool."

"You think?"

"Yes."

"It's come in handy a time or two."

"And you are bringing it up now because?"

"I could smell Miss Fournier's perfume all over you."

"All over me?"

"Yes. You were making love to her, weren't you?"

Ethan reached down and laced his fingers through her hand, stopping her from playing with the chiffon. He rubbed gently over the back of her hand with his thumb. "Tell me why we went tonight."

"To learn what we could. So, you're saying you were using seduction to get information out of her." She tried to tug her hand away, but he wouldn't let go.

"No. We also went to plant listening devices, remember?"

"Yes, but I don't see how putting a bug down her bra is going to help us find out what Prescott is up to."

He laughed. "You've got an acerbic tongue when you want to, Sunshine. I didn't touch her bra. I touched her throat." He brushed his fingertip lightly over a spot on Beth's neck. "Specifically, here. With the correct amount of pressure exerted, you can cause a short blackout in your opponent."

"Are you trying to say you had to fight her off?" Her voice came out husky with an invitation she was trying very hard not to give him.

"No. I'm saying that I used her as a blind to get to the second floor, where I caused her to go unconscious without hurting her so that I could exit through the window and plant a receiver outside the master bedroom window."

"Why do you reek of her smell?"

"Her hands were everywhere after she yanked me onto the bed. She pressed herself against me."

"Did you kiss her?"

"No."

"Is that part of the special training you were talking about me needing?"

"Yes."

"I didn't like the idea of you using your body for the cause."

"We're even. I didn't like the sight of Prescott's hands on you at dinner."

"He barely touched me."

"It was enough."

"Would you have kissed her?"

"I didn't kiss her . . . by choice."

"Would you, if you had to?" She took a breath and then asked the question that mattered most of all. "Would you use your body . . . if it meant getting what we needed?"

"No. Not for the sake of the case and not because of desire. I don't want anyone else. Only you." He pulled their entwined hands so they rested on his thigh, all the while keeping up the soft massage with his thumb.

"But what if—"

His finger moved from her neck to press against her lips. "There are no buts. I couldn't make myself touch another woman with intent right now, Beth. Not for this assignment. Not for anything."

"Even though I said no sex?"

"Even then."

"But I have no hold on you."

"Apparently, you do."

"I don't want to. I don't want you to have a hold on me."

"I know I'm not the kind of man you see in your future, but that doesn't change that right now, we are bound together. Like it or not. Think it is smart or not. You are mine and I am yours."

The words were more seductive than his touch. "But we aren't sleeping together."

"I know and it's killing me."

"Is it?"

"You know it is. Don't play innocent. You know how hard you turn me on, how much you excite me."

"You don't like my intensity."

He laughed, like she'd said something really, really funny. "You are so wrong. I purely revel in it, baby."

"But you said—"

"That it made doing my job harder and it does. I've never been less than one hundred percent focused on my objective on any assignment. It's different this time, Beth. No matter what I'm doing, a little part of me is always focused on you. I thought it was just the sex, but it's not. I'm attuned to you like I've never been with another person. You make me feel needy, damn it."

"You sound angry."

"I am angry. These kinds of feelings are what make great agents screw up." Even angry and frustrated by feelings that clearly blindsided him, the man was ultraconfident in his assessment of himself.

"Are you sure about that?"

"Having my attention divided is always a risk."

"But we aren't having sex."

"And I told you it doesn't matter."

"It sounds to me like you're the intense one." Which was a revelation. A nice one.

"You could say that."

"But it bothers you."

He sighed, frowning. "Yes."

"You aren't bothered by who I am though, are you?"

"No. In fact, I'd feel a lot less like a fool if you shared a little of this intensity, Sunshine."

"You're not a fool." She was admitting to feelings she'd rather pretend did not exist, but living outside her fantasies meant admitting to realities she didn't like as much as being willing to take risks on making dreams real.

He didn't look appreciably cheered by her admission. "I feel like a green agent lately."

"Why?"

"I should have let Prescott walk with you in the maze. Nothing could happen to you with all of us so close by, but I couldn't stand the idea of you being alone with him like that. Even for a little bit."

"Are you sure you aren't just getting into your role so deep, you're internalizing projected feelings?"

"You thinking about taking up psychology, Sunshine?"

"I read about actors doing that . . . even writers feeling the emotions of their characters so deeply it affects their moods."

"I'm not an actor and we hired a ghostwriter to generate the books for my Ethan Grange persona."

"But you do play a role . . . you're playing one right now."

"No, Beth, right now, I'm Ethan Crane and I'm sitting on the sofa with a woman who drives me insane with desire and the need to protect her. That's not a role, that's the real deal."

Beth didn't want to believe him. Because if she did, her defenses were going to crumble. But his green eyes glowed with sincerity. His body radiated both a heat that wrapped around her and a sense of security she could not dismiss.

He meant it. He wasn't talking about forever. Neither of them was. But he was talking about having something more than physical lust in the here and now. He was talking about feelings mirrored in her own heart. The case had brought them together. But it was genuine feeling that kept them both from being able to ignore the intimacy between them.

She licked her lips, feeling wary, nervous, and filled with scared hope. "When you touch me, things go a little crazy."

"When I don't touch you, *I* go crazy."

"I don't want to be responsible for you losing your focus."

"I'm not used to these feelings. I'll admit that. I want things with you that I haven't wanted with another woman, but I'm learning to deal with that. Pretending the feelings aren't there won't work."

"Pretense is never as powerful as reality." She should know. She was an expert on fantasy.

He moved so both his hands cupped her neck. "I'm learning that."

"I'm scared, Ethan."

"Why, baby?"

"I don't want to love you."

"You said that before."

"And you said sex wasn't love."

His thumbs brushed along her jawline, tilting her head just a little. "It's not."

"It feels like it." The words were out before she knew they were on the way, but she wouldn't take them back.

Neither of them was going to hide from this truth.

"Then we'll deal with the emotions when and if they come. I've never run from trouble, Sunshine, and you're no scaredy-cat yourself."

She wondered how he'd worked that one out. "Self-preservation isn't cowardice."

"Sometimes it is."

"I'm not a coward."

"No. You're not."

"You're too good, you know that?"

"Am I?" Even those two words were seduction personified.

"Yes." She met his gaze, the hunger in his eyes matching her own. "Kiss me, Ethan. Kiss me like you mean it."

"I do mean it, baby."

There was no time to answer because his lips were on hers, possessing her with a tender determination that felt different than anything they'd shared before. But then it was different. They were both admitting that it was more than physical. That love might very well be lurking beneath the explosive desire they shared.

The woman she'd known herself to be a month ago would have run from that knowledge and the possible ramifications it could have on her heart and on her future. She'd learned painful lessons from her parents and Alan. But that Beth had not yet known the depth of Ethan's passion, or her own. Even so, she hadn't been able to walk away from Alan and what he represented.

Yet the feelings she'd had for him were a misty reflection of the deep well of emotion Ethan stirred inside her. She had no hope of turning her back on him and what he was offering, but she wouldn't hide from the truth this time either. She wasn't going to weave fantasies in her head about the kind of life they could have together.

Ethan was an agent. First, last, and always. She wouldn't ask him to give that up and she'd never make the mistake of assuming he was going to. If they had a future. And she would not pretend he'd offered that either. He'd used the phrase *for now* more than once. He wasn't thinking in terms of a life together, but he also wasn't dismissing the possibility.

He was being honest with her and she could be no less with herself.

She wanted and needed this man and all he would give her.

He lifted his head. "I feel like you're not with me on this, Beth."

She'd been responding, but he'd sensed her mind was elsewhere. He was so in tune with her, it was scary.

She smiled. "I was thinking."

"About us?"

"Yes?"

"Good thoughts or bad thoughts?"

"Mostly good."

He brushed his lips over her eyes, closing them. "I'm an overachiever, Beth."

"I noticed that about you."

"I'm not going to settle for anything less than great thoughts . . ." He slid his lips along her cheek and bit her earlobe gently. "Spectacular thoughts . . ." He licked her ear, sending shivers along her nerve endings. "Deeply erotic and pleasurable thoughts."

"You aren't?" she asked on a breathy whisper, concentrating on the feel of his mouth on her and keeping her eyes shut so the world she knew was only where their bodies connected.

"No." His lips were back to playing with hers. "Now, think about this."

This kiss was pure carnality. He wanted her thinking about nothing but the passion igniting between them and used his considerable expertise to guarantee it. His tongue was hot and tantalizing against hers, taking possession of her mouth with a marauder's confidence. She'd never kissed a man who could make her feel the things Ethan did with his mouth.

It went beyond the physical response of her body to something deep inside her that responded to him as if he was the other half of herself.

As the kiss went on and on and on . . . she did what she'd been aching to do since he took his shirt off. She smoothed her hands over the hair-roughened contours of his chest, memorizing every indentation and muscular formation with her mind as well as her fingertips. He was so perfectly, utterly masculine. And she loved that. She felt like Eternal Woman simply from touching him.

He shuddered, making a very male sound of appreciation against her lips as she caressed him. His skin was hot satin against her hands. It had only been a couple of days since they'd made love, but she felt like it had been forever. She was so hungry for him. Ravenous. Starving. Her nerve endings each craving the food of their mutual passion.

She pushed him backward, straddling his hard hips and aggressively responding to his kiss, all the while her fingers kneading him like a cat establishing its territory. His body shook with laughter as if he found her assertiveness funny, but she didn't care. He wasn't pulling away and this was what she needed.

She rubbed herself over the hard bulge straining against the seam of his trousers and his laughter abruptly ceased—to be replaced by a low, feral groan. He gripped her hips and surged up toward her, caressing her sweet spot through the layers of fabric with a long glide. She rode him like that, fighting the guide of his hands, wanting to set her own pace.

He let her go and she rocked zealously against him. She was dimly aware of his hands on the zip of her dress and then she was naked from the waist up, her bodice bunched up around her hips. Air cooler than her body brushed breasts swollen with desire and nipples beaded with almost painful desire.

She stopped moving and allowed the sensation to wash over her as goose bumps formed on her sensitive skin.

His big hands cupped her, the shocking difference between their warmth and the air sending pleasure arcing through her to be expelled in a tiny cry against his mouth. She pressed herself into his hold, moving side to side and up and down, reveling in the friction of his rougher hands against such soft flesh. He shifted his hold so her nipples were between his fingers and then squeezed them together, sending sensation zipping straight from the hard buds to her clitoris.

Another scream rose from her throat, but no sound emerged. She could do nothing but begin rocking her hips again in an anguished attempt to assuage the need exploding inside her womb and throughout her body. But it wasn't enough. She needed to have him inside of her, filling her until she thought she could not take any more.

The desire was so strong, she tore her mouth from his and leapt off his lap, her dress falling to the floor with her violent movements. She stepped out of it and stripped her tiny panties down her hips, kicking them off with an urgent flick.

He didn't say a word, but yanked off his pants and shorts, grabbing a condom from the pocket before he let the clothes fall to the floor.

"Thought you were going to get lucky?" she asked, panting.

He shook his head in a single hard denial as he ripped the packet open. "Afraid I wasn't going to be able to keep my hands off you."

"You were right."

"Yes, I was." She went to unhook her suspenders while he donned the condom, but he shook his head. "Don't. Leave them on. Please."

She looked down at herself. The suspender belt and stockings outlined her feminine mound like an erotic picture frame. Lifting her gaze, she smiled at him, feeling sexier than she ever had. "All right."

"Come here, baby." He put his hands out to her, his erection jutting from his body, thick, hard, and intimidating.

A sensual thrill ran down her spine and she reached for his hand, letting him pull her close. When that big shaft rubbed against her stomach, she moaned and leaned forward to bite him softly right beside his nipple. "I need you, Stud."

He laughed, the sound low and sexy. "For the first time, I don't feel like you're calling me that in an uncomplimentary way."

He was right. She wasn't. "You are the ultimate stud to me."

"Good. Because, baby, you are the quintessential woman to me."

Her body trembled against him. "You use big words for being so turned on."

"They're coming from someplace other than my brain, because right now, you've got that part of my anatomy fried with pleasure."

Something in the region of her heart went on meltdown. "I need you, Ethan."

And she wasn't sure she was just talking about making love.

But he took the words as an express invitation and lifted her. Happy to let the disturbing thought go, she spread her legs and wrapped them around him, whimpering when his penis pressed against the entrance to her body. She pushed down, taking more of him inside her, while he surged up with a tortured groan. He was moving, but she was too busy trying to increase the level of his penetration to care where he was taking her.

Her back landed against the wall. He pinned her there with his big body and with the leverage was able to thrust hard, filling her. "You're so tight, baby."

"You're big." She was stretched beyond comfort, but not to the point of pain. It felt so right.

"Is that an accusation?"

"A compliment. I like it."

"Only like?" He thrust into her heavily.

She moaned and moved to enhance the feelings arcing through her like lightning. But there was no question about which of them was in control at the moment. Ethan made love to her, his hands on her hips, holding her against the wall as he pounded in and out, driving her higher and higher until she couldn't think and could barely breathe.

"Just *like*, Beth? You only *like* this?"

"I love it!" she screamed, her body convulsing with the cataclysm of pleasure she only knew with him. "I love it . . . I love it . . . I love it . . . I lov . . ."

The chanting trailed off into a snaking moan as Ethan pinned her to the wall with a final, hard thrust and came. He yelled her name in a hoarse shout, his head thrown back like an ancient warrior, muscles corded along his neck.

Afterward, his head fell forward, nuzzling into the curve of her shoulder. They stayed that way a long time, Beth's arms locked around his neck, her legs locked around his waist.

"We have to move," he said in a gravelly voice that made her smile.

"Yes."

"I don't know if I can."

"Did I wear you out?"

"Are you saying you can walk?"

She didn't think she could make her legs move enough to unlock from around him. "Maybe not."

"So we wore each other out."

"You are so competitive."

"Who me?"

"I don't buy the innocent act, but if that condom is going to maintain its effectiveness, we've got to disengage like now."

"I don't want to."

"Neither do I."

He sighed and lifted her so he could slide out. She lowered her legs, but couldn't quite stand on her own, so stayed leaning against the wall while he took care of the condom. He came back to her and brushed a fingertip along the top curve of her breast. "You look like you could use some help."

"I can and notice, I'm not too proud to admit it." She put her arm around his shoulder, intending to lean on him.

But he swept her into his arms and carried her to the master bedroom. He pulled back the covers and carefully laid her on the bed. Like she was fine porcelain or something.

It made her eyes smart and she had to swallow back silly tears. "You're ruining me for normal men. I just thought I should mention."

He laughed, his eyes filled with a serious look at odds with his amusement. "That's the idea."

"My suspenders and hose are still on."

"I'll take care of it." And he did, his touch gentle yet provocative.

They ended up making love again, though she was positive she was too spent to respond. He proved her deliciously wrong and she fell asleep curled into his body, her own replete with satisfaction.

Chapter 18

Ethan went into the second bedroom to call the friend he'd mentioned to Beth the night before. Hotwire picked up the phone on the first ring and Ethan quickly explained why he'd called.

"I'll ask around," Hotwire said.

"Thanks. How's Claire?"

"Sassy as ever."

"Some men have all the luck."

Hotwire laughed. "That we do. How about you?"

"What do you mean?"

"Your voice changes when you say your partner's name."

"She's not exactly my partner."

"She's working the case with you though, isn't she?"

"Yes. She's my in."

"And she's got you tied in knots so tight she should be a sailor."

"Why do you say that?"

"Instinct."

"And yours is always on?"

"Isn't yours?"

"Usually."

"So?"

"So, don't say anything to Claire."

"Why not?"

"I'm not sure where it's going."

"We never are."

"We?"

"Men . . . when they finally meet the woman who brings them to their knees."

"Hey. I didn't say a thing about being on my knees."

"I hear it in your voice."

"What, you're psychic?"

"Nah. Just a man who's been there."

"I'm not anywhere."

"You keep telling yourself that, buddy."

"She doesn't want long term with an agent."

"Why?"

"She thinks they make lousy family men."

"You've got to admit that it's hard to raise kids today, even harder if you're gone for weeks at a time on a case."

"I know you're right, but I don't know if I can do anything else."

"I felt that way about being a merc. I learned I could."

"You were ready for the change."

"Life has a way of making you ready when it's important."

"Has Claire heard from Queenie this week?"

"Yes. She's got Josie's dad teaching self-defense classes at the local senior center. His wife loved the idea and she plays his sparring mate."

Ethan laughed. "What does Queenie do?"

"She plays the second assailant, or takes pictures. Her newsletter is gaining popularity."

"I'll have to check on distribution."

"Keeping her out of trouble is close to a full-time job."

"Especially with her cohorts in crime."

"Claire says she's going to be just like that as an old lady."

"Lord have mercy."

"He already did. He brought her into my life."

There was a time when Ethan would have razzed Hotwire for the sentiment, but he didn't feel like laughing right now. "Some women are special."

"Bring her to meet us when the case is over."

"We'll see."

"Yeah, we will." Hotwire was laughing when Ethan cut the connection.

Beth came out of the bedroom, her hair a messy cloud around her shoulders and wearing one of his shirts.

"You didn't bring any pajamas?" he asked with a smile.

She blinked her dark, bedroom eyes at him. "I like this better."

"Me, too." He gave her a complete once-over, letting his gaze linger at all the most interesting dips and valleys.

She blushed. "I get the feeling I could wear anything and you'd like it."

"You're right."

"That's pretty amazing considering the kind of women you normally date."

This was one of those tricky, feminine quagmires he just knew he was going to regret getting into. "What kind is that?"

"The put-together, always dressed for both sex appeal and fashion kind."

"*You* don't need to dress a certain way to be sexy."

Her expression filled with pleasure. "Thank you."

He wiped his mental brow. That had gone much better than it could have, but sometimes the truth had a way of getting a man out of potential trouble. At least good truth. "And we aren't just dating, we're living together." He didn't care if it was for the job, he liked the way it felt. "You can wear my shirts any time."

"That's very generous of you."

"Remember that the next time you get irritated with me."

She grinned. "You act like I get mad at you all the time."

"I'm just hedging my bets for the future. Smart men know when to take advantage of a moment."

"I'll remember," she said in a voice laced with laughter.

He leaned back in the chair, waiting for her to come closer, wanting to touch the silky smooth skin exposed below the hem of the shirt. "You sleep well?"

"You mean when you let me sleep?"

He'd woken her more than once in the night, but she'd responded with generous passion every time. "Yeah. When I let you sleep."

"I slept great, thanks."

"Thank you, Beth."

"For what?"

"For trusting me and for not holding my idiotic behavior against me."

She came over to stand beside him, laying her hand on his shoulder. "Idiotic behavior?"

He turned the office chair and pulled her onto his lap, laying one hand on her silky thigh right where he wanted it to be. "The whole intensity thing."

He'd hurt her with his confusion and inability to deal with feelings that were so new to him. He wished he could take it back, but all he could do was not make the same mistake again.

He wondered if he could make her faint again. He almost laughed at his own thoughts. She was right. He was competitive.

"Oh, *that* idiotic behavior. Don't worry about it." She wrapped her arms around his shoulders. "This is new territory for both of us."

"Not you. You loved Hyatt."

Her body went completely still. "Are you saying you think you love me?"

"I don't know, but it's different with you."

"Well, it's different with you, too, whatever it is. Trust me, this"—she swept her hand in an arc, indicating the rest of the cabin—"is very different for me, too. I've never lived with a man before."

"Have you ever wanted to?"

"No."

"So, new ground for both of us." Satisfaction he could not hide filled his voice. He liked knowing that. A lot.

"Very."

"I still like you in my shirt."

She laughed, the sound musical and very feminine.

"I talked to Hotwire. He's going to see what he can see."

"Did you call my dad to have him look into the possibility another agency has Prescott targeted, too?"

"Yes. Earlier. I've also been listening to the bugs I planted last night." He'd have to bring in one of the field agents staying in town to help listen to the bugs in real time.

"The disrupter doesn't stop them sending signal?"

"No, but some of the transmissions are fuzzy."

"Have you heard anything of interest?"

"Something about a UGCV."

"What is that?"

"Unmanned ground combat vehicle."

"A robot?"

"Yes. Our country has reached testing stages for technology that would be your basic war machine of specific to mass destruction that can be controlled by a portable unit within frequency range or via satellite from anywhere else in the world."

"Armageddon."

"We're hoping not, but in the wrong hands that kind of machine could do horrific damage."

"You mean like terrorists who don't care who they kill as long as they win?"

"Exactly."

"And you think Prescott has one he's going to auction off."

"More likely the plans for one, but yes . . . I think that's the merchandise that has so many clients from different nationalities interested in it."

"He really doesn't care who gets hurt by his actions, does he?"

"Beth, baby . . . I have the disturbing feeling that Prescott is the kind of man who likes to hurt other people."

"I'm starting to think you might be right." She shivered.

He rubbed her back. "I need you to put a listening device in the office. I wasn't going to try, but just before we left, I saw Prescott take several of his guests to that part of the house. If the device is found, it wouldn't be automatic for him to trace it back to you."

"I'd take the chance."

"I won't."

She shook her head. "For such a tough guy, you can be a real worrywart."

"Only about some things."

"Besides me, name another."

"I worry about Queenie. My mom. My sister."

"I guess I'm in exalted company."

"If you see my family that way, then yes, you are."

"I'm not family though."

"You're my woman."

"For now."

"Now is when we live."

She nodded. "I'm sure Prescott's personal office is sound-proof, so I don't know if it would do any good to put a bug in the one I use or his secretary does."

"Can you get inside?"

She bit her lip. "Yes, but I don't think you'll like my methods."

Something clenched in Ethan's gut. "You want to flirt with him."

"I think it would work."

"Try other methods first."

She saluted, her eyes dancing with mischief. "Yes, sir."

"Woman, you are a menace."

"I live to serve."

"You live to drive me insane."

"Oh, no . . . don't blame that on me. I have it on good authority all agents are a little crazy. It comes with the job."

"It still bothers you that I'm an agent." She hadn't sounded bitter, but he knew.

She shrugged. "What is must be accepted."

"Oh, very Zen."

"You think so?"

"Sounds like it could be . . . or one of my grandmother's bits of wisdom."

"She's into Zen?"

"She's into old sayings that carry a world of truth."

"I like that."

"I do, too. You'd like her."

"I'm sure I would."

Despite having to spend time listening to the goings-on at Prescott's estate and having another agent there to help, Ethan and Beth spent a lot of time together. And it felt right.

She went to work on Monday morning determined to get into Prescott's office, but was shocked when he called her in to speak to him.

"I trust you had a good weekend, Beth."

"Yes, Arthur. Ethan wasn't working, so we got to spend a lot of time together."

"I see." He frowned, looking concerned. "In the general way of things, I stay strictly out of my employees' personal lives."

"Yes, sir."

"Arthur, Beth. I want us to be friends."

"Thank you."

"I find what I'm about to do distasteful. Not that I am wrong to do it, but it is always distressing to me to have to point out the perfidy of others to someone as sweet and innocent as you."

"Perfidy?" Had Prescott discovered Ethan was an agent? Why would he tell her?

"Especially in relation to someone you love."

"Um . . . I don't think I understand." But her heart was beating a mile a minute.

"Beth, my dear . . . I have something to show you and I know it is going to upset you." He stood up and came around his desk, putting his hand on her shoulder. "You have only worked for me a short time, but I feel that we connect." He paused. "As friends. I want you to let me be your friend right now."

"Thank you, Arthur, but I don't understand what's going on."

He guided her around his desk and pressed a button on his computer so the image from a security tape started running. It was the upstairs hall and Ethan was walking along it with Miss Fournier. Her hand was under his jacket, caressing him. He was guiding her toward a bedroom.

"I don't understand . . . how did you come across this?"

"It's my habit to watch my security feedback after I have guests in my home."

She wasn't touching the why of that with a barge pole. "He told me he was helping her because she wasn't feeling well."

"Is that what it looks like to you?"

"It could be. Women go for Ethan, but that doesn't mean he responds. It's her hands all over him. Do you have cameras in the bedroom?" She didn't think Ethan would have risked going on the roof if that was the case, but she had to ask.

"Not that bedroom, no."

"You have cameras in some of your bedrooms?" she asked, feigning shock, but feeling disgust.

"Some people who stay in my home can be security risks. It is a protective measure only."

She managed to hold back a cynical *I bet*. "I appreciate your concern for me, Arthur. I really do, but I don't think this proves Ethan was doing anything other than what he said he was. Helping the woman out. You don't know him like I do. He wouldn't cheat on me."

"Beth." Prescott shook his head. "You are so innocent and good, only seeing the best in others. Mr. Grange is a very lucky man."

She let him hug her shoulder even though it made her feel claustrophobic to have him so close. She used the diversion to press the listening device to the bottom of the desk near where she stood. Ethan would be proud of her.

"The smarmy, self-seeking bastard." Rage ripped at Ethan's insides and he wanted to pound something. Preferably Prescott's skull.

Beth had waited to tell him about Prescott's attempt to discredit Ethan in her eyes until they were in the cabin after he picked her up from work. She had good instincts, always careful to discuss sensitive stuff behind the wall of their security.

"Don't get so upset," she soothed, her voice soft and so damn feminine it made his dick hard despite his anger. "It's not as if I believed him. I know why you were in that room with Celine Fournier and frankly, I'm glad he thinks it was for the reason he does."

Ethan knew his fury was all out of proportion to the situation. This was a case and as Beth had pointed out, it was a good thing Prescott wasn't wary of his motives for going upstairs. But none of that seemed to matter.

"The idea of anyone trying to undermine our relationship pisses me off," he admitted through gritted teeth.

Her big brown eyes widened, as if his words had really shocked her. "But he's one of the bad guys. We expect this sort of behavior from him."

Uncomfortable with the feelings roiling inside him, Ethan paced away to stare out the window. "I know he's a lowlife slug without a shred of loyalty to his country, but this is getting personal, Sunshine."

"Ethan, you're the kind of agent who takes all your cases personally."

He turned around to frown at her. "I'm a professional."

She didn't even look minutely intimidated. Her eyes were filled with the kind of warmth that could be addictive. "You're a man who cares about your country so much you'd give your life for its safety. You've risked your life on more assignments than I care to think about."

He shrugged. "I'm an adrenaline junky. Everyone knows that."

She didn't smile like he expected her to, but got all serious like a woman intent on knowing and exposing the secrets of his soul. For a man like him, it was a terrifying look, but he couldn't make himself break eye contact or turn away.

He needed to hear what she thought of him. Of why he did what he did.

"Maybe," she said after several seconds of intense silence, "but you're an agent because you care, not because you need your adrenaline fix. You've got a superhero complex and I, for one, find that irresistible."

Then she did smile, but he couldn't match her lighthearted expression. Her attitude touched something deep inside him that no one else, not even his family, had ever come close to. She was right. He did want to be a hero for his country. Not so others would look up to him; he didn't care if anyone ever knew what he sacrificed for the greater good. But he needed to be part of making the world a better, safer place.

It wasn't something he'd ever admitted out loud. Not even when he told his dad he wanted to do something besides ranching. Back then he'd been too embarrassed to admit to such lofty goals and since then, he'd gotten used to hiding his true nature behind his adrenaline junky image.

Beth saw through him though. "I think you're the only person who sees that about me," he admitted quietly.

"I doubt it. A discerning person couldn't know you very long before realizing you want to save the world from evil." Again the smile. So darn sweet. So incredibly beautiful to him.

"But the fact is, others don't see it, Beth. Why do you know me so much better than anyone else?" It really was a puzzle to him.

They'd only been "together" for a matter of weeks and he'd never told her any of this. Or even hinted at it.

"You've been my obsession for two years, Ethan. A woman learns a thing or two about a man when she spends so much time thinking about him."

"So, it wasn't all sex . . . even in your fantasies." Man, he liked hearing that.

She looked startled and then shrugged, as if it didn't matter. But it did. To both of them.

"We've gotten off topic," she said a little primly.

She was running again, but he was a natural-born predator. When prey ran, predators followed. Though sometimes, they bided their time, which was what he planned to do. For now. Beth was cagey and she had a lot of hang-ups about their relationship; he had to tread carefully. But he liked knowing that she'd noticed more than his great body for the past two years.

"Have we?" he asked.

She bit her lower lip and nodded, looking wary. "Yes."

He drew her into his arms. "What were we talking about?"

"The fact that I got a listening device into Prescott's office." She sounded really pleased with herself.

And she had every right to be. "I'm proud of how well you think on your feet, baby, I really am, but I still want to knock the toad's teeth in."

She patted his chest, her small hand settling right over his heart. "Maybe you'll get the chance when we move in for the kill."

"There is no *we* about the collar. You are not an agent and will be far from the scene when we go to arrest him."

"Whatever you say."

He tried to read her expression, but couldn't find any evidence of subterfuge. "You make me nervous when you get agreeable like this."

"I don't know why. I'm not an agent and I don't want to risk the operation by being where I'm not needed. I used *we* strictly in a generalized sense."

"I should feel reassured."

"But you don't?"

"No."

"You need to trust me, Ethan."

"I do."

"I'm glad to hear it. I'm not stupid, you know?"

"I do know."

"Then you should know I would never risk you or the case."

He sighed. "I'm being overprotective, aren't I?"

"Considering the fact that I agree with you, um . . . yes."

"I'm not internalizing projected feelings," he admitted, wishing the psychological phenomenon she'd mentioned the day before could explain his behavior. "I have this caveman-like need to make sure you're safe at all times."

"And here I thought you were the epitome of the modern sophisticated male."

"I did too," he acknowledged wryly.

She laughed, rubbing his chest in what was no doubt supposed to be a soothing gesture, but which turned him on. Everything about her excited him. "Don't let it upset you. I'm learning stuff about myself I didn't know either."

"Like what?"

"I like the adrenaline rush of fieldwork." She said it like she was admitting a deep, dark sin.

His heart stuttered as his head swam with images of Beth taking risks he'd approved for other female agents. "I'm not sure my heart can take that, but it's not a crime, sweetheart."

"I know. It violates what I believed about myself though."

"Does it bother you that your dad might be right?"

"That I'd make a good agent?"

"Yes."

"A little, but mostly it just throws my view of the world and my place in it off-kilter."

"Maybe the job change you need when we get back to D.C. is to take more extensive agent training instead of leaving the city looking for a place you fit better."

"You might be right."

As much as he hated the thought of her ever being in danger, he felt nothing but relief at her willingness to consider staying in D.C. and continuing to work for The Goddard Project. Maybe she would rethink her views on long-term commitments with agents as well.

Chapter 19

They hit pay dirt with the bug in Prescott's office two days later.

"He's planning an auction at the end of the month for controlled technology classified as unexportable," Ethan told Beth. "He's bringing the potential buyers back for a video demonstration of a UGCV along with specs. The auction will happen two days later, but so far we don't have a line on how he intends to pass the plans on."

"You know, I think the man is arrogant enough to store the plans at his house. The security there is tight." She kitty-combed Beethoven's fur while the growing kitten lounged in her lap on the sofa.

"I agree, but I've been over the house plans until I can see them with my eyes shut and there are just too many places he could have a hidey-hole. Going in with a warrant wouldn't necessarily net the goods."

"My guess is that he's got the plans stored on a media device, maybe even his computer. He thinks its foolproof."

"His security is better than most. I've been trying to hack his system and there are so many layers of ICE that my fingers are getting frostbite from the keyboard."

"Ouch."

"You're telling me. The intrusion countermeasure engineering Prescott's invested in is the best. There are several signatures, as if he's got graduating as well as same-level layers of security from different sources."

"You'll get through."

"Maybe we should call Bennett in on this. This is really his thing."

"But you're no slouch at it, Ethan. Besides, he's on assignment in the Middle East. He left three days ago." The cat jumped off her lap and Beth dropped the special brush down on the coffee table.

"You been checking up on the other agents, Beth?"

"I can't help myself. Maude and I talk daily."

"She handling things okay?"

"Of course. The woman is a miracle worker."

"We all feel that way about you."

Beth smiled, clearly pleased. "I'll remind you of that the next time you give me a hard time about turning in your expense reports."

"I never forget it, baby, but I still don't like doing expense reports. I think miracle workers should be able to generate them without any help."

She launched herself toward him as the phone rang.

Ethan grabbed it and her at the same time. He pressed the button to talk while pulling Beth into his lap. "Ethan here."

She gave him a friendly elbow to the ribs before settling against his chest.

"Ethan, it's Hotwire."

"Any word for me?"

"Officially? No. But ten months ago, a young woman in Oregon killed herself. She was attending a community college not far from Prescott's home when they met. They started dating and she stopped attending classes. She'd lost her job for not showing up and had a miscarriage due to drug usage and possible sexual trauma the week before she killed herself."

Ethan couldn't believe what he was hearing. "I didn't find anything about this during my investigation into him."

"Your perp did a good job of hushing his connection to the girl up."

"But you found it." It irked Ethan that he hadn't.

"Her parents died when she was fifteen. Her older sister finished raising her and was helping her through college. The sister is a DEA agent by the name of Rachel Gannon. She confided her fears for her sister and then about the suicide to a friend of mine."

"And let me guess, the DEA agent has taken a leave of absence, her whereabouts unknown."

"Yes. My friend's worried about her, but he hasn't said a thing to their superiors. She's a hell of a sniper and she's more lethal with a knife than Wolf."

"This doesn't feel good."

"I concur."

"Damn. You think Rachel Gannon is planning personal revenge."

"If you can stop her, you'll be saving a life worth preserving." They both knew Hotwire didn't mean Prescott.

"She could have killed him at the party the other night."

"If she was the one who was there. Yes. I'll send you a picture for verification of her identity. But personal revenge plans aside . . . she's still her country's servant."

"You think she wants to stop the plans for the UGCV getting into enemy hands before she offs Prescott."

"That's my guess."

"Whit is going to lose his mind if I pull her into our investigation."

"You don't have to pull her in to stop her, but if you don't, you'll be robbing her of the closure she needs."

"I'll talk to Beth about it."

He got a kiss on his cheek for that and couldn't help taking her lips.

Hotwire was laughing and calling his name when Ethan remembered he was still on the phone. "Save it for when I'm not on the other end of the line. You're making me miss Claire."

"Where is she?"

"She went shopping for the baby with Josie. She and Nitro are staying for a few days before she goes back to classes."

"Where's Nitro?"

"Outside scaring the wildlife."

"I heard that," came from the other side of the room. "I'm going to tell Claire that our Medicine Men believe a woman should stop having sex the last three months of her pregnancy for the safety of the baby."

"The man is getting serious," Hotwire said, sounding far from worried. "I think I need to go kill him."

"I've got a man I wouldn't mind skinning like a snake and staking out in the sun to dry."

"Do tell."

Hotwire swore when Ethan told him what Prescott had done with the video and Beth.

"You watch her, Ethan."

"I plan to."

"I mean it. This man is a sadistic son of a bitch. I have a feeling that young woman in Oregon was one in a long line."

"Beth will be safe."

"If you need us, you call."

Ethan felt something strange in his chest. Beth was right. He didn't have a lot of friends, but because of his need to know what had really happened when his great uncle died, he'd made some good ones. "Thanks. I'll remember that."

"You were there for me when I needed you to help me keep Claire safe from our own government."

"All part of the job."

"You just keep believing that."

They hung up a minute later after Hotwire reminded Ethan to bring Beth to visit Montana when the case was over.

The next couple of weeks were an exercise in frustration on one side for Ethan and pure bliss on the other. He was having no luck cracking Prescott's ICE, but living with Beth was pure pleasure. He liked being with her. Even when she was cranky waking up in the mornings and slapping at his hands when he touched her in front of the agents coming in on rotation to help him listen to the audibles from Prescott's bugs.

She acted like she enjoyed the intimacy of living in the same house, too. She definitely more than liked the pleasure they shared in the privacy of their bed at night. Holding her in his arms was addictive and he didn't relish the thought to returning to living and sleeping alone. The closer the end of the case got, the more he considered what to do about that.

Beth was preparing a report on investment opportunities for Prescott when his secretary told her he wanted to see her in his office again.

He had a complacent expectancy about him that made her leery, but she forced a smile. "You wanted to see me, Mr. Prescott."

"Please close the door, Beth."

She did so, but was glad that their conversation was being overheard by Ethan and the other agents back at the cabin. This was one man she had no desire to ever be completely alone with.

He stood up from behind his desk and came toward her. "Beth, I'm not going to beat around the bush. I care about you. When I met you for your interview I knew you were special."

She backed up toward the door. "I'm involved, Arthur, you know that."

"Yes, I know." Prescott looked pained. "To a man who is not worthy of you."

"You're wrong. Ethan is really wonderful."

"I'm sorry but, Beth, because of my growing feelings toward you . . . because of who you are, how very innocent you are . . . I could not leave well enough alone after the party."

"What are you saying?"

"I had your boyfriend followed by a private investigator."

Her lungs froze for a second in stark, utter horror before her brain started working again. "You've had him followed? But why?"

Now, more than ever, she appreciated Ethan's attention to detail when establishing and maintaining cover for a case. Her heart was pounding wildly, but she was confident Prescott's private eye would not have found anything to compromise that cover.

"I didn't believe his encounter with Miss Fournier was as blameless as he tried to pretend."

"But he explained about that."

"And you believed him. That is to your credit, my dear Beth, but I have evidence that it was not so."

This was getting really bizarre. "What evidence?"

"This will be difficult for you, but I have some photos to show you."

He indicated a file on his desk. "Please. Come with me."

He led her to stand with him behind the desk and then without further preliminaries, flipped the file open.

The picture on top was of Ethan naked, but covered by a sheet. A woman sat on his torso, touching her breasts for his keen gaze. Beth knew that look, he gave it to her when he wanted her. She knew the pictures had to be faked, but even knowing that, pain lanced through her. The very thought of Ethan with another woman was enough to make her physically ill, but Prescott's machinations filled her with fury. The man was worse than a snake.

Ethan had been right about that. Not that she'd doubted him. But he'd been right about something else, too. Prescott had been spying on them. The picture of Ethan's face had to have come from times when they'd been in the living room with the curtains open.

Imagining someone watching them, even though they never did anything really intimate until they shut themselves into privacy, made her skin crawl. And Prescott would be the kind of man who got a kick out of something like that.

Forcing herself to dwell on how it would feel if it really was Ethan with another woman rather than her intense anger, she gave Prescott the reaction he no doubt expected. Tears spurted into her eyes as she put her hand over her mouth.

He patted her back and it was all she could do not to belt him. "You must be strong, Beth."

Then he flipped the photo to reveal the one beneath it. There were six pictures in all, each of them very cleverly done. None actually showed Ethan naked so if he had a birthmark and his body double didn't, she wouldn't see that. His face was superimposed on the pictures with the skill of a true artist. If it were any situation other than the one she was in and any man other than Ethan, Beth would have taken the pictures at face value. They looked absolutely authentic.

And the more she looked, the angrier Beth got. Prescott was pure evil and she'd like to drop him in a rattlesnake pit.

She went to grab the photos. "I have to show these to Ethan."

Instead of looking disgusted, or even disappointed, Prescott looked strangely pleased by her reaction. "You want to give him a chance to explain it, but how can he?"

"He needs to see them."

"I'm sorry. I can't give you the photos. I stepped outside of my role as your employer to have him followed. It would be too risky to let him have a copy of these pictures. He might try to sue me . . . or pay someone to say they are forgeries."

"But I have to show them to him."

"No, Beth. You need to decide if you will stay with a man who has cheated on you."

"But where would I go?" she asked with credible dismay. "I just moved here . . . started working for you."

"You know I'm interested in you. But I would never force the issue in your current state. However, I would be pleased to allow you to stay with me."

"You want me to move in to your home?"

"It isn't an offer I would make to another woman."

"I . . . I appreciate it." The slimy toad. "But I've got to talk to Ethan."

"Yes, I can see that you do, Beth. But consider this . . . if he's cheating on you now, chances are he's been screwing other women all along."

She flinched at the crudity and Prescott's lips curved in a twisted smile. "You are far too innocent for the likes of him, Beth."

And just the type of woman he liked playing his ugly games with. Or so he thought. Beth wanted nothing more than to give him a taste of black belt and teach him not all women were helpless or that easily enthralled.

Innocence did not equate to stupidity and naïveté was something that should be protected, not exploited. But he was going to learn that soon enough.

Ethan was simmering with rage when he came to pick Beth up.

Neither of them spoke until they were inside the cabin.

"That sick son of a bitch had photos doctored to look like I was having an affair, didn't he?"

"Yes. You heard the conversation."

Ethan jerked his head in assent, his body vibrating with incandescent anger.

"He wants me to move in with him." He had to have heard that, too, but she didn't expect him to bring it up.

"No way in hell."

She'd anticipated that reaction. "Ethan, we've got to get into his computer . . . find something more than what we've got right now for an airtight collar. Me being in the house is an in we can't afford to ignore."

"No."

"I'm not going to let him hurt me."

"Neither am I. You are not moving in with him. In fact, I think it's time you quit your job."

She gasped. "We don't have enough intel. I need to be there."

"We've got bugs."

"What if they're found? For all you know, Prescott has a sweep scheduled any day now."

"He's too arrogant to sweep for bugs. He thinks he's too smart to be double-crossed. If he wasn't, he would have swept for them right after the party."

"Maybe. Or maybe it's just part of his routine security and he's got one scheduled soon."

"It doesn't matter . . . we'll make the collar. And we'll make it stick, but we aren't risking your safety to do it."

"And if I were a trained agent?"

"Then it would be different, but I'd still be strongly against it. The man hurts women and he likes doing it."

"You talked to the sister. When?"

"I called this morning, before that jumped-up scene in Prescott's office."

True to his word, Ethan had discussed the option of bringing the DEA agent in on their case with Beth. Beth had felt the woman deserved the chance to help bring down her sister's abuser. Ethan had agreed, but only after doing a thorough investigation of the other woman's background, her strengths and weaknesses as an agent.

He'd concluded Rachel Gannon was someone Beth's dad would be lucky to have working for him at TGP.

"She told me that Prescott plays dominance games with women of the sadistic kind."

"He's into S&M?"

"Yes. She fully expects the auction to include a new sex slave for him as part of the package."

"That's horrible."

"Yes, it is, and there's no way you are ever going to move into the same house with a monster like that."

"But we need an in."

"I'm going to ask Hotwire to help me hack the system."

Beth's mind reeled at the statement. Ethan was not the

type of man to ask for help, ever . . . but especially not out-side the agency.

"Don't look at me like I just said I wanted to get a job table dancing at Hooters."

"But . . ."

"Bennett Vincent is not available and he's the only hacker at the agency better than me."

"You think Hotwire's better than you?"

"He might be, but even if he's not—if we're working to-gether, even Prescott's ICE won't stand against us."

"What about my job with Prescott?"

"You're quitting."

"Do you think Whit would approve?"

"I'm the agent in charge. This is my call, Beth."

"What if you can't crack the ICE, what if what we have isn't enough evidence to put him away?"

"You need to trust me, Sunshine. My gut is telling me to keep you the hell away from him."

"Your gut, or your heart?"

"Does it matter?"

"It shouldn't. It's an assignment. I know that. But it does."

"Both, all right?"

She nodded, her chest tight. "Is Rachel Gannon going to be a problem?"

"No. She was relieved when I called. She'd come to the re-alization that killing him wasn't enough. She wants to see him suffer, see him in prison where his reputation as a woman abuser can precede him, see his assets seized by the govern-ment, see him broken."

"Like her sister before she took her life."

"Yes."

"Why didn't she call her agency?"

"It's not the DEA's jurisdiction. She was getting ready to call the FBI when I contacted her."

"Your timing was good then. They would have compli-cated things."

"It always is, baby, or hadn't you noticed?"

She laughed at his sheer confidence. "If I say yes, it will go to your head."

"Whereas if you say no, my manly ego will be mortally wounded."

"Your manly ego could take a mortar and not be mortally wounded."

"It's the way you respond to me. It makes me feel like Superman."

"You mean Super*stud*?"

He laughed. "Yeah, maybe that."

Ethan made the phone call to Prescott and it wasn't pretty. Prescott kept insisting on speaking with Beth and Ethan told him no. Categorically. He also called him a couple of names and told him he knew he'd had the photos faked, but couldn't figure out why he'd gone to the trouble. If he was that hard up for women, maybe he should buy himself some companionship.

"He's going to send an assassin after you after that," Beth said when Ethan hung up.

"Good. Then we'll have another crime to charge him with."

She shivered. "I'm glad the auction is in only a couple of days. Even you aren't invincible, Superstud."

"Is that my new name?"

"To me."

He grinned. "I like it."

"I know you do."

"I like something else, too."

"But it will have to wait. You just destroyed our in with the perp. Call your friend. You two need to get to work."

"You can be very bossy when you want to be, has anyone ever told you that?"

"Why do you think I fantasized about handcuffing you to the bed?"

"You did that because you secretly longed for a lover who could take all you had to give and come back for more."

"You think so?"

"I'm sure of it. You're a very passionate woman and you need a man who can match that passion. It's not easy, but I'm up to the job."

"You might be up, but you are also on duty. Now . . . get . . . to . . . work." She enunciated each word with careful clarity.

He saluted and then called Hotwire.

Ethan was grinning when Hotwire picked up the phone. He loved Beth in her feisty, take-charge mode. She got that way at the office and it always made him smile and grow hard. He was up, just like he'd said, but he could control himself. For a while.

"Hey, buddy . . . you got some time?"

"Sure, what's up?"

He moved to sit in front of his laptop set up at the dining room table. Another agent was in the spare room listening to Prescott's audibles. "I've got prelim access on a computer, but I'm hitting wall after wall in ICE."

"Give me the ID code and ISP if you've got it."

Ethan relayed the information he had.

He heard clicking in the background and did his own initial sequence for connection.

"You're right, this man has serious ICE, but he's made the terminal mistake . . . the only one that it's impossible to protect against."

"He's got ISP connection."

"Yes. No matter how good the ICE, it can always be cracked, but you can't hack a computer externally that isn't hooked up for outside connectivity."

He didn't know how long he'd been working when Beth started rubbing his shoulders, massaging the kinks out. He turned and kissed one hand.

She kissed the top of his head. "I'm going to make a pot of coffee."

"That's great, thanks." But his mind was on Hotwire's de-encryption program.

It was one of the best he'd seen. They'd connected about thirty minutes into their session and were working on the hack in real time together.

"If we work from three different points, rather than all of us working on each wall of ICE at the same time, we have a better chance of breaking in." Claire had picked up an extension and joined them sometime ago. "Bennett, you stick with encryption. Ethan, you work on circumventing the firewall, I'm going to work on the password for entry. It's a scrolling one and I recognize the pattern . . . I studied its creator in one of my classes."

"Good idea, honey," Hotwire said. "The longer we take on the hack, the bigger chance we're going to be detected."

They'd been careful to cover themselves, but it was taking longer because they had to be so careful to hide their fingerprints in the system. If they were backtracked, the trail would end at three different computers with ISP addresses assigned in China. Any attempt to go beyond would encounter a virus that would keep the backtracker busy if it didn't destroy the hard drive.

Chapter 20

Beth grew fidgety as the afternoon wore on. She was keeping quiet for both Ethan's sake and that of the agent in the other room, but she needed to breathe some air besides that in the cabin. And she wanted to go through her Poom Ses, but there was nowhere inside that she could do it without disturbing someone. The clearing about a hundred yards from the cabin would work great.

For the past two weeks, Ethan had been taking her down to the beach just after dawn each morning, where he worked out and ran while she went through her tae kwon do exercises. But they'd missed yesterday and today because of his efforts to hack into Prescott's computer security.

She changed into clothes that would be comfortable for her workout and then tapped Ethan on the shoulder. "I'm going for a walk."

"Wear a comm unit and stay in sight of the house."

"Aye, aye, sir."

He turned his green gaze on her. "Don't be smart."

"But I am smart."

His lips quirked. "You're also sassy."

"You wouldn't want me any other way."

"No, I wouldn't."

She was smiling when she let herself out the back door of

the cabin. The autumn air smelled fresh and clean, so different to what she was used to and she stopped to drag in a deep breath. They were close to the ocean and she could smell the salt in the air along with wet leaves and moist earth. Even the tree bark had its own unique fragrance that added to the ambiance in the forest.

She was tempted to walk to the beach, but she'd promised to stay in sight of the house. She headed through the forest to the clearing. In the spring and summer it would have been out of sight of the house, too, but the crimson and yellow leaves had dropped from the trees, creating a spongy layer over the ground. The evergreens blocked the view from the house a little, but not completely and she was wearing the comm unit.

It was so different here. Not just clean, but earthy. What would it be like to live someplace like this all the time?

Immediately following that thought another came unbidden. Her and Ethan sharing a small house in Virginia, close enough to D.C. to continue working for TGP, but far enough from the city to catch the flavor of the world she was standing in right now. Ethan hadn't said anything about a future, but he had suggested she train to be an agent rather than leave TGP.

He'd also seemed relieved when she said she would consider it. He didn't want her to go, she didn't think. She wasn't the queen of reading men's feelings, but she was pretty sure Ethan didn't want their relationship to end with the conclusion of the assignment. That didn't mean he'd be open to sharing the kind of future she was dreaming about right that minute.

She kicked at fallen leaves. She'd learned so much about herself in the past few weeks, it was kind of scary. But she realized that if she couldn't have the life she'd always wanted— the loving family that did normal stuff together and shared the same home more than occasionally—maybe the life of an agent would be an okay substitute. It was such a huge transition in her thinking, she was wary of her reasons for feeling this way.

Was she trying again to be acceptable to someone she loved? Did she want the life Ethan had so she could share it with him?

But being an agent didn't necessarily mean they'd spend any more time together. Ethan did not work with a partner. Most agents for TGP didn't. He took high-risk assignments usually, not ones that a new agent would be sent out on. In fact, becoming an agent might keep her in D.C., but it wouldn't guarantee her one more minute of Ethan's time.

So, why was she considering it when she'd fought the idea for so long? Was it because she'd realized that she liked the adrenaline rush? Or simply because she saw that she had an aptitude for subterfuge? Or maybe, more disturbingly because her dad would be thrilled by the prospect? Was she still seeking that elusive brass ring of parental approval?

Yet, her heart rejected all the alternatives her mind tossed up to her. It told her that despite what she'd always been so sure of . . . she was finally finding a life that might fit who *she* was. Or at least who she had become.

"Beth, I'm glad to see you here."

Her head snapped up and she stared in shock at Arthur Prescott. She'd been so lost in her thoughts, she hadn't heard his approach. "What are you doing here?"

"Walking in the woods." But he wasn't exactly dressed for the endeavor. He wore one of his many designer suits and Italian leather dress shoes that looked strange against the carpet of decaying autumn leaves. "I needed some time to myself after your boyfriend called and said you would not be working for me any longer. I'm worried about you, Beth."

He sounded so sincere, but the hairs on the back of her neck were standing on end. She hated the thought of his smarmy technique fooling another woman like the young girl who'd killed herself after tangling with him. There was something coldly evil that surrounded him in spite of his urbane façade.

"I'm sorry about that. I didn't mean for you to be worried, but he insists you faked the pictures."

"What do you think?"

She was using her peripheral vision to scan her surroundings, trying to listen for the sound of anyone he might have brought with him. "I don't know what to think. He asked lots of questions about the pictures. None of them showed his naked body . . . he said that was proof that they were faked."

"Did they look faked to you?"

"No, but I love him. I have to believe him."

"That's an admirable sentiment, my dear, but why would I do such a thing?"

"I don't know." She bit her lip, striving for a confused look. "Ethan says you want me."

"I do, but I don't have to stoop to lying to get women I want." He was moving closer and she backed up.

He stopped and frowned at her, contriving to look hurt. "Are you afraid of me, Beth?"

"If you faked those photos, I have good reason to be. But I can handle you." She said that for the agent monitoring her comm unit back at the cabin.

They were so close to nailing Prescott, she didn't want to risk their cover having the Calvary come riding to the rescue.

Something sparked in Prescott's eyes at her assertion—something like twisted anticipation. "And if I didn't? If you quit your job and let me down . . . all on the word of a cheating swine, what then?"

"That's not true."

"Where is Ethan, Beth?"

"He's working."

Prescott gave her a disbelieving look. "After what you learned today, he's dismissed you to work on another of his second-rate books?"

"His writing isn't second rate."

"Then why has he published with a small press in the Midwest rather than New York?"

"New York publishers require authors to be available for publicity and Ethan is a very private person."

Prescott shook his head pityingly. "You'll make excuses for him no matter what the circumstance, won't you?"

"They aren't excuses."

He was moving again, trying to get closer and she was parrying his moves with defensive postures from her tae kwon do that were second nature to her now. But when he reached out and grabbed her arm, she let him, wanting to know what he planned to do. And not wanting to tip off how easily she could get away from him.

He pulled her closer. "I can't stand to see you waste your life on him, Beth. This is for your best interests."

"What?"

One of his security men came out of the forest to their left. Beth's eyes widened, though deep inside, she was not surprised. As inconceivable as it might be in the world of the sane, she thought Prescott planned to kidnap her. And believed he could get away with it.

"I think you should come back to my house with me, Beth."

"No." She windmilled her arm, breaking his hold and hooked her foot behind his ankle, jerking with practiced ease while she shoved against his chest with all her might.

He went down hard and she ran.

"Get her!" Prescott yelled.

Another security man came out of the forest and the two converged on her. She'd had to spar multiple partners to earn her black belt and she let instincts she'd taken years to hone take over. The one on her left lunged for her and she used his forward momentum and a spinning axe kick to send him flying in the opposite direction.

The other guard didn't mess with trying to grab her, but brought a gun up. She threw herself into a forward somersault landing near enough to kick upward and dislodge the gun before executing an openhanded punch to his groin. He grunted and fell forward, his face losing all color.

She flipped to her feet and sprinted toward the house, using the trees as cover in case the other guard had a gun as well. There were no shots fired behind her, but she heard Prescott curse. She felt the vibration of a pursuer in the ground and leapt to grab a leafless branch above her head.

She swung herself in an upward arc as her pursuer would have crashed into her. He passed her and skidded to a halt in the wet leaves, almost falling. Meanwhile, she had swung back and was coming forward again as he spun to face her. She let go of the tree branch and hit him with both feet solid in his chest. They both went down, but she tucked into a roll, using his body as a cushion for her fall.

She came up on her feet, turned and kicked him in the head, knocking him back to the ground and most likely unconscious. This time, when she ran for the house, there was no one behind her. She rushed in through the back door, slamming it behind her and locking it for good measure.

Ethan looked up from the computer when she came into the main living area from the mud room. His eyes narrowed and he yanked the headset for the phone from his head, pressing the disconnect button as he jumped to his feet. "What happened to you?"

She looked down at herself. She was covered in leaves and dirt. Her hands were scratched and stained green from moss where she'd gripped the tree limb. They stung. "I went to the clearing and—"

"The clearing is not in sight of the house," he interrupted before she could finish what she was saying.

"It sort of is."

"In just the right spot."

"More like lots of spots. There are actually only a few areas completely out of sight of the house."

"Regardless," Ethan said from between clenched teeth. "Why do you look like you've been wrestling bear cubs?"

"Prescott was there."

Ethan's eyes filled with a deadly intent. "He attacked you?"

"No, but he tried to take me back to his house . . . or rather two of his security men tried."

"Damn it, you promised you would wear a comm unit."

"I did wear one."

"Was it turned on?"

"Yes, of course. I'm not an idiot."

"Then why wasn't I notified you were in danger?" He looked ready to kill someone and she had the horrible feeling friendlies would do if the enemy wasn't available.

"Probably because I did not give the distress signal."

Ethan spun away from her and stormed to the second bedroom, slamming the door open.

A younger agent named Vinnie was listening to the audibles from Prescott's estate as well as the output from Beth's comm unit. He eyed Ethan warily, obviously having overheard this latest conversation as well.

"Why didn't you inform me of Beth's danger?"

"She indicated she could handle it, sir."

"Is she a fully trained agent?"

"Uh, no sir."

"Then how in the hell did you take her word in a dangerous situation that she could handle it?"

Looking highly uncomfortable, Vinnie offered no answer.

"You knew she was facing three assailants and you chose not to inform me of this fact?" Ethan asked, sounding even more dangerous.

Vinnie swallowed nervously. "I only heard one other person through the comm unit."

"The battle was mostly silent," Beth added.

"Battle." Ethan drawled the word out like he was tasting it for flavor and turned to face her. "You chose to attempt to fight off three men rather than calling in reinforcements?"

"I did fight them off and if I had felt in serious danger at any point, I would have given the distress signal."

"Did any of them have guns?"

She didn't want to answer this question. She really didn't. "One, but it might have been a tranquilizer gun. It looked like it could be anyway."

"Yet you still didn't give the distress signal?"

"I wasn't thinking at that point . . . just reacting."

"Damn it, Beth." He sighed and ran his fingers through his hair like he wanted to say more, but didn't trust himself to do so. Vinnie wasn't so lucky. Ethan turned back to face him. "She's not trained for fieldwork. Even if Prescott wasn't speaking threateningly, the second you became aware she wasn't alone, you should have alerted me."

The look on the other man's face gave him away.

"He *did* threaten her, didn't he?" Ethan asked in a chilling voice.

Vinnie nodded. "He said he wanted to take her back to his house, for her own good."

Ethan lost it right then. He didn't yell, he didn't even swear, but he ripped down one side of the younger agent and up the other and it all centered around the fact that Beth was not an agent and should never have been left unprotected in a dangerous situation. As a fully trained agent, both in surveillance and fieldwork, apparently, Vinnie should have realized that.

Beth was learning a lot herself. Not all of it pleasant, but in retrospect, she knew Ethan was right.

"I'm sorry, sir. I'll never make that mistake again."

Ethan made a visible effort to rein in his temper and nodded. "See that you don't."

He spun and left the room without another word. Beth followed him.

She took off her comm unit and turned it off before laying it on the dining table near the computer. "Did you get into Prescott's system?"

"We're close, but I cut the call with Hotwire and Claire when I saw you."

Her eyes scanned his computer monitor. "It looks like they're still working."

"We have to call the sheriff."

"But if we have Prescott arrested for attempted kidnapping, he's going to cancel the auction."

Ethan shook his head, his expression still bordering on fury. "He's not going to jail over this. Men like him don't. It's your word against his and he's the kind of man who has CYA down to an art form. But if we don't call it in, we'll look too suspicious to him. We can't afford for him to get leery at this point and cancel anyway."

"You're right, I guess."

Ethan nodded and went to make the call. He did the part of the outraged boyfriend to perfection, but he was scowling when he hung up the phone. "I expected it, but it still makes my blood boil."

"What?"

"The sheriff is sure you are mistaken about Prescott's intent. He's going to go by and ask him about it."

"He's not even going to bring him in?"

"My guess is that the sheriff owes a lot of favors to our information broker."

"I'm sure you are right, but it makes me mad. How many women has he gotten away with traumatizing?"

"He could have made it one more with you."

"He wasn't expecting me to fight back. None of them were."

"And if they'd shot you, you wouldn't have had the chance."

"I fought and I won."

"You should have given the distress signal."

"You're right, I should have. I've never been in a situation like that before and I reacted rather than really thinking," she said again. "I think some part of my brain was afraid that if I called in reinforcements, we would have put the case in jeopardy."

"Better that than the sadistic poser get his hands on you, but worst case scenario is I would have gone out there pretending to be looking for my wayward girlfriend. Not anything to arouse his suspicions."

"I didn't think of that angle."

"You're not the trained agent."

"My instincts told me to handle it alone." She wasn't trying to justify herself, just explain why she'd made the choice she had. "I want to say that in the future, I'd do it differently, but I can't be sure."

"Listening to your instincts when they are on is the mark of a good agent, but part of an agent's training is also learning to follow procedure."

"If I had been fully trained, would I have thought to call in reinforcements?"

"Yes. In cases like this, you learn to conserve energy and diminish danger. We're close to the end of this case and it could have been blown sky high because I guarantee you, if he'd managed to get you back to his place, I wouldn't have left you there. The thought of you in that psycho's hands is making my insides twist like a new rope."

"I'm sorry."

"You did good. I don't want you to think I'm not proud of you, because I am. I'm still pissed as hell at our back-up agent. He had a call to make and he made the wrong one."

"He didn't want to interrupt your work."

"Bad choice."

Beth could see Ethan's point of view on that, too. If he were in danger, she'd want to know and she wasn't the agent in charge. This incident would go into Ethan's report and would not reflect well on Vinnie though. And she felt sorry for him.

"You need to get back to work now that the excitement is over."

"I'd rather take you to bed and assure myself that you are really okay."

"I'll be more okay when that man is behind bars."

Ethan nodded. "Point taken."

He went back to his computer and she went to take a shower. He was waiting for her when she came out of the bathroom though.

He had a bottle of antibiotic ointment and some gauze. "I want to treat your hands."

"What about your hacking?"

"I called Hotwire and filled him and Claire in on what had happened. They're still working and I was, too, until I remember seeing a glimpse of your hands. I wish you'd said something. I could have taken care of them right away."

"I would have just gotten them wet in the shower."

He was gentle in his ministrations, making sure the small scratches were completely clean before applying the ointment.

She sighed when he was done, wishing he could stay in the bedroom with her and knowing he couldn't. "You really need to get back to your computer."

"Come with me."

"Okay."

He moved his laptop to the living room so he could work while she cuddled next to him on the couch. The kittens joined them, snuggling against her legs and she felt contentment like she'd never known.

She was dozing with her head on his thigh when he shouted, "Hot damn, we did it!"

Beth scrambled into a sitting position. "You got into the computer?"

"We got in an hour ago, but we had to get through the security to the files of interest. Not to mention we had to find them."

"And you've got those."

"Oh, yeah, baby . . . we've got 'em. The plans are here and so are his contacts."

"When will you move in?"

"The risk that he knows we hacked in is minimal. Once we got inside, we were able to reset his security measures. The whole situation today worked to our advantage because it kept him away from his office."

"Who knew, huh?" she asked with a smile.

"I'll take whatever help I can get, even when it comes from my target. Hell, especially then."

"So, you're waiting to move in?"

"We've got proof that the plans are on his system right now, but I want to raid the bastard's house when he's doing his little video presentation. The buyers need to be brought down as much as Prescott."

"I agree."

Ethan knew she would. Beth was like that. She saw the bigger picture, even when it wasn't comfortable. Like agreeing to play agent when it was the last thing she wanted to do so they could bring down the enemy. She was such an intriguing mixture of soft heart and just mind.

She was strong, but her innocence and often shy personality fooled others like Prescott into believing she was a pushover.

Ethan knew better and he liked what he knew. A lot. He was proud of the way she'd handled herself in the clearing, but he was still jittery from her near miss. Her instincts were right on, but the one time they were off could spell disaster. He knew it. He'd been there. And he'd survived, he reminded himself.

He wanted Beth to know her own potential and live up to it, but if he had anything to say . . . there was a certain type of assignment she would never get offered. It probably wasn't fair, but he wasn't New Man when it came to her. His instincts were strictly primal where she was concerned and the first one roared with a need to protect her.

That instinct was filling him with rage the next morning when the sheriff called.

"Mr. Prescott denies being anywhere near your cabin yesterday, Mr. Grange."

"He was here with two guards from his estate."

"Did anyone besides Miss Whitney see them?"

"No."

"Whereas Mr. Grange's staff assured my officer that he was in his office the entire afternoon."

"Did he tell you that Beth quit her job yesterday?"

"Yes, he did. Something about an argument regarding you."

"He didn't tell you about the photos he had faked to try to prove I'm having some kind of sleazy affair?"

"Did you see the photos, Mr. Grange?"

"Beth told me about them."

"Just as she told you about Mr. Prescott attacking her?"

"Yes," Ethan gritted out. He was so going to enjoy raking this small-town idiot on the carpet once the collar was made.

"Does it seem likely to you that a man of Mr. Prescott's wealth and personal appearance needs to go to such lengths to attract a woman?"

"Stranger things have happened."

"Maybe between the pages of your books, Mr. Grange, but here in the real world, multimillionaires do not stoop to such measures to get a date. I'm sorry to say this, but I think your girlfriend is creating drama to ensure your interest. Have you been fighting a lot lately?"

"My personal life is none of your affair, but if you think I won't expose your incompetence to the world, you're a fool."

"Be very careful what kind of insinuations you make, Mr. Grange. Mr. Prescott is not taking action at this point, but if Miss Whitney persists in her accusations, he could sue her for slander."

Ethan hung up the phone, promising himself he would rub the sheriff's nose in his idiocy and if the cop was dirty, he was going to do time. Once charges were laid against Arthur Prescott for illegal brokering of technological secrets, kidnapping would be added to them, no matter what this hick small-town sheriff thought.

Ethan was still steaming an hour later when he got a call from a bookseller in one of the bigger coastal cities to the south. The owner of the shop said that he had just found out Ethan was living along the coast. He had a group of readers who were fans of his work and would be meeting for a discussion group the next morning. Was there any way Ethan could make it?

"I'm sorry, Mr. Jackson, but I'm far too busy with my current book to take on any publicity events right now."

"I'm sure your publisher would appreciate your cooperation in this event."

"My publisher understands my reticence to meet the public. I am confident they would not give you my personal tele-
phone number and since it is unlisted, I have to ask how you
came by it."

"I'm not at liberty to divulge that information."

"I really must insist."

"Perhaps if you came to the discussion group, I might be
persuaded to tell you."

"I told you, I'm too involved with my current book."

"It's not a good idea to alienate readers, Mr. Grange."

"Have you read my books, Mr. Jackson?"

"Actually, no."

"If you had, you would know that I do nothing to avoid
alienating anyone. Good-bye." He hung up.

"Who was it?" Beth asked, coming from the spare room
where she'd dropped off coffee for the secondary agents.

They'd both come in today and neither one had said boo
to Ethan since their arrival. Vinnie had given him a particularly wide berth.

"A bookstore trying to get me to come to a discussion
group tomorrow."

"You think Prescott put him up to it?"

"I'm sure of it. The man is tenacious."

"He's used to getting what he wants."

"He can't have you."

"No, he can't."

But Ethan's blood curdled at the thought of how far the
man was willing to go to get what he wanted. Rachel Gannon's
sister had not had a chance. How many other women had
fallen into his dangerous web?

Chapter 21

Ethan waited for Beth to come into the bedroom where he was gearing up for the take-down at Prescott's.

She was feeding her cats and talking to them, trying to act like everything was normal, but he knew she wanted to go along on the collar. Though she didn't try to talk him into it. She accepted his judgment as agent in charge and that increased his respect for her. But he'd decided after how well she handled herself when Prescott tried to nab her that she should be there. If part of it was the desire to show her how well she fit in the world of agents, he wasn't ashamed of that fact.

Beth was a natural and nothing would please him more than to see her using those talents for the good of their country.

Besides, tonight was going to go down without a hitch. He could feel it in his gut. He and an elite team would parachute in and secure the premises. His plan was for Beth to be part of the second team let in through the gates.

She walked into the bedroom, her beautiful brown eyes almost black with emotion. "You'll be careful tonight? You won't take any unnecessary risks, will you?"

He'd never liked anyone worrying about him, but her concern felt good. "I never do."

"I'm not sure I believe that."

He smiled. "Maybe you should come along and keep an eye on me."

"Are you serious?"

He indicated a second set of gear on the bed. "Very."

She gasped. "You are serious."

"So, get geared up."

She grinned. "You got it." She lifted the Kevlar vest off the top of the pile. "Wow, it's heavier than I expected it to be."

"You're in good shape. It won't slow you down."

"Not that I'll be chasing anyone. This is a straightforward sting, right?"

"Right. Alpha team chutes in and takes out the guards at the gate and on the grounds. Beta team comes in through the gates as backup to help secure the premises and cuff the prisoners."

"Is there a third team on the beach, in case Prescott runs?"

"Why the beach?"

"He's a pirate. And he's done everything to make his house authentic to period, you know? The maze, the grandeur, all of it. I wouldn't put it past him to have an escape tunnel to the beach."

Ethan felt something inside him slip into place at her words. "You're right. I should have thought of it."

"You don't read books about pirates."

"And you do?"

"Sometimes."

"Among other things." He'd never forget the spicy content he'd skimmed in the book beside her bed when he'd been doing personal recon in her apartment.

"Among other things," she agreed with a blush.

His heart contracted. She was so damn sweet. "I'll assign an agent from the Beta team to beach-watch."

"Good idea."

"But I don't plan to give Prescott the chance to reach any tunnel."

She waved her hand. "The best laid plans and all that."

He laughed. "Are you casting aspersions on my abilities? Because I'll have you know that someone I care for very much told me she thought I was the best of the best."

Beth paused in donning her dark camo shirt over the vest. "Someone you care for very much?"

He nodded, wishing he had more time to say what really needed saying. "It was harder than it should have been to decide to include you tonight, and it wasn't because I doubted your abilities."

"But you care for me too much to hold me back?"

"Yes."

"I feel the same way about you," she said in a low voice, her expression hiding her thoughts from him.

"So, I don't have to quit my job and become a plumber to keep you in my life?" he asked, only half joking.

If it came between being an agent and having Beth, he didn't think his job would win anymore.

"I never said anything about plumbers . . . they can keep really bad hours."

"Beth . . ."

"No. I don't want you to quit your job. It's part of who you are and I like that person."

"Like?" he asked carefully.

She turned and peeled out of her jeans before slipping on a pair of regulation pants. "I think you know it's a lot more than like or I wouldn't be willing to compromise my dreams for you."

Everything inside him went still. "Are you willing?"

"Yes." But her voice was quiet and he couldn't see her face. He didn't know how she felt about that.

He crossed the room and took her shoulders, turning her to face him. She met his gaze, her own unflinching, but still giving nothing away.

"We need to talk," he said.

She licked her lips and nodded. "Later."

"After we take down Prescott."

"Yes."

"If I kiss you, I'm going to want to make love to you."

"But you'll wait for that, too. Your self-discipline is legendary."

"It goes right out the window when I touch you."

Her smile was soft and wholly feminine. "I like knowing that."

"I thought you might."

"Are you going to kiss me anyway?"

"You know me . . . I live for risk."

She was still smiling when his mouth claimed hers and he molded the curve of her lips, taking that smile inside him like a talisman. He didn't risk using his tongue, but he did pull her against his body. The Kevlar vests kept them apart, but it still felt good to wrap his arms around her.

He broke off the kiss, but not the hug. "This is a good way to get ready for a mission."

She laughed. "If you say so, but I can't imagine doing it with a different partner."

"Me either."

"Really?"

He pulled back so he could look into her face. "I told you at the beginning of this assignment I don't want anyone else. And I can guarantee you, I've never gotten ready for a mission like this before."

"I'm glad."

He broke the hug and moved away. "Now, it's time to get a move on."

She saluted him. "Yes, sir."

She was adorable when she was being sassy and it took that famed self-discipline of his not to pull her back into his arms and kiss her until they were both writhing, naked on the floor.

The jump from the gliders went like clockwork. Using their heat-sensor goggles, Alpha team was able to identify and neutralize all outside guards before opening the gate and letting Beta team inside.

Ethan sent three agents to the back of the house in case anyone tried to run and took control of the premises by kicking in the front door and identifying his team as federal agents.

It was almost too easy. A guard opened fire, but one of Ethan's agents took him out with a stun gun. Using his knowledge of the house plans, Ethan led the way to the underground movie theater where Prescott and his clients were watching a video of the UGCV. They moved fast in case the guard upstairs had been able to alert the others.

But the single guard outside the door to the underground theater looked stunned to see them. He lifted his weapon, but was taken out with the same efficiency as the guard upstairs.

Ethan didn't bother with subtlety when blasting through the door to the room since it was locked via a biometric alarm. He simply blew it with C-4 and infiltrated the room before the dust cloud had finished forming.

There were six clients in the room and the DEA agent. She dove for Prescott when he jumped and ran for the back of the room. She caught him behind the movie screen.

He fought, but she had a snub-nosed revolver pressed against his skull when Ethan caught up with them. "Give me an excuse to use it, you bastard. Please."

Prescott went utterly motionless, his hand still against something on the wall. And darned if Beth hadn't been right. A secret door in the wall was cracked and if it didn't lead to an escape tunnel, Ethan would hang up his Lone Ranger star.

The others in the room weren't as quick as Prescott to realize the futility of attempted escape and more than one had to be brought down with the stun guns. Ethan's agent upstairs commed-in to say that he'd secured the premises, having found one more guard in the house.

Beth cuffed the Ukrainian and read him his rights like she'd done it a hundred times before.

Pride swelled up in Ethan, almost choking him. "All right, people, move the prisoners upstairs one at a time."

The Arab was making noises about diplomatic immunity, as were a couple of others.

"We'll let the lawyers work that out," Ethan said. "If you can prove your status, and it can be established that you are not working in the capacity as espionage agents for your respective governments, you will be deported without incarceration, but all rights of return to this country will be revoked."

No one looked all that smug after his announcement. In essence, the men and women in this room were spies and they knew it. Some might get off without doing time, but none would be allowed to return and all would be stripped of diplomatic status for perpetuity by the U.S. government.

Something happened on the way up the stairs and Beth tripped with her prisoner. She ended up racking him with her knee before dragging his limping form up the remaining steps.

The prisoners had all been put in secure transports to a federal facility in Portland and he and Beth were following in his car when he asked her about it.

"I told him he should be ashamed of himself for not only abusing the hospitality of our nation but also betraying his own people by being willing to provide a sex slave for a man as depraved as Prescott. He said that one woman's plight was nothing compared to the power of a nation."

"So you tripped him and racked him?"

"Yes."

"Don't admit that to anyone else."

"As if I would."

"You shouldn't have told me."

"But you're more than my superior on the case, aren't you? You won't put it in your report."

"You're right, I won't—except the part where he confirmed his intention to you."

"That was pretty dumb on his part, wasn't it?"

"In more ways than one. I've been racked once or twice in my life and it's not an experience I ever want to repeat."

"Well, you don't have to worry about it coming from this

quarter. I'm far too fond of your equipment to allow it to be in anything but full working order."

He laughed out loud. "You're pretty darn bold for a shy woman."

"I'm not shy around you, or hadn't you noticed?"

"Are you saying I bring out the best in you?"

"You know, Ethan, I think you do."

"You were right about the tunnel, too."

"I was?"

"Yep." He told her about the secret door Prescott had attempted to escape through.

"But you were right, he didn't get to use it."

"It could have happened. If DEA Agent Gannon hadn't been so quick, I would have had to chase him down the tunnel." And chasing suspects in enclosed spaces was dangerous.

"She's good. Are you going to tell Dad about her?"

"You mean recommend her for acquisition by TGP?"

"Yes."

"Yes. Not only is she a good agent, but as much personal baggage as she had on this assignment, she didn't use it as an excuse to do anything stupid."

"That shows a lot of integrity."

"Yes, it does."

"I hope Dad acquires her."

"Me, too." But his thoughts were not on the other woman.

He'd never wanted to be done with an assignment so badly. There was so much unresolved between him and Beth and he wanted it taken care of now.

Twelve hours later, Ethan had finished interrogating suspects and filling out paperwork. He was exhausted and wired at the same time. There was nothing new in that, but what was different was the need to get away from all of it with someone else. With Beth.

He insisted on driving back to their cabin and she fell asleep about ten minutes into the drive. By the time they got there, he was ready to go to bed, too. He'd gone more than twenty-four hours without sleep and he could think of nothing more appealing than twining his naked body with hers and rectifying that problem.

Beth woke up to autumn sunshine streaming in through the bedroom window and wrapped in Ethan's strong arms. It felt right—being there, with him—everything about the night before and waking up next to him this morning.

She was glad he'd brought her back to the cabin because she wanted privacy for their discussion. And she just plain wanted time alone with him. Her dad would expect them to return to D.C. that day, but she planned to talk Ethan into taking a couple of days off before heading back. They had to arrange return transport to the East Coast for his car and the cats anyway.

She carefully extricated herself from Ethan's arms so she could go take a shower.

When she came out of the bathroom, Ethan was sitting on the side of the bed, an expression in his green eyes that made her heart melt. Her gaze flicked over the bed and then stuttered as it encountered a set of hand restraints attached to the brass headboard.

"What are those for?" she asked in a voice gone breathless.

"We never got around to my turn . . ."

"Restraining me?" she squeaked.

"Yep." He grinned. "You sound nervous, Sunshine. Don't you trust me?"

"Yes, I do." And to prove it, she let her robe fall from her shoulders to the floor and walked naked to the bed.

She lay down and put her hands toward the headboard. Ethan straddled her, his flesh already erect and tempting, his body heat transferring to her with the sizzle of an electric charge.

"Now, that's one of the things I love about you, Beth. You've got a real sense of adventure." He secured the cuffs to her wrists and brushed his thumbs against the palm of her hands.

"*One* of the things . . . *love?*"

His expression so sincere it brought tears to her eyes, he nodded. "Definitely love. I love so many things about you I can't count them all, but that's because I love *everything* that makes you Elizabeth Whitney."

"I love you, too," she choked out past a tight throat. She'd never imagined she would tell a man she loved him for the first time in such a situation, but then with Ethan, life was going to be an exciting journey into each new day.

"Enough to be my partner?"

"Partner?" she asked, afraid to guess what he meant.

He nodded. "In everything."

That sounded promising, but she waited in expectant silence for him to go on.

"I've never worked with a partner, but I want that to change." He cupped her cheek. "I want that partner to be you."

"But I'll be a new agent."

"And I'll take responsibility for training you, but there's just one thing, Beth."

"What?"

"When the babies start coming we have to promise each other we'll leave fieldwork. It's hard to raise kids in today's world and they're going to need us home, not gallivanting around trying to save the world."

"Do you mean it?"

"Oh, yeah, I definitely mean it."

"So, you want to have babies?"

"In a couple of years . . . maybe five at the most. You okay with that?"

"More than okay." Her heart was so full, she felt like it was going to burst from her chest.

"I want these babies to carry my last name."

"You want me to marry you?"

He got a chagrined expression and then said, "Wait a sec."

He jumped up and dashed into the other room. When he came back, he was carrying a small box. He climbed back on her so he was straddling her hips and opened the box to reveal the most beautiful marquis-cut yellow diamond she'd ever seen.

He cupped her face with both hands this time, his thumb brushing her lips. "I love you, baby. Will you marry me?"

Her eyes filled with tears, emotion coursing through her in a tidal wave, but she couldn't stifle a burst of giggles. "I never thought I'd be proposed to while I was naked with my hands tied to the bed."

"Are you telling me that even your rich imagination didn't stretch that far?" he teased.

"Yes."

"Well?"

"You win hands down."

"That's not what I was asking, but what did I win?"

"The most unique marriage proposal."

"Good. I wouldn't want to remind you of anyone else."

"You couldn't . . . no matter how you had asked. Everything about us is different . . . bigger, deeper, more."

He inhaled a deep breath, his eyes closing for a couple of seconds as if he was savoring her words and then they opened, fixing her with a glittering green gaze. "So, are you going to answer, or am I going to grow gray sitting here?"

She looked down at his still erect penis. "Um . . . I don't think you've got the patience to wait for that."

"I agree. Now answer me before I have to get nasty."

"I might like you nasty."

His eyes narrowed. "You're pushing me, Sunshine, and I gotta believe you're doing it on purpose. I think it's time I taught you what happens to feisty little agent hopefuls who give their trainers a hard time."

"Something looks hard, definitely."

He burst out laughing and then leaned forward to kiss her. His hands twined with hers while his tongue claimed rights to her mouth she'd never give another man again. He kissed her until her body was hot and needy, until her lips were swollen and her heart was pounding in her chest.

When he sat up she felt the ring on her finger, but couldn't hold the thought long because he was trailing his fingertips down her arms. He brushed over her armpits and she shivered, a convulsive movement that shook her whole body.

"You're so responsive," he praised.

"Your touch is too perfect." She was panting and didn't care that he knew she was so excited from the molten kiss and little bit of caressing he'd done.

He cupped her breasts, rubbing his thumbs over her already erect nipples. "Touching you gives me more pleasure than I would have ever believed possible."

A lump of emotion formed in her throat. "I'm glad."

"I love your body, Beth."

"I'm nothing special."

He laughed. "Not special?" He shook his head. "Baby, you are more woman than I've ever known. You are it for me. The most sexy . . ." He squeezed her breasts. "Most sensual . . ." He leaned forward and gave her a love bite right over the pulse beating so frantically in her throat. "The most imaginative . . ."

He ran his hands back up her arms to trace the cuffs holding her wrists. "Most fun . . ." He kissed her again, using his tongue to trace at her lips. "All kinds of fun . . ." He kissed her again, this time nibbling at her and teasing her tongue with his.

"Most delicious." His voice was going ragged. "Most beautiful." Another kiss while his body rubbed hers, like a big cat of prey marking her with his scent. "Most caring." Several nibbling kisses. "Most adventurous." A long drawn out kiss that sent her connection to reality rocketing off into the ether.

Then it was just his body pressing against hers, words spoken in her ear that she couldn't make sense of and eventually hands and mouth everywhere, bringing each individual nerve ending to tantalizing life. Without knowing how they got there, her legs were wrapped around his hips and trying to draw him to her. He said something, cursed, and yanked away.

She lay, dazed with desire, watching as he donned a condom with trembling hands and then he was back where she wanted him to be, on top of her and surging into her.

He ripped the Velcro straps on the handcuffs open. "Hold me, baby. Hold me hard."

She didn't need a second bidding, but wrapped her arms and her legs around him with all her strength and even so, he rode her with powerful thrusts that sent her careening into orgasm and him with her.

Afterward, he took care of the condom and then lay down again, pulling her until she was sprawled on top of him. "Tell me *yes*, Beth."

"I'm fairly certain I said that word several times in the last hour," she said in a voice hoarse from her screams when she climaxed.

"Say it with the words *I'll marry you* attached."

She lifted her head so she could look straight into his gorgeous green eyes. "Yes, I'll marry you, Ethan Crane. I love you."

"I don't want you to give up your dreams, Beth, I want to give them to you. Every last one."

"You have." Tears she made no attempt to control burned her eyes. "You've made me dream bigger and promised a future that fulfills my every fantasy, but one that is very, very real."

"I always want to be your fantasy man, Beth."

"You always have been and you always will be."

"You're my fantasy woman."

"Am I?" She didn't really doubt it, not after all that he'd said when he started making love to her.

"When you meet my mama, you ask her what kind of woman I always said I'd marry and she'll describe you to a T."

Beth didn't doubt him, only she didn't think anyone else in the world saw her like he did. But that made them equal, because according to him, no one else saw into his heart the way she did.

"My dad is going to be over the moon about this and Mother is going to be so relieved I'm getting married. She thought my aborted wedding attempt put me off marriage for life."

"I'll be there, Beth. No way would I leave you standing at the altar."

"I know. With love comes trust."

"And passion," he said with a suggestive grin.

"You can't be thinking of making love again so soon. I'm wiped."

"Baby, when it comes to you, I will always be thinking of making love."

"I guess that's only fair . . . since I've spent more than two years dreaming of making love to you."

"Reality outdoes fantasy, no matter how good . . . doesn't it?"

"When that reality is with my fantasy man, every time, Ethan. Every time. I love you."

"I love you, Beth, and I always will."

And then he proved once again just how much better reality was than fantasy.

Epilogue

Whit sat in his office chair and congratulated himself on a job well done. Ethan and Beth were getting married, just like he'd planned.

Bringing Alan Hyatt in to make Ethan jealous had worked like a charm. So had assigning his daughter to work the case with Whit's top agent. They'd nabbed Prescott, gotten some good leads on further technology espionage, and gotten engaged to boot.

He'd have to wait a few years for the grandkids because his daughter was training to be an agent. Finally. He had to admit, he hadn't expected that outcome, but he liked it just fine.

Ethan had made it clear that from this point forward, he went on assignment with Beth, or he didn't go. Whit didn't blame him. He'd always planned to marry another agent, or at least someone in the business, but Lynn had derailed his thoughts. He'd never regret marrying her, but he thought maybe they could have handled some things in their life a little differently.

He liked knowing both Ethan and Beth planned to stop fieldwork once she got pregnant. Whit had missed out on too much of Beth's childhood. He couldn't get those years back, but he planned to be a hell of a grandpa and a better father to his grown daughter than he was to her as a child.

He was proud of his matchmaking skills though. It seemed a shame to waste them.

His gaze slid to the computer where an image of a red-haired actress filled the screen. Jillian Sherwood. There was something about her eyes that spoke honesty and integrity and mischief. Just the kind of woman Alan Hyatt needed since he'd lost out on Beth. You had to feel for a man who had lost his chance with Whit's daughter.

Hmm . . . if Whit played it right, he could get Hyatt and that pretty little redhead together. It would require a little judicious information on his part and assigning Hyatt to a case that wasn't strictly his area of expertise, but he had faith in the agent. Hyatt was smart and knew how to think on his feet. Whit was willing to bet the pretty little redhead in the picture shared those qualities, too.

He typed up the assignment orders while whistling the tune of "Matchmaker."

If this worked out, he was going to have to turn his eyes to some of the other agents. Most of them were single and he thought it was time they found the bliss he'd known with Lynn all these years.